Proceed With Caution

Selected Stories

Melanie Wyllie

ISBN 978-0-9956431-0-9

Book design by Barbara Wyllie

Published by Melanie Wyllie, London, 2017

Contents

Once Upon A Time   1

The Wind Grows Colder   74

Demons Seldom Sleep   82

A Wedding Has Been Arranged   141

Scorn   164

Proceed With Caution   272

Once Upon a Time

1

When the following morning the bleeding was still heavy, she phoned Miranda.

She had lain all night stiffly cold, not daring to move, a confused mesh of pain and fear distancing her from the enormity of what she had done.
The much wanted child torn away with metal spatula and rubber gloves.

Dan had buried the curly blond head in his hands and wept. He couldn't leave Jackie — what would she do without him?
Overcome with love and compassion she had stroked his hair, feeling it springing under her fingers.

She had no choice. She couldn't have this child.

She had told no one except Giselle, who had been incredulously scornful.
'For Christ's sake!' she said. 'Get yourself fitted with a cap. You knew he would never leave his wife. They never do.'

Leila had wanted to protest. Dan was different — he really loved her — it was just that he couldn't bear to hurt Jackie.

Sharing a flat with Giselle hadn't been a very good idea. She left her Dutch cap in the bathroom basin, and draped wet stockings and underwear over the backs of chairs.
Her boyfriends put their feet on the furniture and drank beer from bottles. As there was only one bedroom and Leila slept on a divan in the living room, she was unable to go to bed until Giselle's varied guests had left or had made the transition from the sofa to her bedroom.

It was a garden flat, which meant that the living room window was on a level with the paved terrace, and it was possible to see the overgrown square of garden, a tangle of unpruned roses and rotting shrubs.

Her feet were cold — she kept as still as she could in case the bleeding got worse.

Dr Lieberman had given her some large white tablets.

Giselle had brought her a cup of tea before she left for work. 'You'd better stay where you are,' she said, 'and if it gets any worse you'll just have to call someone.' She avoided looking at her. She thought Leila was a fool. 'Take what you can and move on,' she said. 'Getting emotionally involved with married men is a useless waste of time. Make them pay for their adultery, have some fun and wave them goodbye!'

'I'm not feeling very well,' she said to Miranda on the phone. 'Please could you come, and bring some milk and a sliced loaf?'

The beautiful Miranda — small and slender with shiny short dark hair — glossy red lips — glossy red nails — long silky legs — very high heels — always in black, high-necked, long-sleeved, wafting perfume as she moved.

Nick was crazy about her. They had been married for three years... and now...

'I've fallen in love with someone else,' Miranda had told her, scooping the froth off her cappuccino with a spoon. 'I told Nick. He won't talk to me. I don't know what to do.' She didn't look at Leila.

She didn't know what to say. In love with someone else? It was unthinkable. She couldn't be serious. What about Nick? She saw him taking off his glasses, pushing back the lock of hair.

Miranda lit a cigarette — her delicate beauty smudged with fatigue.

'I don't know what to do,' she repeated.

Nick had come in late for supper.

They were already at the table.

Their mother, with her habitual tight-lipped disapproval, fetched his chop from the oven — the covered vegetable dishes concealing the pallid cabbage and plain boiled potatoes.

He had taken off his glasses and rubbed his hand across his eyes.

'I'm getting married,' he said.

There was a stunned silence — even their father raised his head.

'What did you say?' asked their mother. 'Did you hear what he said Father? Really Nicholas...!'
Leila looked at her brother in astonishment. 'Who are you marrying?' she asked.
'Exactly,' said their mother. 'Who are you marrying Nicholas?'
'You don't know her,' said Nick. 'Her name is Miranda...'
'Miranda who?' demanded their mother. 'Really Nicholas...!'
'Miranda DuCane,' said Nick, the lock of dark hair falling on his forehead. He pushed it away and put his glasses back on.

'That's quite a famous name,' said their mother. 'Of course she wouldn't have anything to do with *that* family.'
'Yes,' said Nick. 'She is that family. Her mother is Lady DuCane. Her father is dead...' He began to eat his food.

'I don't believe you,' said their mother.

She hadn't believed him. She had put on the awful brown felt hat and ill-fitting tweed coat and gone to the Library to look Miranda up in Burke's Peerage. Sir Basil and Lady Sybille DuCane. Two daughters. Miranda and Camilla.

Nick refused to invite them to the wedding. Leila was very hurt. 'I don't want Mother there,' said Nick. 'So I can't ask you or Father.'

2

At the last minute Leila had put on her black and white checked dress and gone to the Registry Office in time to have her photograph taken with the small group of laughing friends.

Nick was overjoyed. Miranda smiled and laughed. She wore a lemon yellow silk dress with a long swaying skirt, and held a bunch of yellow roses. Nick kissed her and hugged her, and everybody kissed and hugged everybody else. They piled into taxis, and went to a party in Hampstead, at one of those houses that Leila never thought she would ever enter. The garden was a soft mass of white and mauve lilac, with goldfish darting about in a reedy pond dribbled with water from over moss-covered stones.

The hosts, DeeDee and Buzz were friends of Miranda's, casually elegant, DeeDee wore powder blue with a diamond choker and several bracelets, Buzz a dark blue silk scarf in the open neck of his white shirt.

The food was laid on a white-clothed table on the lawn. Delicious small mouthfuls — crab tarts, prawns in a creamy sauce, little strawberry and raspberry tarts, morsels of chicken in aspic.

The table was strewn with flowers, and there was pink champagne. Miranda loved pink champagne. 'Oh Wonderful Nick Darling!' she would say, her voice caressing his name, holding up her glass of pink bubbles.

There were two waiters in white jackets handing round the glasses on silver trays.

The girls took off their shoes, and stood barefoot on the smooth green velvet lawn. She remembered it in a haze of golden summer light.

She had met Miranda's sister Camilla for the first time. She was tall with long blonde hair, usually wearing slacks and cashmere sweaters, she was dazzling in a frock of electric blue and green zigzags. She was quite drunk.

A friend of Lady DuCane's was lending Miranda and Nick her flat in Paris for their honeymoon. It was near the Arc de Triomphe, all guilt and crystal, hung with claret velvet and sombre portraits. Her maid Celeste would take care of them. Nick was walking on air, she had never seen him like this, her solemn brother transformed. he kept touching Miranda as if to reassure himself she was real. A magical day.

Leila was overwhelmed with unaccustomed luxury, the abundance of food and drink, the smart expensive people, the beribboned hats and glimpses of gold, the discreet glitter of jewels.

They had left in an open car, in a flurry of coloured streamers and rose petals.

How could Miranda be in love with someone else? It couldn't be. She could almost feel Nick's pain.
'He won't talk to me,' said Miranda.

Leila didn't really like this sort of coffee. She sipped a little and added more sugar.

Miranda knew about Dan. Leila had had to tell somebody.
'Daniel?' she had said. 'Daniel! Does the incredibly successful, fabulous Jackie know? How on earth did you get involved with Daniel?' And then gently, 'He won't leave her you know.'

It had taken Leila a long time to get to know Miranda. She was used to girls who came from the same privileged background.

They were frequently promoted ahead of her at work. 'Daddy' being an old school chum of the Chairman, or having been at Balliol with the Managing Director. She was not used to them on an equal level.

Miranda and Camilla had both gone to an expensive, exclusive boarding school — to be prepared for their futures as exemplary wives of men in high places, and mothers of sons who were to become men in high places, or, failing that, to serve the community with selfless dedication, bestowing the benefits of their superior wisdom on the less fortunate.

They were taught how to curtsy in preparation for their presentation at Court, and were adept at all forms of ballroom dancing. Able to distinguish between the Quickstep and the Foxtrot, the correct formation of the Eightsome Reel and the Gay Gordons, mastering the new Latin American rhythms of the Samba and Rhumba, although the Tango was somewhat frowned upon as 'unladylike'. They learned the exact position of the hand on their partner's collar.

They were required to read *The Daily Telegraph* and to memorise the names of cabinet ministers, and to discuss the latest theatrical productions and be familiar with the stars of opera and ballet. At mealtimes, they were supposed to discuss with knowledge and intelligence a variety of subjects. Thursdays the conversation had to be in French.

Their reading matter was strictly monitored. Nothing sexual, politically subversive or controversial was allowed. Careful study of Sir Walter Scott, Grey's *Elegy* and Wordsworth. Novels by Georgette Heyer and Monica Dickens. Copies of *Jamaica Inn* and *Frenchman's Creek* banished from the shelves.

Afternoons sliding on the muddy lacrosse pitch, or in summer endangering life with cricket practice.
Every self-respecting wife of a 'Superior Englishman' has to be familiar with the subtleties of cricket.

Then to expensive exclusive secretarial college in Kensington.

Neither Miranda or Camilla fitted the expected image of this carefully structured programme.

Camilla worked in an art gallery in Cork Street doing very little. She spent her time at parties — drinking and dancing. 'Wine, Men and Song,' she would say, scattering ash as she passed. Camilla didn't have opinions.

Miranda had opinions on everything from the latest plays, housing conditions in Notting Hill Gate, the exploitation of coloured people, the best place to buy lobster, the right time of year to prune fruit trees to how to make chocolate truffles. She worked for a theatrical agency in Shaftesbury Avenue, a job she enjoyed very much.

She belonged to CND and marched with them from Aldermaston. She argued passionately for the abolition of the death penalty and the easing of the laws on homosexuality.

She was arrogantly self-assured, sweeping aside contrary opinions, crushingly abrupt.

Camilla collected people together and descended on the house in Ennismore Gardens, finding only half eaten packets of Ryvita and Weetabix and solid home-made jam with a thin layer of mould.

Florence, Lady DuCane's faithful servant since before the war, kept the storeroom key on a black velvet ribbon round her neck, so that no one could rifle the tins of gammon, jars of consommé, pickled peaches, and the brandied Christmas puddings in their white-clothed bowls ready for steaming.

*   *   *

Having verified that Miranda was a bona fide member of the aristocracy, their mother became determined to find fault with her. 'She'll have to take us as she finds us,' she said. 'We have no time for airs and graces.'

She was suspicious that the wedding was to take place so soon, in barely four week's time, on the last Saturday of July.
'Why are you in such a hurry to get married?' she said. 'Have you got her pregnant?'

Leila had never seen Nick so angry, for one awful suspended moment she thought he was going to hit her. He got up abruptly, scraping his chair harshly on the brown linoleum, and without speaking slammed out of the house.

Leila was shocked by her mother's uncharacteristic behaviour. It was not like her to use such language.
Red patches had appeared on her neck, spreading to her face.

That was before they met Miranda. Nick had agreed to bring her for tea, really to please their father, who distanced himself from the acrimony, and the chill atmosphere of the house, standing in the small vegetable garden smoking his pipe, and pretending to do something with the garden twine.

Leila was embarrassed by her mother's meanness. She wasn't going to put herself out for some hoity-toity slip of a girl. She put out the everyday crinkly red and white check cloth and matching napkins. Plain bread and butter — a glass plate of Peak Frean's Teatime Assorted.

'Haven't we got any cake?' asked Leila.
'We don't need cake,' said her mother. In the end she produced a piece of stale Lyons swiss roll, cut in thin slices on another glass plate.

Miranda took them all by surprise. Delicately lovely in a long black linen coat, her mouth a startling red.

Nick put his arm round her shoulders as he introduced her with such tenderness that Leila spilt the sugar.

Then she had understood why Nick didn't want his mother at the wedding, she hadn't realised before how much he disliked her.

She poured the tea without looking at either of them. Father folded the paper on his knee, and sucked at his unlit pipe. Miranda had beautiful manners, asking about the garden, and where were they thinking of going for their holiday.

'We don't go on Holidays,' said their mother, making it sound a dirty word. 'Life is too short to be frittered away on Holidays.'

Miranda's mother didn't attend the wedding either. She was on a cruise in the Greek Islands.

She didn't approve of her daughter's choice of husband. A young man with no position and no 'class', virtually no money and few prospects. They hadn't even anywhere to live. What a waste of her expensive education!

'I don't know what your father would have had to say,' she said, rummaging in the wardrobe for her sun hat and canvas beach shoes. 'Girls nowadays have no sense of responsibility.'

3

Leila had met Dan at Camilla's Birthday Party.

She had been going out with Heinrich for nearly two years. He was tall, which made her less conscious of her height. She was the same height as Nick, and felt awkward with shorter men.

Miranda said it must be wonderful being so tall, but it just made her feel large and clumsy.

She was not in love with Heinrich. She had never been in love, she thought she would never fall in love.

Sometimes on the narrow divan in his bedroom of the flat he shared with Quentin, he had tried to persuade her to 'let herself go' — pulling at her clothes as he panted and groaned, she tried not to turn her head away from his wet-lipped kisses.

He was a useful escort, and he had a car, a beige Hillman, and could drive her home after their meetings, sparing her the interminable late-night waiting for tubes and buses, and the walk to the far end of Willow Road — where there were no willows, in fact no trees at all, many of the square front gardens concreted over. A road of terraced working-class houses for the respectable men and women who kept the wheels of industry turning — shoulder to shoulder rebuilding their country after long years of war — uncomplaining.

It suited their mother to whom all pleasure was sinful. The wireless frowned on — buttered crumpets — a glass of sherry — even the humble comfort of a hot water bottle occasioned a feeling of guilt.

She sat in her thinly cushioned chair beside the dimly flickering gas fire, unpicking old sweaters to knit socks and scarves. Her scrambled eggs like rock cakes on the brittle toast. Margarine instead of butter — the Sunday piece of topside cooked until it was grey and tough — their father going through the ritual of sharpening the carving knife and cutting thin rubbery slices.

Sharp toilet paper and Lifebuoy soap.

She used no make-up, not even a smidgen of lipstick on her small bloodless mouth.

The bedrooms were always unheated.

It was the first time Leila had been to the house in Ennismore

Gardens. Nick and Miranda had a flat in Frognal, full of plants and flowers and pictures, the small kitchen a jumble — glass jars of herbs and sugar, a red tin of tea, a dish of lemons, strings of onions, bright teacloths printed with roses and recipes, and Miranda in black ballet slippers stirring a large pot of lamb and apricots, adding bits of this and that...

The house in Ennismore Gardens was a pillared mansion in need of a coat of paint, the brass bell polished to a mirrored shine.

Camilla had raided the cellar — uncorking priceless bottles of dusty port and vintage wine, to pour into the bowl of fruit cup, adding a bottle of gin and the remainder of some crème de menthe, decorating the top with slices of orange.

The two boxes of Twiglets she had found in the sideboard hardly seemed adequate, so she had phoned Hamish, one of her latest admirers, and told him to go to the Corner House — or Fortnum's — and get some pies and sausage rolls and stuff...

There were two huge reception rooms. One full of sofas and armchairs, little tables covered with silver nick-nacks, ashtrays, cigarette boxes, candlesticks, framed photographs, piles of books and magazines, a heavy-legged black grand piano with a large bowl of flowers on the lid. Tapestry footstools and Persian rugs, worn through to the backing, scattered over the thick-piled carpet. There was an air of neglected grandeur, the cushions and covers threadbare. The high ceilings were yellowed and there were cracks in the plaster mouldings. The curtains at the tall windows, perished and striped by the sun.

The other room had been cleared for dancing, the carpets rolled back and the furniture pushed against the walls.

It was the first time she had met Lady DuCane. She stood by the marble fireplace in the drawing room, a few coals smoking in the grate. There was a gilt clock on the mantlepiece crawling with gilt trumpet-blowing cherubs and a high ornately decorated mirror with bits of gilt frame missing which reflected the back of Lady DuCane's head, and Leila's anxious face with Heinrich tall and bony behind her in a blue velvet jacket.

Lady DuCane was tall like Camilla with shoulder-length silver-blonde hair in a 1940s pageboy bob. She wore long black crepe with flappy sleeves, and managed to hold a glass and cigarette holder in one hand whilst she shook the guests' hands limply with the other.

'How nice,' she murmured in a languid drawl. 'So pleased you could come,' her washed out blue eyes blankly unsmiling. She found these events incredibly tiresome.

Leila saw Dan first, her heart giving a little leap. He was standing by the drinks table with Jackie — in a figure-hugging plum-coloured low cut velvet evening dress, her dark red hair thick and tumbling. Dan, blond and tanned, dashingly handsome in dinner jacket and frilly shirt front.

The floor was crowded with dancers, some jiving, others cheek to cheek. Miranda and Nick were dancing with eyes closed, in a world of their own. Camilla, dramatic in silver, was jiving with abandon, the long blonde hair falling over her face. It was Camilla who introduced them. She was very tipsy, the sliver sheath strapless and revealing.

She dragged Leila with one hand — her impossibly long nails painted silver, and tottered against Dan, who put his arm round her and kissed her bare shoulder.

'This man you have to watch!' she said. 'Dan, you gorgeous hunk, this is Leila — my sister's husband's sister!' and she chuckled, pretending to push him off as he kissed her neck.
'Better not let Jackie see us!' she said, 'Here,' pulling Leila forward, 'have a go at this English rose, ripe for the picking, as they say... should be some sort of fruit... She has a Hun in tow, but he seems to have lost himself.'

In fact Heinrich was dancing with Jackie. Camilla was swept off by a tall man with thick black hair and a tartan shirt. The music was very loud.

'Like to dance?' asked Dan.

He held her firmly close, their faces touching. His hand burning an imprint on her back. She could hardly breathe. She hadn't believed there was really love at first sight except in romantic novels and Hollywood musicals. When he kissed her she didn't even protest.
He was a married man.

He had met Jackie at a barbecue on Bondi Beach.

The seductive warmth of a summer evening — the softness of the fine white sand — the glow of charcoal — appetizing smells of grilling food — steak and spiced sausage — potato salad — the beer cooling in buckets of iced water. Somebody had brought some vodka.

So many golden bare limbs — revealing bikinis. He had the pick of the girls.

Jackie had sat beside him, feeding him mouthfuls of steak.
Her black bikini top barely decent — a very short black pleated skirt. He had had a lot to drink. He was feeling great. This was the life! He was a lifeguard, spending his days on the beach — riding the tumultuous waves — alert to anybody getting into difficulties in the giantly rearing sea.

Jackie was in Sydney working for a British TV company on a documentary about life in the city.
To Dan she was just another pretty girl, a good lay.

They went to her hotel — one of the luxury ones overlooking the beach — the curtains floated in the breeze — gold taps in the bathroom.

was not something nice girls should enjoy, that the disgusting intimacy involved could only be tolerated in the dutiful confines of marriage when absolutely necessary. It had been so easy to fend off Heinrich, to stop his greedy fumbling.

She hadn't wanted to stop Dan, even though it was wrong, even though he was married, even though she risked getting pregnant.

When he made love to her she was hurled over the exploding foam, swept away by his exuberance and passion.

4

Howard found her on the bathroom floor in a pool of blood. She had not been feeling very well for a while — the cramping pains getting worse, more frequent. She hadn't taken much notice. Things were hectic at work, and she was dreadfully tired.

They had planned to take a holiday in the spring — get away — have a good rest.

Howard fancied Sorrento or Amalfi. He was eager to visit Pompeii. They could take a trip to Capri — should be a good time of year. Or they could go to Madeira. Howard's mother was very fond of Madeira — or Florida, see where the millionaires go. Or perhaps a cruise?

He came home laden with brochures and travel information. It was good to think about the spring.

Winter clutched the garden in its bony grasp. The trees gaunt against the washed out sky. No green shoots yet in the dormant earth — not a single snowdrop — only the bush of winter jasmine by the drawing room window, white with starry flowers.

She had gone to bed early with a book about mosaics. Going into the bathroom to clean her teeth, she felt something break inside her, and she collapsed on the newly carpeted floor, Howard's favourite blue.

They gave her a transfusion, and did various tests. Ovarian cancer. Inoperable. A matter of time.

This then was to be her retribution for destroying the child she should have had — all those years ago — that her own life should end this way.

She had never told Howard. Good, kind Howard.

They had never had a child.
Howard had said it didn't matter, they were fine as they were.

Leila was glad she had had no children.
She hadn't wanted Howard's children.

She had wanted Dan's children. She longed for Dan's child. It would be almost grown up now.

All these years she had resolutely refused to remember those days — shutting out the memories — the shafts of regret — in case they engulfed her.

But now — now she could let them in. Now she could think of Dan — wished she could talk to Miranda, could tell her 'I'm dying...'

She could listen to the voices from so long ago.
'I'm in love with someone else...'

Throwing in the pebble, sending tremors across the calm surface of the water, splitting the reflection of the sun into fragments.

'Nick won't speak to me...'

She had always known Dan would not leave Jackie, he had too

They had breakfast on the balcony, looking down on the swimming pool — bluer than the sea.

There was a spare bathrobe.

She wouldn't leave him alone. She was very persistent.

He was flattered by her attentions. She was good-looking — good in bed — hungrily passionate — refreshingly vulgar — often taking the initiative in a way he was unused to.

She wanted him to go back to London with her.

She was rich and successful. He could be too.

She had a flat in Knightsbridge, and could get him a challenging job in the expanding world of television.

Together they could achieve anything. She had enough ambition for both of them.

She was most persuasive, stopping his objections with her mouth on his.

They were married. It seemed a good idea at the time.

'I would never have met you,' he said to Leila as she lay in his arms. 'If I hadn't married Jackie. I'd still be in Sydney sunning myself on the beach...'., as he kissed her.

She wanted to ask why he couldn't leave Jackie. If Jackie wouldn't divorce him they could always live together.

She shut her mind to her mother's horror, her father's discomfort, to society's disapproval.

Trying to respond to Heinrich's agitated fervour, she had almost come to believe her mother's opinion that 'That sort of thing' much to lose. His tears were for himself, not for her or the baby. He would not give up his smoothly easy sensual life with Jackie for thrift and nappies. The new black Jaguar — 'Isn't it a beaut sweetheart...' — the silk pyjamas, handmade shirts, gold cufflinks, whisky clinking ice, scented women. He had become used to having them all.

5

Leila was still living at home when their father was taken ill. He collapsed at work and was rushed to North End Hospital. She had not yet met Dan.

Heinrich took them to the hospital in his car. Their mother ramrod straight in the back between Nick and Miranda.

Leila had been with her mother the night before, going straight from the office to get there in time for visiting hour between seven and eight.

The hospital was an uninspiring one-storied concrete building, with a flat roof which extended over the front entrance, supported by white poles, the forecourt badly drained, a network of puddles. A notice saying x-rays had a large arrow underneath pointing down a coke path to a square red brick building surrounded by scrappy variegated laurel bushes. It was badly lit.

Their father was in a long ward, the high windows uncurtained. He had looked pretty bad — his small frame shrunken — they had removed his false teeth, and he had difficulty speaking. There was no doctor, or anyone to ask how he was.

Miranda said she thought it was disgraceful that they had not seen a doctor, had received no information whatsoever about his condition.

'I'm sure they know what they're doing,' said their mother huffily.

She objected to Miranda's scarlet nails, her high heels.
'We're visiting a hospital,' she said. 'We're not going to a party.
You didn't have to dress up.'
'Oh for God's sake,' Nick had said.
'And there is no need for bad language,' said their mother.

Miranda said she had come straight from work, that she wasn't
dressed up! There was an uncomfortable silence, and Heinrich
crossed an amber light.

Their mother had disliked both Heinrich and Miranda.

Heinrich because he was German. The fact that he had been
brought up in Tunbridge Wells and spoke impeccable English
made no difference. He was 'foreign', wearing cologne and suede
shoes, greeting her with a little bow. She had to grudgingly admit
that he was very polite, and had an excellent job with the Kroger
Bank in the City, but she still regarded all Germans as the enemy,
also 'foreigners' were known to have excessive fleshly appetites.
She issued dire warnings about men's uncontrollable urges, and
the need to keep oneself 'nice' for one's future husband.

Her dislike of Miranda was more complicated. She came from
a class she was used to looking up to, and resented this 'slip of
a thing' with her painted face and black clothes, being, in some
way, superior to herself. She held extreme views. Nicely brought
up girls didn't have views. She dismissed other people's long held
beliefs and opinions with a silencing gesture of a red-tipped hand.
She had the effrontery to criticise the government — the royal
family! Now she was preparing to criticise the hospital.

She also wished Nick would not embrace her so ardently in
public. It wasn't decent.
Their father seemed to be asleep when they arrived. His breathing
shallow and wheezing. He was a dreadful colour. As they stood by
the bed, mutely distressed, a crackling sister appeared, her white
frilly cap attached to her head with kirby grips, a gold fob watch
pinned to her pocket.

She said she would like to speak to the 'wife' and perhaps 'the son', her eyes travelling from Nick to Heinrich and back again.

Nick and their mother followed her out of the ward, and into an office at the back of the hall.

They came out, almost immediately, pale and shocked.
'So? What did they say?' asked Miranda.
'He's dying,' said Nick. 'Lung cancer.'

They stood in a little group in the dingy hallway.

Their mother pressed a handkerchief against her mouth.
'Who says he's dying?' demanded Miranda. 'Have they done tests?'
'She said there was no point,' said Nick.
'You should insist on seeing a doctor,' said Miranda.
'Don't make a fuss,' said their mother. 'They know what they're doing.'
'How do we know they know what they're doing?' said Miranda. 'Can't we get a second opinion?' She turned to Heinrich. 'We can ask for a second opinion, can't we?'
'Yes of course,' said Heinrich. 'It's always a good thing to have a second opinion.'
'I'm sure they know what they are doing,' said their mother.

The sister reappeared, letting the swing doors clash together behind her. 'Come along!' she said. 'I can't have people standing about blocking the doorway.'
'Are you sure that nothing can be done for Mr Thompson?' said Miranda.

The sister regarded her with disdain. 'If you have been told there is nothing to be done,' she said, as she swished past them into her office, 'then there is nothing to be done.'

'What a cow!' said Miranda. 'How do we go about getting a second opinion?'

Their mother's friend Ivy was waiting at home with the kettle on — piously anticipating the thrill of bad news.

'I don't think you should question the doctors,' she said. 'They know what they are doing. When I was at the Hall, nobody would have questioned the doctor, not even Her Ladyship...'

Ivy had worked for Lord and Lady Dartford at Beardsley Hall. All her conversations were interspersed with anecdotes from those wonderful years. 'I rely on you Ivy,' Her Ladyship had said. 'We don't know what we would do without you!'

She glared at Miranda, who made her feel inferior, disapproving of the crimson lips and nails, the pale silk legs. Her Ladyship had never painted her nails.

Miranda said 'Rubbish!' and lit a cigarette.

'You young people think you know everything,' said Ivy, trying to sound indulgent. Little Miss Know All — who did she think she was, laying down the law, telling other people what to do.
'Who are we to question a doctor's judgement?'
'When someone's life is at stake,' said Miranda, 'one questions everyone.'

Heinrich said he had a friend he could ask about getting a second opinion, and went to telephone.

'Her Ladyship had complete faith in her doctor,' said Ivy. 'She wouldn't have dreamt of having a second opinion.'

Leila was afraid Miranda would say something about her family's doctor, an austerely correct person with consulting rooms in Harley Street, but she just crossed her long silky legs and blew smoke at the ceiling.

'Gwyneth doesn't like people smoking in here,' said Ivy, struggling to keep her voice pleasant.

She sat with her heavy legs slightly apart — the tan and green wool skirt stretched wrinkling across her thighs. She wore thick lisle stockings and an awful felt hat like their mother's pulled closely over her ears.

Miranda removed her gaze from the ceiling and looked at her. 'This is quite delicious tea,' she said, 'and such pretty china!'

Leila wanted to laugh. She didn't dare look at Ivy. Perhaps that would shut her up for a bit.

Nick had gone with their mother into the kitchen. They seemed to be arguing. Then she heard Heinrich's voice joining them, and prayed that his friend had been at home, and that it had been possible to arrange something.

So it had really been Miranda who had save their father's life. He did not have lung cancer, just very severe pleurisy and water on the lung — several pints of liquid were removed, and he was transferred to another hospital where he slowly recovered.

Their mother's attitude towards Miranda didn't change. The temporary truce caused by their father's illness was soon over, and they ceased to visit.

'Pride comes before a fall,' her mother said, referring to Miranda's cool composure, her conviction that she was always right.

Nick said his mother was narrow-minded and ignorant.

They quarreled about Miranda.
How she would have gloated to know that Miranda had broken his heart.

6

When Leila moved out, their mother was sure it was Miranda's idea. She was a bad influence.

'No mother,' said Leila, 'it was nothing to do with Miranda. I just think it's about time I left home. I should be more independent.'

Of course it was really because of Dan. Her mother must never know about Dan.

'Fancy wanting to leave your nice home,' said Ivy. 'Silly girl. I hope that Miranda hasn't put you up to it. She'll come to no good — flaunting herself around!' She heaved herself up in the low hard chair and accepted another slice of 'next door's' fruit cake. It was rumoured that 'next door' was 'carrying on' with No. 80's lodger! 'Stuck up little Madam,' she added, and their mother nodded in agreement.

Leila was glad to leave the comfortless house — cold and carpetless, except for the two brown striped mats in front of the fireplaces, with their empty black grates and shiny brown tiles — the calendar of the Lake District in the hall — the skirting boards dark brown — the walls a sludgy brown — the linoleum — just BROWN. The brass pot of artificial flowers on the table in the dining room — faded paper blooms on green wire stalks.

Her bedroom so cramped, it was difficult to do anything in it except go to bed — the cheap plywood wardrobe taking up the rest of the space.

'Nothing like home comforts,' said Ivy, wiping the crumbs from her mouth with a freshly ironed handkerchief. 'Don't know when you are well off. I expect you'll soon be back.'
Her mother said nothing, pursing the thin bloodless lips in unspoken disapproval. It was a good thing she had never met Giselle, who was certainly not what a *nice* girl should be.

It had been a piece of luck that Giselle, who worked in the records office, should have been looking for someone to share her flat just at the right moment.

After Leila met Dan, she knew she must leave home.

It had happened so suddenly — at first she tried to resist — to hold back the torrent of emotion that threatened to engulf her, but it was no use. She couldn't say no to Dan. She didn't want to say no to Dan. She could never say no to Dan.

She was filled with joy and wonder that he should love her.

She was reluctant at first, to go to the flat in Cadogan Court — to lie in Jackie's bed, with its quilted satin headboard and slippery peach pink sheets — the bathroom royal blue and gold — the kitchen a gleaming array of stainless steel.

Jackie was frequently away on business trips. A few days in Aberdeen, a week in Stockholm, overnight in Paris, working late in the office.

Dan was persuasive and insistent. There could be nothing shameful in their love for one another. It was something special. There was no use trying to fight it. It was stupid not to use the flat. Jackie would never know.

They always entered the building separately. There was always a porter on duty in the foyer, in a long bottle green overcoat and cockaded top hat, opening doors with a flourish.

'Good morning Madam.' — 'Good evening Madam.' — 'Good night Madam.'

Leila was sure they knew why she was there, and who she was visiting. They knew she was not a resident. She crossed the silent thickly carpeted floor, trying to walk tall, holding in her stomach, trying to suppress her guilt.

Of course he had realised his marriage to Jackie had been a huge mistake. The lucrative, exciting job had never materialised, partly because Jackie didn't want to risk him becoming financially independent. She might lose her hold over him. As it was he enjoyed their affluent life-style, had come to expect it.

He had a job three afternoons a week at a private health club in Lancaster Gate, frequented by the bored wives of businessmen, who with a few lengths of gulping breaststroke hoped to retain their youthful firmness, and whittle away the extra inches gained by consuming too many coffees and Danish Pastries, too many cocktails and savoury snacks, so that they could stroll the sunlit beaches of fashionable resorts, and still feel the men's eyes on them.

The clientele increased considerably after he had started working there. He was in great demand for coaching and advice. Supporting and guiding flaccid bodies with his strong brown arms.

Unease nibbled Leila's heart. She didn't like the thought of him with all those women — predatory and cunning. He was so good looking.

She told herself not to be silly. After all, it was her he was in bed with, taking her breath away with his kisses.

Jackie was more forthright. 'And don't think this job gives you Carte Blanche to screw as many of the bitches as you want,' she had said.

Leila lying in his arms — his hands straying — strong brown hands. She thought of Jackie in this bed — her pale skin against his golden tan — the blond head buried in Jackie's auburn curls — murmuring words of love — the jealous nibbling tore the edge of her heart into strips.

Dan said Jackie was a selfish cow — incapable of love — that their relationship was almost platonic.

Leila wanted to believe him — she knew it wasn't really true. Whenever she had seen them together Jackie had certainly not been cold and unloving. She wished she could believe him.

7

It had been a long wet summer. A summer of umbrellas and macs, cardigans and ruined shoes. They spent as much time as they could together. She did not go on holiday. she could not bear to leave London if Dan were there.

'Why on earth don't you go away?' said Miranda. 'He might find he can't live without you.'

Or he might find someone else. She shivered at the thought. No, she wanted to be near him as much as possible.

They went boating on the Serpentine — Dan's blond hair plastered dark by the rain — water accumulating in the bottom of the boat. He rowed with effortless ease, fooling around, making the boat spin in circles.

They squelched across the park — sitting briefly on waterlogged seats — taking refuge in steamy cafes.

Jackie and Dan were to go for three weeks to Portugal. Jackie had friends who had a villa on the Algarve, with its own pool. They were all going together.

'I'd rather go with you,' said Dan. 'Cheer up, sweetheart — I'll soon be back.'
It had seemed interminable. She tried to shut the image of him making love to Jackie from her mind — lying by the still blue waters of the pool in the heat of the unclouded sun — their tanned bodies entwined.

He came back exuding health and vitality, lean and bronzed. He said he had missed her — couldn't wait to see her — couldn't wait to hold her.

His eyes had been so blue.

8

Miranda arrived with a pint of milk and a sliced white loaf, her eyes bruised from lack of sleep. She wore a black polo neck and black drainpipe trousers.

She stood by the bed and Leila tried to smile.

'Whatever's the matter?' she asked. 'You look absolutely awful.'

Leila gave up trying to smile and told her about the abortion.
'Oh God!' said Miranda. 'Oh my God, Leila! You could go septic. Should we call a doctor?'
'No... No!' said Leila, her voice sharp with alarm. 'We can't — I mean — its illegal — they could send me to prison.'
'Oh rubbish!' said Miranda. 'How could they?'

She moved restlessly around the room, picking things up and putting them down, angry and helpless.

'For Christ's sake!' she said. 'How dare Daniel leave you in this mess. Do you want me to phone him?'
Oh, no!' said Leila. 'Jackie might be there.'
'Not very likely at 11 o'clock on a Thursday morning,' said Miranda.
'I don't want to worry him.' said Leila.
'Honestly Leila! Don't be so feeble! Why shouldn't he be worried? Of course he should be worried!'
Leila felt the tears clogged behind her eyes. She was careful not to move her legs.
'Please God let the bleeding stop,' she prayed. 'Please God forgive me. Let the bleeding stop. Why hadn't Dan phoned?'

Miranda brought her tea and poached eggs on toast.

'You'd better try and eat something,' she said, fetching cushions from the sofa to prop her up.
'I suppose Jackie doesn't know about you and Daniel.'
'Oh, no!' said Leila. 'He can't tell her. He couldn't bear to hurt her.'
'Nonsense!' said Miranda. 'Jackie's as tough as old boots. He's probably too scared.'
'Oh, no!' said Leila. 'Really! He's afraid she might to something stupid.'
'Oh come off it!' said Miranda. 'Cut her wrists? Take an overdose? Stick her head in the oven? You must be joking! More likely to stick a knife in his heart. What a swine! I'd like to kick those wonderful white teeth in. Honestly, Leila, you can't really believe that rubbish.'

No, thought Leila. No, I don't really believe it, but I want to believe it. Otherwise it means he doesn't love me enough to leave her, and I don't want to know that. I don't want to know it — and yet I do know it — I know it already, and I have committed this monstrous act knowing it. He hadn't even phoned.

She took a mouthful of tea, grateful for its warmth.
She was so cold.

'Try and eat,' said Miranda. 'Are you sure we shouldn't call a doctor?'

Leila shook her head, and forced herself to eat a mouthful of toast, tears blocking her throat.

'I have these pills to take,' she said. ' I expect it will stop soon.'

Why hadn't Dan phoned? She loved him so much. Surely he could have phoned.

Miranda stayed until it was dark, holding her hand and trying to comfort her — her own sadness weighing her down.

She had taken a few days off work to try and sort things out, but Nick refused to see her. He had gone to stay with friends.

'He won't speak to me,' she said. 'Nick won't speak to me.'
Nick didn't want to speak to her either.

She rang him at the office and said she would like to meet — have a chat.
There was a long pause, and then he said 'I'm rather busy'.
Leila said she thought it was important, and he said 'Nothing is important'.

They met in the Bell and Whistle, not the best place to have a personal discussion — crammed with city-suited brokers and jobbers from the Stock Exchange, noisy and jocular, the air thick with bonhomie and cigar smoke.

'Miranda wants to talk things over,' she said.

He took his glasses off and pushed back the lock of hair — he didn't look at her — replacing them carefully.

'There is nothing to talk about,' he said, his voice hardly audible in the hubbub.
'I'm sure you could work something out,' she said.
'There is nothing to work out,' he said. He had ordered whisky, drinking it in one gulp, placing his empty glass with studied care on the cork mat in front of him.
'You can't just let it happen,' she said.
'Why not?' he said. 'Why not? What else is there to do...?' His voice cracked.
'She's confused,' said Leila. 'I'm sure she doesn't want anything drastic to happen. Really she doesn't.'
He didn't answer.
'Do you want another drink?' he said.
'No thanks. Look — please won't you talk to her? There's no harm

in talking to her.'

'I can't,' he said. 'I can't talk to her...' He was struggling to control his face. He removed his glasses again, wiping them on his handkerchief, pushing back the lock of hair.

'Look,' he said with an effort. 'I know you want to help, but there is nothing you can do — nothing...'

His desperate unhappiness was almost visible, she could feel it touch her. He was so difficult to get close to. When he was a child he had never cried when he hurt himself — falling and twisting his ankle, he had been sick with the pain, but had not made a sound, or shed a tear. She had run to fetch her mother who had scolded him for tearing his trousers.

He had always kept his feelings to himself — self-contained, quietly determined. Only with Miranda had she ever seen him show any emotion. His love for her transformed him.

9

Their childhood had been cheerless and inhibited. The war years dark with blackout and enforced austerity.

They grew vegetables in the front and back gardens, cultivating every available space, and exchanged cauliflowers and cabbages for eggs from a neighbour who kept chickens. Frugality — pinching and scraping — suited their mother's thrifty nature. She enjoyed eeking out the rations, counting the clothing coupons, allocating the few sweets.

They had both done well at school, going to the respective boys and girls grammar schools in Enfield.

Dutiful and hard-working — trudging up the long dismal street, a piece of bread and red sticky stuff that passed for jam for tea — they did their homework at the table in the icy front room, heated in exceptionally cold weather by a smelly oil stove. It was cold even in summer — two ugly china figures in ball dresses on the windowsill.

They were in their early teens when the war ended.

The factory where their father worked changed from producing munitions to processing fertilizer.

They rebelled against the boredom of Sundays, refusing to accompany their mother to church, wandering around Enfield looking in the windows of shops, and going to the ABC Tearooms for a sloppy cup of tea and india-rubber bun.

Leila had hated going to church. Their mother in the awful felt hat — even in summer, when she wore cotton mesh gloves, carrying her Prayer Book against her chest. The purple-nosed, purple-handed Vicar, droning on in the pulpit about God and Sin and Brotherly Love! She would sit hands neatly folded, saying all her 'Times Tables' backwards and forwards, and as many French verbs as she could remember.

Their father never came to church. He stayed at home with his pipe and *Sunday Dispatch*.

'He works hard enough during the week,' said their mother. 'He needs a rest on Sundays.'

Nick started being late home from school — going out after he had finished his homework.
He bought a trumpet and went to a friend's house in Enfield to practise. He saved to buy a record player, and played records of Louis Armstrong and King Oliver in his bedroom. Their mother was horrified. Jazz music, associated with drink and drugs and BLACK people and Sex! What did he want to play a trumpet for? He should be concentrating on his School Certificate. He wouldn't pass the Civil Service Exams if he didn't work hard, and then what would he do? What good would a trumpet do him then? She nagged and scolded, but Nick took no notice, finishing

his tea, fetching his trumpet case from upstairs and going off into the twilight.

They both passed the Civil Service Exams. They both had good *pensionable* jobs.

Nick came in later and later. Sometimes he didn't come in at all. He played with a band in jazz clubs in Soho! Leila never went to hear him. She knew little about music, going to the occasional concert. Handel's 'Messiah', Tchaikovsky's '1812' Overture, the First Piano Concerto. She knew nothing about jazz.

*   *   *

Nick spent two years in the RAF doing his National Service,. Excluded from flying because he wore glasses, he was trained as a radar operator.
Stationed in the windy expanses of Norfolk, he was not sent abroad so he could still manage to get back to London as often as he could to play gigs with his friends.

There were enough musicians on the base to get a band together, and they became quite famous, playing at parties and for the weekly hops in the village hall. Girls came in by the bus load, chattering and giggling, in Jane Russell sweaters and spindly heels, waists widely, tightly belted, newly shampooed hair.

There were refreshments — orange squash and ginger beer, and plates of petit beurre biscuits.
Bottles of beer and vermouth were smuggled in to spike the drinks. The girls were crazy for uniforms. The back of the hall was lined by embracing couples, tripping over each other in the darkness.

Nick did not go with the girls, he preferred to play his trumpet. If he went out with any girls he kept it to himself. He never mentioned any girls.

Their mother was pleased at his seeming lack of interest in girls. She was deeply suspicious of girls, particularly pretty ones. She hoped Nick would soon settle down and stop playing his trumpet and smoking cigarettes. She liked the idea of his staying at home, he didn't want to get himself mixed up with one of these flighty modern girls with their faces covered in muck.

She was not so happy about Leila's lack of enthusiasm for the young men she met — she didn't want her daughter being an Old Maid. A woman ought to be married, even if she did have to put up with the indignities of married life.

10

Dan had come out of the bathroom to answer the phone, a towel round his waist.

Picking up the receiver and turning away from her towards the window — lowering his voice. 'Hi! No, not now — perhaps tomorrow. OK, I'll call you. No, everything's fine. Yes — of course.'

She had tried not to listen, deafened by her own heartbeat. 'Private coaching,' he said. 'I seem to be in great demand. Its good, it means I earn a bit extra.'

She wondered what these extra coaching sessions really entailed.

How could she think such things? Didn't she have enough proof of his love for her?

Wet summer became wet autumn — the sky a solid block of grey, darkening to winter. The wind blowing the leaves from the trees in flurries of sodden brown to stick to their feet.

And then she realised she might be pregnant.
Her old school friend Sara — she couldn't remember her other

name — had got herself pregnant. She had been a nurse at the Highgate Hospital, and had got involved with a medical student. He had refused to marry her.

She had tried the usual remedies — gin and hot baths — to no avail. She couldn't afford an abortion.

Miranda was fiercely angry. 'One rule for the rich and one for the poor as usual.'

Leila said perhaps she hadn't wanted an abortion —

'I don't suppose she wants to give it away either,' said Miranda.

Sara's parents wouldn't help her. They were horrified, had forbidden her to come home.

Miranda asked DeeDee and Buzz if they would take her in until she had the baby.

'Their house is big enough,' she said to Leila. 'They won't even notice she's there.'

Leila had been so sorry for her. It must have been terrible having to cope alone, rejected by her lover and her parents. They couldn't even knit little garments for her — turning sadly away from prams, children playing on swings.

Sara hadn't seen the baby when it was born — a little girl. She was never to see her, or give her a name. She was taken away to go to her adoptive parents. She was told it was better that way. Make a clean break.

It had been an unforgettable bereavement.

Sara had taken a nursing post in Toronto, and she and Leila had gradually lost touch.

Now it was her turn.

Maybe she was just late. It had happened before.

It was Christmas. Not the miraculous snowed, tinselled Christmas of story books and films, but the dreary, mild, wet of a London Christmas. The pavements dirty and draggled, people hurrying, heads down against the wind, clutching their bags and parcels. The wheels of buses spattering their legs with oily water.

The office was strung with sagging paperchains. Everybody drank too much at the Christmas Party, sweet sherry, beer and whisky, and ate too many of somebody's home-made mince pies and tinned salmon and cucumber sandwiches. Leila was sick. There was an artificial Christmas tree in the foyer where Geraldine sat at the reception desk, smiling her meaningless bright smile.

Dan and Jackie were spending Christmas with her parents in Leeds. He would not be able to get in touch with her whilst they were away.

He had bought her a large bottle of Ma Griffe perfume. She couldn't really get him anything — Jackie would be suspicious.

They had lunch in the Queensway before he went to the Club.
The fear of her pregnancy a growing certainty with each day that passed.
She couldn't remember what they ate.

She had decided to wait until after Christmas to tell Dan she was pregnant — by then she would be completely sure. At first she thought, when I tell him, he will surely leave Jackie. He will want our child, created by our love — we shall be together.
She had not really believed that. No, she had not. Of course she had not.

He said he would much rather spend Christmas with her.
'We could have such fun, sweetheart,' he had said, eating whatever he was eating. 'At least Jackie's mum is a great cook, and there are plenty of pubs!'

His eyes smiled at her, and he reached over and patted her hand.

'I'll have to yank Jackie out for a walk on the moors — if it's not pouring with rain. It's always raining in this Goddam country.'

Leila tried to smile, to hide her misery. She would have to go home for Christmas, sit in front of the badly focused television screen, hoping she would not be sick, that her mother would not suspect anything. There would be chicken, dry and sinewy, and a small 'shop bought' Christmas pudding full of candied peel. Ivy would come for tea and eat sandy Christmas cake, and talk about her Christmas at the Hall.

Her Ladyship had always given her Yardley's Lavender Soap, and a box of Meltis Berryfruits.

Her mother would give her something sensible. Woollen gloves, a pair of 30 denier stockings, perhaps a diary. They had always had sensible presents — pencil cases, handkerchiefs, a new bicycle torch...

She had bought her father a book on gardening, and her mother some linen teacloths, bright like Miranda's, with poppies and cornflowers and sheaves of corn.

Of course Nick and Miranda would not be there.

Giselle was having a drinks party — the living room crushed with people. Giselle — shrilly flirtatious, hanging over her American boyfriend Marvin, gold chains swinging in her cleavage.

Cherry, knees bulging below her short skirt, her prominent teeth giving her a permanent look of surprise, wriggled coyly as she passed the drinks.

Giselle had bought paper cups and plates, which she had scattered with cheese biscuits and crisps — a fair amount already trodden into the carpet.

There were several Americans — all middle-aged — paunchy and bullet-headed, wearing unseasonal seersucker and cotton plaid jackets.

Margot, busty and bouncy, who always felt it her duty to jolly people along, chortling lewdly, attempted to jive in the small space by the record player. She was wearing a button-through dress which refused to stay buttoned. There were others who Leila didn't know. A serious couple who sat together on the sofa, paper cups on their knees, not speaking — a blonde in red with scuffed high heels.

One of the Americans approached Leila — he had thick glasses. He was short, barely reaching her shoulder — he had dandruff. He was 'in Hamburgers'. 'Can't resist a big sassy woman,' he said. 'You can keep your skinny girls, nothing to get hold of.' Lucky skinny girls, thought Leila, trying unsuccessfully to back away — the room was too crowded to back anywhere. He started to tell her about the art of making Hamburgers.

His name was Dexter. He was going to Milan for the New Year. 'We're looking to open outlets there, great possibilities, all those moped riding Itis. Meals on wheels!' He seemed to find this excessively amusing, swaying back and forth.

'Do you get it? Meals on wheels... Itis on their mopeds! And are they greedy for American dollars.' Saliva gummed the corners of his mouth. 'We should get together when I get back Honey, we could take in some *night* life. We could have a swell time.' He put his hand on the upper part of her arm, giving it a squeeze — spreading his fingers.

There was a buzzing in her head. How was she to get rid of this odious person? She smiled feebly, aware of the potential child within her — Dan's handsome face, his strong brown arms. Oh God! What should she do?

She took advantage of a small gap in the crowd — pushing her way through — sitting down on the divan — which was her bed, spread with Giselle's fringed Indian shawl.

There was already a couple lying among the cushions, their clothes in disarray, his hand in the girl's blouse.

Dan was with Jackie at her firm's smart Christmas Dance at Grosvenor House. Swirls of colour and perfume, jewels and furs. Dancing to a real orchestra in black tails. She imagined Dan holding Jackie close — the plum-coloured velvet gown — her creamy shoulders. When she closed her eyes the image remained, taunting her.

*   *   *

It had been difficult to meet after Christmas. Jackie had no imminent business trips, and Leila could not tell Dan about the baby over the phone. She had to see him. She said it was important.

They arranged a meeting at the Flying Fox in Seymour Street. Leila took the Central Line from Bank to Marble Arch. She arrived first, and sheltered from the rain in the doorway of a hairdressers. She didn't like going into pubs on her own.

When she saw him coming, she felt the usual shock of recognition, the quickened heartbeat — his collar turned up against the rain, his hair wetly curly.

'I think I'm pregnant,' she said.
'Jesus! Are you sure?' He took a long pull at his pint of beer, and wiped his mouth with the back of his hand.
'Pretty sure,' she said. The smell of her sherry made her nauseous — her breasts painful and heavy.
'Have you done anything?' he said.
'Not really,' she said. What had she expected? That he would be overjoyed? That he would rush home and ask Jackie for a divorce? She swallowed, trying to control the tears and rising sickness.

He didn't look at her. 'Oh Jesus!' he said again. 'Look! I'll ask around — Jackie had some tablets which were very effective — I'll try and get hold of some.'

Leila wanted to cry out — 'But it's our baby!' — 'You don't want to get rid of our baby!' — 'You can't want to get rid of our baby!'...

Dan looked at his watch. 'I'll have to go,' he said.
'Jackie will be home by 7.30 and I'd better be there. She thinks I'm having it off with someone at the Club. I'll call you...'

11

The nurse came in with more flowers — freesias and fern.

'My, it's like a florists in here!' she said. 'You have got some lovely flowers Mrs Dewsbury.' She handed Leila the card that came with them, a Get Well wish in silver lettering. She let it fall on the sheet — suddenly sickened by the sweet smell of the freesias.
Howard picked it up. 'It's from Dotty and Ken,' he said. 'That's nice isn't it dear?'

Leila didn't really like Dotty and Ken. They ran the Conservative bazaar every November, and expected her to man a stall. Last year they had raffled a bag of golf clubs. They were keen golfers.

'You ought to play,' Dotty had said to Leila. 'It's wonderful exercise — really keeps you fit.'
Dotty bulged in all the wrong places — firm fat — her short suede jacket accentuating the heavy hips. Ken carried his stomach as if stuffed for a pantomime.

'Very kind,' she murmured, fighting exhaustion, nausea and pain to smile encouragingly at Howard's anxious face.

She didn't like being involved with the Conservative bazaar. She didn't really think she liked the Conservatives much — but it would not do to say so. Everybody in Howard's world — their world — was Conservative.

She yearned suddenly for Miranda. She would have been contemptuous of Leila's acceptance of her husband's opinions. Caustically dismissive of self-righteousness and hypocrisy.
'Their education makes them more able to fiddle their taxes,' she would say. 'They think drinking too much brandy is somehow superior to drinking too much beer. They're disgusting!'

Leila had always respected Howard's views — agreeing politely when she didn't agree. She had never had the courage to disagree. She hadn't wanted to upset him.

She missed Miranda — the thin black figure with the tense white face and gash of scarlet lipstick — her fierce championing of the underdog, the displaced, the needy.

Leila remembered her anguished with fear that Nick might be involved in the trouble over Suez. He could be called up. He had only recently completed his National Service.

'No... No, My Darling!' he had said, taking her hand clenched on the table and holding it in both of his. 'They won't want me — certainly not to do any fighting.' He kissed her cheek. 'I promise you I won't have to go.'

It had been over before it had started.
But there were other unhealed sores breaking open — no end to tyranny and oppression.
Black-edged newspapers reported the crushing of Hungary. Bodies sprawled in the street, on the pavements, hanging out of windows, wherever they had died.

The foolish who had glimpsed freedom and rushed towards it. Halted, hungry and tattered by grim bare huts — by queues for soup, bitter porridge, rough bread. Huddled against the cold, desperate for papers which would open the doors to a new life.

Wondering if it would have been better to have stayed in their homes, stuck it out, hoping that one day things would improve, that the Russian troops in their high boots and swinging greatcoats would go home to the vastness of their own country.

Leila had gone with Heinrich to hear the whirlwind Red Army Choir, who came once a year and filled the Albert Hall with tumultuous sound to wild applause.

This same army had stormed and ravaged — tearing the heart from the remnants of their enemy — enduring the searing cold, the hunger and bloodshed, merciless to those who had caused their suffering.

The West had turned away determinedly unseeing.
The spark of rebellious hope snuffed out by blind lumbering tanks.

Miranda appalled, shaking her Red Cross tin in pubs and cafes and cinema queues, wherever she happened to be, pleading for help for those brave abandoned people. She had wanted to go — to help.

'We have to do something,' she said. 'Surely we could do something?'

One of her old school friends had hired a plane and was flying people out. 'Perhaps I could help in the refugee camps.'

Nick dissuaded her. He could not go with her. She spoke no German. There was nothing she could do that was not being done already.

12

Leila wished she had stood up for things she believed in like Miranda. Always worrying what people might say. She was a coward.

If she hadn't been such a coward she would never have had the abortion.

The pills had given her backache and made her sick, but that was all.

She took the Underground from Mansion House, changing at Charing Cross for Elephant and Castle.

She had had to leave work early to get to the doctor's — Doctor Lieberman — at 5.15. Dan had arranged it all.

She said she had a dental appointment. Moyra was not pleased — they were very busy — somebody had mislaid a file — everybody in the office was looking for it.

It had nothing to do with Leila. She worked for the Director and didn't have to ask Moyra's permission to go to the dentist. All the same Moyra protested. She made it clear that she considered Leila's going to the dentist in the middle of a crisis most inconsiderate.

'It has to be found, you know,' she said. 'We shall all have to stay until it is found...'

The sky had been overcast all day — a fine persistent drizzle covering everything with an inescapable blanket of dampness. It was beginning to get dark when she left the office in Queen Victoria Street — lighted windows in the surrounding buildings, squares of familiarity. Even though it was still too early for the rush hour, she was jostled by hurrying people — the points of umbrellas — sharp corners of briefcases. They were intent on getting their trains to their various suburban havens — their homes, suppers, children, perhaps to finish the row they had started this morning. Perhaps even to an illicit meeting — snatched pleasure...

The surgery was a short walk from the station. There was a church on the corner, the gravestones toppling and broken. The houses in the street solid and respectable Victorian red brick — now rundown and neglected.

There was a brass plate on the gatepost — Dr Lieberman and a lot of letters after his name, obviously a well qualified abortionist — a lighted globe over the door.

A yew tree overhung the path, quietly sinister in the fading light, it had shed its needles on the gravel — a spiky brown carpet.

Her feet were cold, her hands hot, her heart thudding. She had difficulty breathing. She was tempted to turn and run.

She had hoped, right up to the last minute, that Dan would phone and tell her not to go through with it, that he wanted their baby, that he loved her, that he would leave Jackie. What a fool she had been.

There was an elderly woman in the waiting room with badly swollen legs. She wore broken down bedroom slippers and a grey coat with only one button, hanging from a thread.

There were old copies of the *Illustrated London News* and *Punch* on a scratched table and a notice saying No Smoking.

The nurse, a solid woman in a white coat over a yellow jumper and brown skirt, came in holding some papers. She gave the woman a prescription.
'Doctor will see you again on Thursday,' she said. 'Take the tablets *before* your food.'

Leila had shut the rest of the ordeal away — this was one door she did not ever wish to open again.

Dr Lieberman had bushy eyebrows and needed a shave.
She had been allowed to stay on the couch in the side room for nearly an hour. The nurse had brought a cup of strong, stewed tea. She avoided looking at Leila — grimly hostile.

She didn't speak.

Leila was filled with shame and overwhelming grief. Somehow she had got to the end of the street, and sat on a seat outside the church, welcoming the soft touch of the rain, keeping her feet carefully together, until she saw a taxi.

Dan had given her the money for the abortion in the Pink Parrot coffee bar off Sloane Square.

Jackie was at home. He had slipped out on the pretext of getting cigarettes.

They sat opposite each other at the round pink formica-topped table, on spiky pink metal-legged chairs.

She was lumpen and sick with misery — the smell of the coffee made her queasy.

He said he couldn't stay long — Jackie would wonder what he was doing.

Leila noted the new red silk tie — the sheepskin jacket. She longed for him to reach out and take her hand. Could he not see how much she loved him? Surely their love was more important that all the material things Jackie could give him — did Jackie love him? And Dan? Who did he love?

She watched the strong tanned hands take a cigarette from the packet and light it.

'Smoke?' he asked, avoiding her eyes. She shook her head. She didn't smoke, he knew she didn't smoke, she had never smoked.

They stood hesitating on the pavement. Taxis were pulling up outside the Royal Court — so many couples, groups of people, talking, laughing, serious and silent, searching for change, for tickets.

'Well...' he said. 'So long, sweetheart...' They didn't touch. He moved with long easy strides. He didn't look back. She watched him go, following him in her mind up Sloane Street, into the shiny entrance of the flats — the bronzed doors of the lift, the short walk up the thick maroon carpet to 15A.

Jackie waiting for him — elegant — the lustrous auburn hair curling down her creamy neck, wearing one of the many lace negligées that crammed the mirrored wardrobes, lying back on the wide bed, kicking off her satin slippers.

Oh, God! Don't think of it. How could she bear to think of it?

She had put the long white envelope containing the money in her handbag. She didn't like to think how he had got it. It was a lot of money. He could hardly have asked Jackie for it. She was being knocked by the crowds.

Marvin was at the flat, lying on the sofa drinking whisky. Giselle came out of the bedroom tying the sash of her shiny salmon pink dressing gown. She sat on the sofa beside Marvin, drinking from his glass, giggling. Giggling didn't suit Giselle, she was a cold schemer. Men paid well for her 'favours'. The dressing gown came open showing the tops of her stockings, her suspenders.

'We're just going out to eat,' she said. 'How about coming along? Dex is dying to meet you again. I could phone him.'

Marvin was stroking her hip, the fleshy fingers exploring...

Leila muttered about forgetting to post a letter. She put her coat on and went out into the rain, walking all the way to Finchley Road. When she got back they would be gone.

13

Howard stayed all the afternoon.
He sat by her bed and watched golf on the television.
She drifted in and out of sleep.
'Is there anything you need dear?' he asked, as he prepared to leave. 'I'll bring Mother tomorrow afternoon.'
Leila didn't really want to see Howard's mother. She was a dreadful snob — in the old musquash coat impregnated with stale perfume and cigarette smoke, the mascara-matted eyelashes, her thin lips a cyclamen mauve.

They had never been comfortable with each other.

Leila knew she thought her dull and unsophisticated — deplored her lack of class, her inability to be smart, her lapses as a hostess, the fallen soufflés and paper napkins, her childlessness.
The least she could do would be to provide Howard with a son!

She had never forgiven Howard's father for failing to rise above the lowest rung of the legal ladder. She had fancied herself as the wife of a QC.

And Howard had failed to get into Oxford.
She had had to make do with artificial pearls and only one proper maid.

Miranda's mother had had real pearls, and rubies set in diamonds which she wore as if they were trinkets from Woolworth's. Travelling first class to the Aegean — the battered much-labelled leather luggage engraved with gold initials. She only drank champagne cocktails, picking at breast of pheasant and passion fruit sorbet, smoking Turkish cigarettes in a long ebony holder, wearing whatever came to hand, expensively dowdy in pre-war chic.

They would have had nothing to say to one another.

Later she realised that she had known that there was something wrong between Nick and Miranda, long before Miranda had told her she was in love with someone else. There was a tension between them — a subtle withdrawing of contact. Nick looked as if he had not slept, grey and drawn.

It was early in the summer, the beginning of June.

Dan had gone with Jackie to Monte Carlo to a Festival of European Television Drama. They were away for a week. How could a week be so long?

It was unexpectedly sunny and warm. Warm enough to discard raincoats and tentatively bring out last year's summer frocks.

Leila bought herself a pair of white sandals, hoping the good weather would last until after Dan got back. She thought about him constantly — a churning mixture of jealousy and desire.

Miranda got tickets for 'Candide'. She often got complimentary tickets working at the Agency, usually for obscure plays and productions which were not doing very well.

They had been to 'Tales of Hoffman'. The gondola had got stuck half way across the stage leaving the singers open-mouthed, swaying dangerously as it restarted with a series of jerks. They had lowered the curtain. Also 'The Magic Flute' in which the flautist appeared to have got the hiccups...

Miranda had said she thought they would give opera a rest.

'Candide' had opened to mixed reviews. Leila asked Heinrich if he would like to come. She still saw him occasionally — he was a useful escort — he knew there was somebody else, and because she was so secretive had probably guessed he was a married man. He had other girls too, so it was quite amicable.

Nick was playing his trumpet somewhere.

Miranda had been what their mother would have called 'strung up' — like a tight spring waiting to be triggered. She looked particularly lovely. She was wearing a slim dress of lilac linen and several ropes of large pearls. Leila, so used to seeing her in black, was quite taken aback. She almost made a remark about it, and then, for some reason, checked herself.

It was a very dreary musical. The singers hooted or whined, nasally breathy or piercingly sharp.

In the interval they all had double gins.

Several people spoke to Miranda. She was unnaturally bright and sparkling, her pale skin flushed.

'Dreadfully boring, darling!' said a young woman in an orange suit, her hair unnervingly blonde. 'Can't think how Julia got the part — I mean — everyone knows Martin is a frightful poof, so she wouldn't have gone to bed with him. Oh, thanks,' to Heinrich, 'I'd love another drink. And the clothes — what a ghastly dress — the lacing keeps coming undone...'

A floppy young man said the orchestra was all over the place, the ragged chorus looked like something out of Cinderella, except that Cinderella was vastly more jolly.

'Its not supposed to be jolly,' said somebody else. 'Its a moral tale — a fable...'

There were hoots of mirth.

'What about the dishy Rupert?' said the girl in orange. 'He should just stand about looking dishy. His singing is awful!'

They went round after the performance. Leila always looked forward to this bit. She enjoyed seeing the performers — still in their costumes — smoking, arguing, sometimes quarrelling — the make-up cracking and oily from the heat of the lights. Tantalisingly seedy...

There was a small bar — the walls papered with theatrical posters, some elaborately autographed.

One of the ragged chorus poured them each a large gin.

'There's no bloody ice, I'm afraid,' he said.

A buxom girl in a peasant's dress asked for a drink.

'If that snooty cow pushes me aside once more,' she said, 'I'll fix a trip wire — hope she breaks her bloody neck...'

The leading lady appeared briefly, holding a massive bouquet of flowers wrapped in cellophane.

'You were wonderful tonight darling,' said the peasant girl. 'Just wonderful!'
'Thanks, sweetie,' said the leading lady. 'Has anybody seen Desmond? He has to do something about my dressing room — its an airless hole — completely airless. It is doing terrible things to my throat. How am I supposed to sing with a fossilized throat? For God's sake, give me a drink Greg.'

'There's no bloody ice, I'm afraid,' said the ragged young man. 'No lemon either...'

And then the 'dishy Rupert' appeared from the narrow, dark passage where the dressing rooms were. He had changed into shirt and slacks. He came straight to them and swept Miranda into his arms.

'Wonderful to see you darling,' he said, kissing her on the mouth, and then kissing her again. 'Wonderful! Can you stay a bit? You must be able to stay a bit — please?'

Leila and Heinrich had stood watching — disconcerted.

At the time Leila had thought it was just theatrical behaviour. Everybody kissed everybody — everybody called everybody darling. She dismissed the shimmer of unease — of course it meant nothing. Miranda was radiant. Rupert had not let her go. He held her against him whilst he shook hands.

'Hope you enjoyed the show,' he said.

Miranda had almost pushed them into a taxi.
'I have to get home,' she said. 'Don't want Nick to worry...'

Of course she had not been in a hurry to get home to Nick, but to meet this other man, the 'dishy Rupert' as the girl in orange had called him.

Then it had seemed unthinkable — that anyone should come between Nick and Miranda, that Miranda could be unfaithful to Nick, that she could love someone else — that she would have to turn away, so that she wouldn't see the pain in her brother's face.

14

Mist hung softly in the white hospital room — the strip of fluorescent light too bright. There was a picture of snow-capped hills over the white table, now a garden of flowers — blue irises, red bending tulips, musky pink carnations, long-stemmed roses (from Howard), a pot of rusty chrysanthemums...

It was quite a nice room, as hospital rooms go — they had given her extra pillows.

Howard had always insisted on private medical care.

He had left the television on — a murmuring window of changing images, an unobtrusive companion.

There was no Miranda to demand a second opinion. This time the diagnosis was final.

Her mother and father would not be coming to see her.
Since they had moved to the squat pebble-dashed bungalow in Leigh-on-Sea, they never went anywhere.

They hadn't got a car. They didn't drive.

They lived their mean shuttered existence, the greying nylon net curtains shielding them from the sunlight and the incurious gaze of passersby.

Their father taking his daily walk to the newsagents for the *Daily Mail*, and tobacco for his unsmoked pipe.

He read gardening magazines, dreaming of vegetable gardens — clotted cream cauliflowers, rosy carrots, yellow-flowered emerald-skinned marrows.

Their mother tidying and retidying, darning socks on the wooden mushroom, complaining about the obscenities on the TV.

Leila and Howard visited regularly. Howard had a strong sense of duty even though they would always be Mr and Mrs Thompson to him.

Her mother viewed him with her habitual chilly disapproval.

They would take them to lunch at the nearby Steak House.

Her mother didn't like 'fancy' food.

She said the steak was tough, that the skimpy-skirted waitresses were 'indecent' and nagged her father for choosing Black Forest Gateau.

'I don't want to be up all night,' she said. 'You know it won't agree with you.'

She thought Howard's black BMW ostentatious. 'What's wrong with British cars?'

Howard did his best. He talked to her father about fruit trees. Next door had a rather splendid plum...

She talked to her mother about — well — about nothing, nothing at all. It had been wet, cold, hot. They had no meeting point.

Nick never visited. Since his Department had been transferred to Edinburgh, they hardly ever saw him.

Debbie sent their mother pictures of the children, which she put away in a drawer, and presents at Christmas — tartan scarves and tartan-lidded shortbread and mugs painted with thistles. Their mother never used mugs.

She wanted to talk to Nick. She longed to see Miranda, to know what had happened to Dan, to see him once more, to feel his arms around her, to wipe out the bitterness and the sorrow...
She would never see him again. Very soon she would not see anyone again.

'Are you comfortable Mrs Dewsbury?' asked the nurse.
'Yes, thank you,' said Leila. 'Quite comfortable.'

There had always been a coldness between Howard and Nick.

It was as if Howard knew they shared a secret — a protected memory of past experience of which he knew nothing.

Dear considerate Howard — an undemanding and careful lover — almost apologetic.

Somewhere inside her, she held the breathless exaltation of Dan's passion, the panorama of stars.

She had found the snapshots in an envelope at the bottom of a box in the cupboard under the stairs, whilst she was looking for Howard's maps of Italy. They fell, loosely scattered on the floor beside her — fragile ashes, glimpses of brief captured moments.

Her wedding day, holding Howard's arm, wearing the stupid straw hat — hats never suited her, her face was too round...

There was a lunch at the Hyde Park Hotel.

Howard's mother in ruched sapphire blue satin. Her mother in the dreadful felt hat, declining champagne, which had not really been champagne, just sparkling wine.

Her father, uncomfortably squeezed into his only suit, trying to be pleased, wishing her happiness.

Howard in Florence, sitting at an outdoor cafe, purposefully casual in his open-necked shirt and Freeman Hardy & Willis sandals. So many Madonnas in the Uffizi gallery.

The shower water lukewarm. There were separate beds.

She hadn't known how she was going to get through the nights — dreading Howard's body — unable to escape now.

To her relief she found that she felt nothing, absolutely nothing. She had no emotion left, no responses, no tears, no desires, and when Howard returned to his bed, she lay awake watching the shadows on the ceiling, an empty shell, knowing she must not think of Dan.

Nick and Debbie's wedding.

Nick unsmiling, looking straight ahead. Sensible, sturdy freckled Debbie in a white taffeta dress with a square neckline — too tight, too short, unaccustomed to the high heels. It had been cruelly sunny...
Debbie and Nick with the children — sturdy and freckled like their mother. Thank God they were boys!

Nick looking away from the camera — the younger boy sucking his thumb.

Nick with Miranda on their wedding day. Radiant, kissing in front of the wondrously perfumed lilac. Laughing people raising their glasses.

Dan leaning on an elbow, lying on the grass, grinning — the corner of Jackie's hat, her bare arm...

Camilla had organised a picnic. Several cars crammed with jolly people and picnic baskets — proper glasses and silver, champagne in buckets of ice, white damask napkins.

It had been somewhere on the Downs — high and grassy with clumps of trees and wind-broken bushes.

It had been at the beginning of their affair. She was shaken and breathless just being near him. His was the casual strength of the conqueror.

It was agony seeing him with Jackie.

When it had begun to rain, they had piled back in the cars and gone to Ennismore gardens. Somebody had gone for fish and chips and they had rolled back the carpets and danced, and drank a lot of wine and danced.

As it got dark Camilla had lighted lots of candles, and they had managed to slip away and make love in the library.

It might have been different if Camilla had not seen them together.

She had taken the morning off work, and they had spent it together making love among the silken pillows on Dan and Jackie's bed.

They walked across Hyde Park — round the end of the Serpentine to the Fountain Gardens and out on to the Bayswater Road.

It was a fine, pale spring day. The trees hazed with green, a slight chill breeze ruffling the water, beds of velvety jewelled polyanthus.

He kissed her and hailed a taxi to take him to the Club.

She was about to cross the road to take the Underground from Lancaster Gate to work, when she saw Camilla coming towards her, vivid in a fuchsia pink coat, her blonde hair tucked up under a fuchsia pink pillbox hat — she had long matching gloves.

'Weeell!' she said. 'I had no idea you two were such good friends! Let's go and get a drink. I need one!'
She gripped Leila's arm with her sharp hands and propelled her across the street, round the corner to the Golden Acorn, a pub with hanging baskets and racing prints.

She had been delivering the proofs of the catalogue of a forthcoming exhibition to the artist, an eminent RA who had a studio in Brook Mews.

His studio was hung with pictures of young girls in various states of undress, their legs apart. 'Disgusting!' she said and ordered them both a double vodka and tonic, peeling off the long fuchsia pink gloves and laying them neatly on the bar.

He had suggested she should model for him.

'You have a lovely body, my dear,' he had said, crossing and uncrossing his thin legs — his trousers were caked with paint. 'You should share its beauty.'
Dirty old man! Who the hell would want to strip off for him? Now if it had been someone sexy like Dan — that would be quite a different matter.

She finished her drink and ordered another.

'If I were clever,' she said, 'I could write a book about pornography masquerading as art! Do you want something to eat? I'm starved — perhaps they have sandwiches.'

She asked the barman. 'Anything but cheese,' she said. 'OK we'll have ham.'

Leila found she was very hungry. The sandwich was freshly made with thick crusty bread — hot with mustard.

'And what about *your* brother and *my* sister? What a tangled web we weave and all that stuff...'
Leila said it was very upsetting.

'Upsetting?' said Camilla, 'Really Leila! That is a chronic understatement. There's Miranda besotted with this poncy actor and Nick completely shattered. But completely! And you say its upsetting! I suppose Jackie will find the situation between you and Dan "upsetting" too.'

Leila felt distant and lightheaded. She shouldn't have drunk the vodka so quickly. What was Camilla saying? That she was going to tell Jackie? It had not been the kiss of friendly acquaintances that Camilla had seen, but the passionate embrace of lovers.

'Jackie doesn't know,' she said quickly.
'Oh!' said Camilla. 'Really! Jackie doesn't know. Poor Jackie!

Well really Leila, I wouldn't have thought you were the sort to have illicit affairs with married men! They always say you have to watch the quiet ones. All the same, I would have thought it would be wiser not to demonstrate your affection for one another on the teeming pavements of the Bayswater Road! I mean — you never know who might see you...!'

Leila tried to speak, but could only think of meaningless platitudes, feeble excuses.

Camilla ordered them another drink.

'Actually,' she said, 'I think Jackie is a selfish bitch, but that is no reason for sleeping with her husband. She thinks he's playing around with someone from the Club.' She gurgled with amusement. 'Perhaps he is. Well, here's to Love and all that stuff...' She raised her glass and made a slight mocking bow towards Leila.

15

Of course it might not have been Camilla who had told Jackie.

She always talked too much, especially when she had been drinking, which was often.

Leila was to meet Dan outside Knightsbridge station.
Jackie was away for two days in Manchester.

They would have a meal and go back to the flat. There would be no hurry. She had gone shopping in the lunch hour and bought a new lacy slip and bra, the colour of creamy coffee.

She changed at work, wriggling in and out of her clothes in the small confines of the toilet cubicle.

The soft fabric felt wonderful against her skin — almost a caress.

She waited for three quarters of an hour. He hadn't come. There was a cold wind briskly gathering the rubbish into dirty heaps, tripping people's feet.

Why didn't he come? What was wrong? Perhaps he was ill. He had been fine that morning when he had phoned her at work. Perhaps he was with someone else — someone at the Club — a late coaching session? He couldn't be with someone else. Oh God! Please, God don't let him be with someone else.

She fumbled in her bag for change and went down the steps to find a telephone.

Jackie answered. Leila was so shocked to hear her voice that she replaced the receiver without speaking.

She went home and waited for the phone to ring.

There must have been a change of plan. Jackie had not gone to Manchester after all, and he hadn't been able to let her know. The phone didn't ring.

Giselle came in and changed into a low-backed red dress and red stilettoes, spraying herself liberally with perfume, powdering her shoulders, her décolletage. She was in a hurry. Gerry was taking her to 'Annabelle's'. He was a friend of Marvin's, another American. Marvin had gone home to Boston. Giselle had said 'Thank God for that —he was getting a real bore.'

Gerry was very tall and skinny — younger than Marvin — polite. He wore button-down collars.

Giselle often stayed out all night.

Gerry had a flat near the American Embassy, in Grosvenor Street.

'Very posh!' said Giselle. She kept clothes there so that she could go straight to work and 'not spend half the night in taxis...'

The phone didn't ring.

Leila drank a tumbler of Giselle's whisky and lay on the bed and wept.

They never discussed the abortion.

'Phew!' Dan had said. 'That was a close thing, sweetheart!'

They never spoke of it again.
She suppressed her feelings of grief and loss, telling herself to think of it just like any operation — having your appendix out, a D and C. It was over now. She should be grateful that she had recovered so well, that Dan still loved her.

There were no phone calls. After two days of desperate silence, Leila phoned the Club. She had to wait. When Dan finally came to the phone he sounded cold and formal. She realised that there were other people in the office.

She said she had to see him.

'It's difficult,' he said. 'Not round here. It'll have to be a lunchtime...'

They met in a pub in Cranbourn Street. It was so crowded they had to stand crushed against the bar.

'Jackie's found out about us,' said Dan. 'She went crazy — completely crazy.'

She had tried to tear the sheets with her teeth, fetching a knife, slashing them to shreds, tipping the contents of the laundry basket down the waste chute.

She attacked him with fists and nails — biting, scratching — drawing blood.

'It's got to be over,' he said.

'Why don't you leave her?' said Leila. 'Oh, Dan, please won't you leave her?'

'I can't,' he said. 'I can't. I don't know what she might do.'

He had wrestled the bottle of sleeping pills from her grasp, pinning her to the bed. Leila could tell they had made love, though, of course he was not going to tell her that. He said they had drunk a great deal and that she had passed out, and that he had promised her that it was over.

'I had to...' he said. She had threatened to kill him — to kill Leila — to kill herself.

She screamed and screamed until he had promised that it was over — that it would never happen again.

There were two long scratches down the side of his face, and a purple bruise on his neck.

She stared back down the empty tunnel, slimed green, crusted with sickly fungus, to the distant circle of light — watching Dan walk away towards Leicester Square, the bright summer sunshine making her blink after the dark interior of the pub.
There were no tears then.

She couldn't remember feeling anything at all. She had not grasped the reality — that he was not going to turn back — to come to her — to be with her.

She made her way automatically back to work — a sleepwalker, afraid to waken.

It did not seem possible that nobody noticed that she had changed, that nothing would ever be the same again.

She took the tea tray into Mr Prescott who was having a meeting with two men from the Ministry — remembering the chocolate digestives that were Mr Prescott's favourites — told Corinne not to paint her nails in the office and typed two reports on the effect of unemployment on pension rights — expecting someone to ask if she were ill — was there something the matter? It was strange how the world could collapse in dusty debris around you and nobody noticed, that you could look exactly the same, neat and proper, performing the usual mundane tasks — telephoning the Adelphi to book tickets for Mr Prescott's wedding anniversary next Thursday — listening patiently to Moyra complaining about Corinne chewing gum and coming in late.

16

She realised she was crying — the tears warm on her face, trickling on the white hospital pillow — dampening the collar of her white bed jacket. She didn't try to stop them. It didn't matter now how much she cried.

The nurse had brought her supper on a tray. They had taken the trouble to make it look tempting. There was an embroidered tray cloth and a single daffodil in a pretty glass vase — a proper linen napkin.

There was creamed chicken, mashed potatoes and peas — and some sort of pink mousse pudding.
It was cold and congealed now.

The nurse said 'You haven't eaten a thing Mrs Dewsbury. Is there anything you'd like? I can go down to the kitchens and ask...'
'No,' said Leila. 'No — thank you — that's very kind — I don't feel like anything.'
The nurse asked if she might like a hot drink and Leila said 'Yes, that would be nice. A hot chocolate — with lots of sugar.'

She and Miranda had drunk hot chocolate in the Chocolate Shop in Regent Street. It had a thick layer of froth.

They had been shopping in Liberty's.

Miranda had bought some material for a dress — deep pansy purples and blues — soft cotton satin — and she had bought a pale pink paisley print scarf. (Almost the same colour as the pudding!)

She was meeting Dan later.
She didn't know there was trouble between Nick and Miranda, remarking gaily that Nick would love the dress.

'I don't suppose he'll notice,' said Miranda.
Leila laughed. 'Don't be silly! Nick never takes his eyes off you!'

Miranda shrugged and lit a cigarette, leaving the chocolate to form a skin.

The phone on the bedside table shrilled impatiently.
She groped and fumbled to pick it up. It was Howard.
He had called to say goodnight. 'Are you alright?' he said.
'I'm fine,' said Leila. What a ridiculous phrase — I'm dying, but I'm fine — just fine!
'I hope they're looking after you well,' he said. 'Do ask if you need anything.'
'They're looking after me very well,' said Leila. 'Everybody is very kind.'
Howard said he would come in the morning. Was there anything she wanted him to do? 'Anything you want me to bring you?'
'Have you told Nick?' she asked.
There was a pause. She felt him withdraw — frown.
He said he had phoned Debbie. 'She's going to write. She doesn't think she will be able to come. It's difficult with the boys...'

But I don't want to see Debbie, I want to see Nick — I want to see Miranda — I want to see Dan...
It must be the sedatives that made her feel so weird.

'I didn't expect Debbie to come,' she said, holding her voice steady with an effort.

'Well,' said Howard, 'I'll say goodnight then, dear. I hope you can get some sleep...'

The nurse brought the hot chocolate, and she managed a few mouthfuls. It was too hot — it stuck in her throat. The nurse turned off the harsh overhead light. Leila told her to leave the television on — she didn't want to be alone in this unfamiliar room, deliberately arranged to look comfortable — an easy chair by the window, a shelf for photographs, a few books left behind by departing patients — Dick Francis, Joanna Trollope, Ruth Rendell. A copy of last August's *Ideal Home*...

It had been Miranda's idea to arrange the meeting.

Leila was reluctant. She had not seen Nick since they had met in the pub in the City.

She had phoned the house in Camberwell where he was living with three friends several times, but he was never in.

She knew he didn't want to speak to her or see her. He didn't want to discuss Miranda with anyone.

She telephoned him at work and managed to persuade him to meet her again in the same pub.

'Its ages since I've seen you,' she said.

They were to be already there and Miranda would come, as if by chance — Surprise! Fancy seeing you! — and join them, and after a suitable interval Leila would excuse herself and leave them together.

Nick had a whisky and ginger. The amber liquid untouched in front of him — the bones of his knuckles clenched white. He took his glasses off and pushed back the lock of hair. He looked exhausted and ill.

Leila suggested a sandwich, but he shook his head without speaking. He didn't look at her. She was not hungry either. She was sure that this was a bad idea. She should never have agreed.

'Please, Leila,' Miranda had said. 'I must see him. I must talk to him. I can't think of another way. He doesn't even answer my letters.'

She came towards them — a slight figure in her long black coat — the thin white face gashed with scarlet.

Nick looked up. It was as if he had been struck a damaging blow — all the remaining colour drained from his face. He got unsteadily to his feet, and like a blind man, groped his way to the door.

Miranda gave a little cry and put out her hand, as if to try and stop him. A gesture of despair. 'Nick — Nick, please!' But he had gone out into the street, already mingled with the lunchtime crowds.

It was the longest winter of her life.

The cavernous split between Nick and Miranda spreading dark tentacles of unease — the frightening fragility of love.

The dreaded confirmation of her pregnancy, the ordeal of the abortion. Trying to convince herself it was for the best. Dan's tears as he gave her the slip of paper with the doctor's name and address. She didn't ask how he knew of such a doctor, or who he knew — who knew such a doctor..?

Nowadays it was different.

Everything was different.

She could have had the baby. People even chose single parenthood. She could have kept Dan's baby... No, she must not think of that now, she could not bear it.

Sara could have kept her little girl. Would not have had to live with a dark patch of regret — lingering. Perhaps Nick and Miranda would not have divorced — could have talked things through, sorted things out, rewoven the magic with stronger thread.

She had often wondered what kind of relationship Nick had with Debbie. She could detect no spark between them — not that she saw them very often.

Debbie was perpetually hearty, solid and safe. That was it really. Safety. She was safe with Howard, dear dependable Howard. There were no unexpected emotional shocks or uncertainties.

Briefly she and Nick had walked enchanted paths, had glimpsed bright-winged birds touching the sky, out of reach of their outstretched hands. They were bound to the earth. They had not been born to climb rainbows.

No — it was better to be steady and safe than to wander into the unknown, along bitter-sweet paths of fragrant soft-petalled flowers — hiding sharp thorns — glossy-leaved bushes concealing poisonous berries, appetisingly red and yellow.

Oh yes, it was better to be safe — to eat the daily toast and marmalade, to murmur about the weather.

Now Death approached, stealthy on slippered feet — not to disturb.

There was not much time.

Perhaps they would let her go home. But she didn't want to go home. Here she did not have to feel guilty that her thoughts

were not of Howard, of their well-ordered life together. Seamless
days — routine marking out the years — ignoring the surprise of
Spring — the scents of Summer — the sadness of Autumn.

Carefully planned holidays — tips and taxi fares precisely
calculated — the required number of baggage labels — always
punctual.

Death took no notice of punctuality.

No — she didn't want to go home. Here she was free to dream.
She could let all the aching memories out to wander through her
mind.

17

She had met Nick just before Christmas.

They had lunch at L'Hirondelle.

Nick had suggested it. Leila refrained from remarking on his
choice. She knew it was where he had taken Miranda on their
anniversaries.

He was thin — gaunt really.

He took his glasses off and rubbed his eyes, pushing back the lock
of dark hair in the familiar gesture. He looked desolate.

As they ate he watched the door.

She had felt so sad for him — for herself — for Miranda —
wishing too that she would come through that door, bringing
lightness and warmth.

She carried on talking about the holiday she and Howard were
planning in the Spring.

There would be no holiday in the Spring. There would be no more holidays.

There was a young couple at the next table. They held hands, heads bent together. The girl wore a wide-brimmed lemon yellow hat — such a pretty hat with silk-petalled roses.

She saw Nick's face bleak across the table.
It was the same colour as Miranda's wedding dress.

They were drinking pink champagne. 'Lovely pink fizz, Nick darling.' Miranda's voice so clear, so close, as if she were beside them.

She broke her roll into pieces, dropping crumbs on the pink linen cloth, and asked about Debbie and the boys.

Nick seemed to hardly hear her, muttering something, pushing his food to the side of the plate.

She said she wouldn't have a sweet — but had another glass of wine — holding the sharp-scented liquid in her mouth before she swallowed.

She could sense Nick's terrible loneliness — the black void which she shared — long bitter years.

She saw him avert his eyes from the lemon yellow hat, the pink champagne, the gold-caged cork lying by the girl's hand.

He had not been able to cope with the catastrophe of Miranda's betrayal — but now, now she was sure he would give anything for her to be with him — leaning her head on his shoulder. 'Let's go home, Nick darling — I'm tired.'

She went to the powder room.

The face in the mirror looked back at her. There were lines now round the eyes. The naturally curly hair still dark, the small nose and well-shaped mouth. Perhaps she had been pretty.

Dan had loved her face — or maybe that was just part of the game — a sophisticated game she should not have tried to play.

All the same she longed for him — just as Nick longed for Miranda.

They stood outside the restaurant like strangers. They had nothing to say to each other — brother and sister, so unalike and distant.

Once upon a time — once upon a time...

She said 'Well, have a good Christmas. Love to Debbie and the boys...'

Christmas. Another Christmas. Another year gone.

Howard's mother finding fault with everything. Drinks with Dotty and Ken — dog hairs on the sofa — wiser not to wear black.

The Conservative Club — determinedly merry. Fruit cup — nothing like Camilla's potent brew — oversweetened orange juice and cheap white wine.

She wondered what had happened to Camilla.

They didn't embrace. She watched him walk up Jermyn Street, past the smart shirt shop, the back of Simpsons, towards the Haymarket, moving quickly, eyes down.

Perhaps she would not see him again.

The cramp hit her as she hurried towards St James' Street.

Howard had asked her to get some plums in Armagnac from

Fortnum's for his mother. They came in a special glass jar that she liked.

She had to stop to catch her breath. She had been getting these cramps more frequently lately. She bent double with the pain.

She shouldn't have eaten the seafood salad — the taste sour now in her mouth.

She wanted to sit down, but she would be late for work and there was an important meeting at 3.30. She thought she was going to be sick.

As the platinum sheen of dawn began to push back the inky weight of the night, she slept.

18

The ceiling of the long dark-panelled room was painted with cherubs and expansively naked women, draped with wispy cloths, reclining among bolsters of pink cloud. The cherubs hovered with sprouting wings, holding little gold harps, pulling wide ribbons across the bright blue sky with fat-creased arms.
Leila held the guidebook open. 'This impressive example of early 19th-century decorative art is in almost perfect condition...'

She had pinned the dark blue rosette to the lapel of her charcoal grey pin-striped suit — her smartest outfit. Howard had said they must show which party they supported.

Miranda was sitting by the window on a straight-backed chair. She was knitting — a long black garment, spread on her black stockinged legs.

'Honestly, Leila!' she said. 'What are you wearing that thing for? You're not a horse!'

Leila took the rosette off and dropped it behind the brass fender of the large brown-mottled marble fireplace.

Above it there was a full length portrait of Lady DuCane. She wore a beaded flapper dress tied at the hip with a large bow, and a jewelled headdress with two white feathers. She stared down contemptuously with her pale eyes.

And Camilla was beside her — in a white sleeveless mini dress and long white gloves, her blonde hair loose on her shoulders. She carried a long white umbrella which she pointed at the ceiling.
'What a load of crap!' she said. 'Fancy eating under that! Very indigestible!'
'Oh, Camilla!' said Leila. How lovely to see you — you haven't changed at all.'
'I should hope not,' said Camilla. 'You only saw me yesterday.'

Florence entered carrying a tray of macaroons, her severe housekeeper's dress buttoned to the neck.
'Her Ladyship says there will be eight for tea,' she said.

Camilla grabbed a macaroon and twirled up the room holding the umbrella like a dancing partner. 'Tea for Two' she sang. 'Two for Tea...'
Miranda got up and walked out through the window — the black wool trailing on the floor behind her.

'You should have a coat Miss Miranda,' said Florence disapprovingly. Leila came after her. 'Wait! Please wait, Miranda! I must talk to you...'

But she had gone — a lonely black figure in the avenue of beech trees stretching into the distance.

And then Dan was there, coming up the steps two at a time. 'I'm sorry I'm late sweetheart!' — hugging her to him — 'Hey, don't cry! There's nothing to cry about!'

They walked hand in hand across a field of long grass — the rough stems dragging against their legs. His grasp was warm and strong.

'Just a bit further sweetheart,' he said. 'Then we will see the lake.'

It spread beneath them, faintly green, glassy smooth, spiked with reeds, swept by supple willows.

They sat among golden celandines and tousled pink flowers.

Far across the other side paper lanterns hung from feathery larches — globes of pink and red and orange. There was the gentle thump of dance music — couples swayed together, the girl's dresses butterfly wings among the dark trunks of the trees. How was it night the other side of the lake, when they sat on the coarse grass in the sunlight?

'Let's go and dance, sweetheart,' said Dan. 'We have time to dance.' His arm was warm and heavy around her shoulders.

There was a flat-bottomed boat tied to a broken wooden jetty among the reeds, its planks holed and rotten. He held it steady for her, pushing it away from the bank with an oar, rowing strongly through the weedy water.

She felt it was sinking, sliding down into the grasping reeds. The lights had gone out among the trees, the music fading. The water closing over her was unexpectedly warm, the oars floating past towards the rushing weir.

She was in the drawing room at Ennismore Gardens.
It was lit by candles — tall thick candles on pewter stands — foggy with smoke, crowded with strange people in strange clothes.

'Where's your Fancy Dress?' said Camilla. 'This is a Fancy Dress party...' Her hair was sprayed with silver, combed high like a crown.

'Really, darling, you knew it was Fancy Dress.'
The chandelier was made of fruit — grapes and cherries and small yellow plums.

The french windows were open — a cold wind billowed the tattered curtains, guttering the candles on the table of food, bowls of trifle and green jelly, and twisted brown things on a blue dish.

'Calamari,' said a pirate, offering her a glass of red wine.
He had a black patch over one eye and gold earrings. 'Fruits of the Sea!'

The wine tasted unpleasant, of cough mixture and aniseed.

She went out onto the terrace, magically shadowed by moonlight.

Dan was kissing someone. He had his back to her. She couldn't see who it was.

She cried out, the glass slipping from her hand — shattered — spreading a bloody stain on the white stones.

The wind flattened her cry, rustling the leaves of the scented viburnum, scattering the petals of the orange blossom.

Confetti for a bridal path.

Dan was no longer there.

She shivered and turned back into the house.

The room was empty now — dusty and shabby — the open door to the hall shedding a dim pathway of light.

There was music somewhere — a haunting melody — a surge of memory — a desperate longing.

Dan said 'Where have you been, sweetheart? I looked for you everywhere...'. And then they were dancing, the room filling again with dancers, turning and twirling, the music wrapping them in its nostalgic beat.

They were so close — faces touching — his hand burning on her back — like the beginning — just like the beginning...

19

The nurse said, 'You've had a nice little sleep, Mrs Dewsbury, and its a lovely fine morning'.

The winter sun spread weak fingers on the bedcover — splinters of pale primrose light touching the flowers on the table, the tulips already shedding glossy red petals.

The nurse took her pulse, slipping a thermometer into her mouth, writing on the chart.

Surely her pulse rate and temperature could be of no interest to anyone. Soon she would have neither...

The nurse gave her some tablets to swallow.
'We'll get you up later and make your bed all nice for you,' she said.

She had a pink face and red hair — the gingery kind that went with a freckled skin — too young to deal with terminal illness. But what had age got to do with it? Death didn't care about age...

'I'll bring your breakfast. Is there anything you'd like?'
'Thank you,' said Leila. 'I'll have some tea...'

It was only to please — she didn't want any tea — she didn't want her bed made — she didn't want to see Howard — or his mother — she didn't want the nurse standing there, talking...

She didn't want anything except to go on dancing with Dan —
just to go on dancing with Dan.
She turned her head away, and closed her eyes against the
sunlight.

Suddenly a wave carries the moon away
And the tidal water comes with its freight of stars
(Yang-ti)

The Wind Grows Colder

The edges of reality blurred — streamers of ragged colour caught in her mind.

The young woman in the sharp black suit and high heels, with the shiny long legs and satin-coiled hair, swinging down Bond Street glancing in the windows, saw the reflection of a haggard face with wispy hair — a long black shabby coat — bent flat black shoes.

Piaf in her pain-wracked voice singing *je ne regrette rien*. How could she regret nothing? It was not possible to regret nothing. The path of her life winding behind her was littered with regrets — silly decisions — missed opportunities — leaving everything too late — tomorrow all would be well — but tomorrow had not been well — to live was to regret.

She should have married Geoffrey, with his crinkled blue-black hair and long white hands — spotless white shirt and knife-pressed trousers.

'Marry me — please marry me Bobs,' he had begged her.
'I don't want to get married,' she had said. 'Marriage would be so dull.'
And she had put on her peach satin dance shoes and gone to Annabelle's with Hamish.

Scotch Woodcock at dawn — why was scrambled egg called Scotch Woodcock?

Hamish, lean and tanned — thick wavy fair hair — who clasped her so tightly when they danced, and in the taxi home.

She had been very tempted to marry Hamish, enduring a freezing, uncomfortable train journey to stay on his estate in Scotland. Striding through the purple springy heather in his mother's boots

— at least two sizes too big — lashed by bracken and brambles. A variety of slavering dogs taking up the hearth. The blazing log fire defeated by the high, cold room — the draught moving the heavy velvet curtains.

They ate Scotch pancakes kept warm over a dish of hot water — served by Higgins from the trolley.

'Get down Trogs — sit! He's only being friendly — aren't you Trogs? There's a good boy — look, he's smiling!' Trogs growled and bared his gums.

She shrank into the worn billows of the sofa, keeping her feet tightly together — balancing the plate of indigestible pancakes. She should have brought more appropriate clothes with her. Her London clothes were completely inadequate.

She borrowed Hamish's pyjamas — stripey and warm — not that he had allowed her to wear them for long.

He had been very keen, but the thought of the icy house with its icy bathroom and tepid, brackish water — the crackling, stiff starched sheets — the permanent presence of the dogs, shedding hair and saliva on the Aubusson rugs — and Hamish's mother, bulky in her heavy tweeds, dismissing Robyn as an arty nincompoop with no stamina — had made her decide against it.

She preferred the thick-piled towels and scented soaps in the flat in Cheyne Walk.

She stood in front of Asprey's looking at the glistening stones comfortable on their velvet cushions.

She was wearing a new frosted pink lipstick and matching nail varnish. She turned to greet him, smiling. Husky in his Burberry with the collar turned up.

They hugged and linked arms, swinging down to the Ritz for tea.

The man in the Saville Row stripes lifted his bowler slightly, and stood aside to let her pass, and the haggard woman stopped smiling, and mumbled 'Thank you so much...'

So many weddings — marquees and grand rooms — chandeliers — footmen with white gloves — stilettos spiking manicured lawns — trampled with sticky wedding cake and cigarette ends.

She was engaged once — to Teddy — dear Teddy — so very sweet.

She had had a beautiful ring, a large square diamond in a very simple setting — long gone now, with her Father's silver cigarette box and brandy flask, which they had managed to conceal from his many creditors — brought down by too much drink and too many bad investments.
Her mother had hidden the remaining valuables under her mattress.

She had urged Robyn to stop gallivanting about — find a rich husband. But she had shrugged — there was plenty of time — and she had gone out to buy new dancing shoes and a dress with a skirt that rustled and swirled with every step.

She had intended to marry Teddy, but he had gone to work in Australia, and she didn't want to live in Australia — kangaroos — corks hanging from hats — beer — and so far away.

Her mother moved into a reasonably priced retirement home just outside Guildford — a cheerless red brick building, but perfectly comfortable, with a resident's lounge and dining room. Of course her mother complained — it was not what she was used to — but she had no choice — it was all they could afford.

She had quite a nice-sized room, adequately furnished. The food was monotonous but perfectly acceptable — meat pie Thursdays — fish Fridays — macaroni cheese for supper on Wednesdays...

The lounge had easy chairs and a large television and tables for card games — or she could walk in the gardens — well kept, with gravel paths and beds of shrubs.

Robyn had visited regularly.
Teddy had a wonderful dark green Armstrong Siddeley, and they would take her mother to tea at the nearby Swan Hotel.
After Teddy had left for Australia, Sandy would take her down in his red roadster.
He wore checked caps and fringed scarves with his tweed jacket and twill trousers. Bluff and boring with his persistent proposals of marriage — but he was much too sporting.
She got tired of shivering at rugby matches and muddy race meetings — her shoes got ruined — there was plenty of time for marriage.

It was almost dark when she reached the top of Bond Street to catch the bus to Notting Hill Gate.
It was chilly too. She felt the cold through her thin coat — a good coat once — Jaeger — cashmere — now worn to the weave with frayed collar and cuffs.

She liked this time of day when the lights came on and the shop windows were suddenly alive.

Hailing a taxi to take her to Quaglino's for dinner — lobster salad and something chocolatey for dessert — or perhaps cocktails at the Ritz — White Ladies at the glittering bar — arranging her hair in the pink powder room.

She had left everything too late.
She had not noticed the time slipping by, faster and faster.
Her mother had urged a proper job — perhaps the Civil Service — she would certainly meet someone suitable in the Civil Service — and she would have a good pension.

Robyn had had no thought of pensions, or a tedious job in the Civil Service. Besides, she couldn't even type.

Her mother had died in the same resigned way that she had lived. Everything was too much trouble, even dying. Everything had always been someone else's fault.

Her own life was full of parties — lolling on yachts in the South of France — sipping cool drinks on the terraces of villas in Crete or the Tuscan hills — dinners at Maxim's — beneath the chestnuts on the Champs Elysees — shopping in Rome and the chic boutiques of Juan les Pins.

She did not notice the time speeding by — the dashing young men becoming serious — marrying, buying houses, having children...

Now there were invitations to christenings — tea and cake in chintzy drawing rooms and respectable hotels with leather furniture — lunches at Simpson's — roast beef and Yorkshire pudding — hearing tales of woe — of extravagant wives — crippling mortgages — outrageous school fees...

She was not interested in clandestine liaisons — furtive afternoons in hotel bedrooms — even luxurious hotel bedrooms.

She had had to move from the smart flat in Kensington when Malcolm had married Arlene — a wealthy American divorcee — to a more modest flat in Shepherd's Bush, and then when the money from selling her engagement ring ran out, to a mournful bed-sitting room in Notting Hill Gate.

She had become adept at collecting bars of soap from the toilets of department stores — wrapped sugar cubes, paper napkins — sometimes butter and tiny jars of jam from cafes and coffee shops — anything was welcome to help sustain her meagre life.

She shuffled awkwardly onto the bus — her ankles were swollen — glad to get a seat next to a Chinese lady with a lot of shopping bags.

Perhaps tomorrow she would got to Wigmore Street. She had always liked Wigmore Street — so civilised. The staid decorum of Debenham & Freebody's which had sold correct clothing, of such high quality — for every conceivable occasion — now a bathroom showroom and dreary offices.

The coffee bar on the corner of Duke Street with its shiny, hissing coffee machine, so new then, where you could sit for hours over a cappuccino, with its hat of white froth and scattering of chocolate, and large flaky croissants — now another dreary office, or was it a shop selling medical appliances, she couldn't remember.

She could go to the Wallace Collection. They had washbasins in all the toilets with soap and towels. She could look at all the pretty things in the shop, and sit on the long seat in the ornate, dim hall where it was warm.

It was Wednesday, so she would stop at Giorgio's cafe for something to eat — egg, bacon and chips — tea and bread and butter. She would take the bacon and bread and butter home with her for tomorrow, wrapped in the white paper napkins from the glass on the chipped red formica table.
Rosa, Giorgio's ample wife, always gave her extra bread and butter, and sometimes an extra slice of bacon.

It was quite dark when she left the cafe.
It was only a short walk to her cheerless room with the dilapidated furniture — the sunken bed — the dressing table propped steady with a piece of cardboard.

In one of the drawers her remaining treasures — many pairs of gloves — short, long and elbow-length, satin and suede, embroidered and beaded, some with rows of tiny buttons, so difficult to do up. Silk scarves — soft lengths and brilliant squares wrapped in tissue paper — faded, and perished along the folds — a collection of gold embossed invitations — a scuffed red leather address book and a small pair of mother-of-pearl opera glasses.

Sometimes she would take them out and spread them on the stained eiderdown, remnants of another life, of dance music and wonderful clothes — champagne and laughter — crisp rolls and orange juice — freshly laundered sheets.

Now she shared the bathroom with its worn, rust-marked bath and erratic geyser with Mrs Simms, whose cooking filled the house with nauseating smells — going to bed in her clothes to try and keep warm — she never had enough money for the ineffectual gas fire — and downstairs Miss Elliot's wretched cats, always miaowing round the steps, and in the dim dusty hallway, their smells mingling with the captured rancidity of yesterday's meals.

The young man was tall.
He wore a dark, hooded coat.
At first she thought it was Teddy.
He had come back — come back from Australia.
He hadn't been able to live without her.
After all these years, he had come back.

She went towards him — eagerly — starting to speak, to exclaim…

The young man grabbed at her bag.
It wasn't Teddy. He was a stranger.
Instinctively she clung to it.
She couldn't let him have her bag.
There were her keys — the bread and bacon for tomorrow — a precious stub of lipstick — the blue enamelled compact that Hamish had given her — so many years ago — a little money in her leather purse — a ragged lace handkerchief.
'Please,' she said. 'Please — Teddy will give you some money…'

Why didn't Teddy come? He couldn't let this happen — she was sure he would come — but there was no one else in the street — no one at all…

She clung on desperately, battling with the young man, but he was much too strong, wrenching the precious bag from her, swearing, shoving her aside.

She fell awkwardly, hitting her head on the hard slabs of uneven pavement.

She tried to reach out to grasp the nearby railings — what would she eat tomorrow without the bread and bacon? — but she had no strength — her limbs were too heavy.

She would go to sleep here, and then when Teddy came he would find her, and they would have something delicious to eat tomorrow. Perhaps brunch at the Savoy — they did a wonderful kedgeree...

The headline read: 'Woman fatally mugged in Notting Hill Gate... The woman, aged about 60, was already dead when she was found by a couple on their way home from Bingo. The dead woman has not been identified.'

Demons Seldom Sleep

1

The scream filled her head with fear — sharp, white fear.

Madeleine's skeletal fingers bruising her arm as she pulled her into the darkness. The smell of paraffin and sacking — chicken feathers and sawdust — suffocating darkness.

She woke and switched on the light — filling the room with a rosy glow from the pink silk pleated lampshade — the pink carpet — the pink flowered quilt and curtains.

The scream clung, twitching — bat's claws embedded — webbed wings flapping...

Madame Dubois had had flowered curtains — blue irises entwined with green creepers — the polished parquet scattered with rugs — blue and green and white — and bowls of flowers — pollen dusting the shiny surfaces of small round tables with curly legs.

Madame Dubois' house was on the outskirts of the village. In the summer its front cascaded with bunches of mauve wisteria — the window boxes bright with geraniums.

They had tea — daintily balancing their cups — small, delicate cups with fragile handles and gold rims — gold-rimmed plates of little biscuits — light and crisp.

She was wearing her best plum-coloured velvet dress with the floppy lace collar.

Bernadette had green velvet — her long brown curly hair held back with a green velvet ribbon.

Their mother wore black. She said, 'We don't know where he has been taken...'

She was telling Madame Dubois that they had had no word from their father since he had left the village — rounded up with others — loaded on a truck by snarling soldiers — the blades of their bayonets gleaming in the afternoon sun, butterflies fluttering pansy-soft wings dancing among the buddleia, branched with purple flowers.

'Bernadette is very talented,' said Madame Dubois. 'A true, natural talent. If it were not for this dreadful war, I should insist she went to Paris to study — but now everything is so uncertain — I feel it would not be safe...'

She pushed the plate of biscuits towards Michelle. She was a tall woman. She wore white canvas shoes, and a braided jacket buttoned to the neck.
'Take another dear — I was lucky to get a little extra sugar...'

Bernadette played the cello as if it were part of her — the rich sound flowing through her into the instrument. Their mother had told Madame Dubois that they could no longer pay for her lessons, but Madame Dubois said it did not matter.

'Someday, perhaps, when this dreadful war is over, Bernadette will be famous enough to pay me back herself. You must not worry my dear. All will be right in the end...'

It was winter. Now it always seemed to be winter. The black twisted arms of the trees scratching the sad sky — black birds searching the sodden fields for food — spitting out pebbles in the waterlogged earth.

The soldiers in grey — jumping from their grey vehicles — helmets over their eyes — grey coats slapping black boots — the clatter of rifles — gutteral commands — bringing fear and death.

Her mother had gone to fetch Bernadette from her cello lesson. She didn't like her coming home alone in the dark.

She put on her ankle boots with the fur lining, and her black cloth coat. She tried not to look too shabby when she fetched Bernadette from Madame Dubois.

Michelle was doing her homework. She had to learn a poem. Next day they had to recite a poem for Mademoiselle. She ate a hunk of rough bread spread with her mother's homemade blackberry jelly. She hoped her mother and Bernadette would not be long.

But it was Madeleine who came — her face stretched taut — a colourless mask.

'Quick — get your coat. Hurry! Where are your boots? Hurry!' Her voice gagged. She grabbed Michelle by the arm, dragging her painfully out into the darkness, up the street to her house. Madeleine's mother was rolling pastry — her plump hands white with flour. She looked up — alarmed — fearful.

'You can't bring her here,' she said. 'They'll take us all.' 'She's a kid,' said Madeleine. 'Just a kid...'

'You'll have to hide her,' said Madame Bronchard. 'Hurry — take her out the back. Please God they don't search — they have a list — they'll know she's missing...' 'We can say she's visiting an aunt — friends — we don't know where...' said Madeleine. 'For God's sake, Maman, they've already taken Bernadette and Madame Leger.'

Michelle wanted to ask where they had taken Bernadette and their mother — why they had taken them — but she was afraid.

Madeleine was Bernadette's best friend. Why hadn't they taken Madeleine? 'Hide her quickly,' whispered Madame Bronchard. 'We will have to think what to do. Hurry!'

2

She got out of bed and pulled on her pink robe. The pretty gold clock on her bedside table said half past five.

She was used to rising early, to get to the shop as the van came with the flowers from the market. She seldom went to market now. She left that to Hélène and Gerard.
She made out a list the night before, so they only had to select the best blooms, and buy anything unusual or unexpected.

The shop was her life, an extension of herself — the only place she could allow the demands of memory to hold her, unchecked, where the emaciated spectres of the night stood beside her, welcome companions in the scented day — filling the spaces in her empty heart.

She closed her door quietly so as not wake Philippe, and went into the kitchen to make herself a cup of tea. She had it very weak with a slice of lemon. Philippe had bought some brioche, but she couldn't face it.

She had been hidden in the loft of the Bronchard's barn, behind bales of straw. Sometimes she had to spend days and nights in the woods — careful to change hiding places. Madeleine brought her food — sour porridge made with water — small dry pieces of cheese, an occasional hard-boiled egg. The Germans had taken all the livestock — their patrols regularly scouring the houses and yards for food and wood.

Sometimes, after dark, Madeleine would bring her into the house, and Madame Bronchard would fill her a tub to wash in, and she would have a bowl of hot soup. She had no clean clothes — Madeleine found her some odd things she had grown out of. Madeleine had saved her life. She yearned for Madeleine...

Later she would walk to Notre Dame and pray — she would light candles for her mother and her sister — her father — for all souls searching for their loved ones in the darkness. She would light a candle too for Madeleine, hoping that she was still alive, that she had escaped — that she had grown up to find happiness...

She walked to the shop. It was not far down the Boulevard Haussman. It was going to be a lovely day, the June sun already warm.

At the time she had not known that it was because she was Jewish that she was being hunted. She had not even been aware that she was Jewish. She went to Church like all the other children in the village. She learnt about Jesus and the Virgin Mary, singing hymns and psalms, decorated the crib at Christmas and sang carols dressed as a shepherd, draped in an old striped bathtowel.

It was her blood that was Jewish. 'You have Jewish blood,' she was told.
Like the stick of pink peppermint a friend had brought her back from a holiday in England, with the name of the town written through the middle — cut open she would have 'Jewish' written all through her in indelible ink.

Two girls cycled past her, their laughter catching her unawares.

Bernadette and Madeleine had cycled ahead. She had to pedal hard to keep up on her small bike.

They were talking and laughing — zigzagging across the road — the autumn sun warm and golden — the sky hazy blue.

They were looking for wild mushrooms in the woods, and had filled the basket almost full with cèpes from under the oak trees, before they stopped to eat their picnic — flopping down on the moss and burnished leaves. They had bread and chicken — pain au chocolat and apples.

'I would love to go to the seaside,' said Madeleine. 'I have never

been to the seaside — it must be lovely...'
Bernadette said she would like to dance under the stars with trees full of fairy lights — with somebody incredibly handsome of course.

Later, when they came to the woods to gather chestnuts, their feet sank into rotting slippery leaves — the trees ominously bare — dark clouds scudding — the grey goose-stepping army had marched the land making them prisoners — stifling them.

They were stopped on the way home by two German soldiers on motorbikes. They prodded the bags of chestnuts with their rifle butts — plunging their nail-bitten hands into the glossy brown contents — tipping them onto the road. One of them held the handlebars of Bernadette's bicycle — leaning towards her — leering — insolent — the German words incomprehensible — alarming...

3

She stood in the workroom at the back of the shop, gentled by the wonderful mingling scents — wet leaves — crushed stalks — the masses of soft-petalled flowers.

Long white boxes lay open on the tables, full of sweetpeas and carnations. Misty balls of pale green maidenhair fern and waxy orange blossoms the colour of clotted cream stood in green tin buckets.

Tall vases of long-stemmed roses, and a flat basket of violets pushed to one side.

Hélène had an armful of lilac almost the same shade as the violets.

'Bonjour, Madame,' she said. 'Chantal is late again.'

Chantal was always late, arriving breathless and untidy, gasping apologies. However, she had a magic touch with flowers, so Michelle shrugged and said 'Never mind' and 'She is young...'

'We have all the flowers to do for Savorin's wedding,' said Hélène severely. 'Bouquets for the bride and three bridesmaids, and *eighty* buttonholes...' She waved distractedly at a box of white carnations. And there were the flowers for the Étoile Filante — she thought she would do sweetpeas today, and some of those fat pink daisies.

'Madame Robarts wants yellow flowers for her sister in hospital. Monsieur Seguin wants another dozen red roses delivered to Madame Cortez — that's the third time this week...'

Chantal arrived, pulling on her green overall, making explanations that nobody listened to.

Hélène managed the shop with Chantal. On busy days like today, Nathalie came in to help — leaving the baby with her mother. She was already working, stripping leaves from a rainbow of asters.

Michelle went over to the counter, and stood looking at the rolls of transparent paper — the reels of satin ribbons — the cellophane boxes and little baskets — the selection of cards for every occasion — Birth, Marriage, Death, Illness, Recovery, Thanks, Apologies, Love...

'I'm going out for a while,' she said, interrupting Hélène's angry monologue complaining of Chantal's unpunctuality and thoughtlessness. 'I won't be long.'

She would walk to Notre Dame.
The walk would do her good. She would go down the Boulevard Malsherbes to the Madeleine and across the Place de la Concorde.

Madeleine said they would have to move her — it was getting too dangerous. All the neighbours had been questioned. They had said truthfully that they had not seen her. She had not been in the village. She had not been to school. They didn't know where she was.

Some of the men were taken — arms behind their backs — up the slope outside the village to be shot — a heap of coats and boots sticky with blood.

She heard the fusillade of bullets as she crouched numbly in the darkness of the loft.

Madeleine said they would go to Montrichon, to Anne-Marie and Jean Claude. Their farm was a long way from the village. Perhaps they could help.

It was well know that Madame Tigny, whose Chateau could hardly be seen from the avenue of beech trees, had a German lover. A Gestapo officer — an important Gestapo officer, who came in a long sleek car with flying pennant and two black-uniformed outriders.

The men spat and swore — the women shrugged. Their village was left in peace — no dawn raids — shootings. Their houses were not searched or their livestock and vegetables looted.

So what if Madame wished to take her pleasures from the enemy? Who was going to complain?

Anne Marie helped at the Chateau — cleaning and preparing meals. 'Only the best,' she said. 'Champagne — foie gras — sucking pig! There was music and dancing — the women dripping with jewels!'

Madame Tigny's daughter, a student at the Sorbonne in Paris, came at the weekends in another sleek car with flying pennant. Monsieur Tigny had escaped to England to join the Free French Army. It was a long war. You couldn't expect a lovely woman like Madame to remain alone for such a long time.

They had often gone blackberrying at Montrichon. The hedgerows were laden with black-purple fruit. Afterwards they would go to the farm — their fingers stained with purple juice, and Anne-Marie would give them milky coffee and slabs of plum tart with dollops of whipped cream.

She gave them baskets of plums to take home. The trees in the orchard were so heavy with plums, their branches brushed the ground — ferocious with wasps drunk on the sweet juice.

Madeleine said they had to leave straightaway. The side of her face was bruised and swollen. She had got in the way of one of the searching soldiers, and he had struck her with his gloved hand.

They went out into the night — across fields — sliding in the mud, whipped and scratched by brambles and branches.

Her legs were weak from lack of exercise, and Madeleine had had to give her a piggy-back.

She owed her life to Madeleine.

4

Anne-Marie had put the oil lamp in the centre of the comfortably worn kitchen table.
She had a shawl over her nightdress — her hair hanging loose — grey and stringy.

Jean Claude sat with his elbows on the table. He was wearing a cardigan over his pyjamas.

Madeleine, her bruised face darkly shadowed by the lamp, was trying to explain what had happened — her speech jerky and incoherent. Anne-Marie and Jean Claude had heard about Bernadette and her mother being taken. They had thought Michelle had been taken as well. They had not known about that night's searchings — the burning of several houses.

'Your face!' said Anne-Marie. 'What happened to your face?'

She had opened the front of the stove — poking the embers — putting on more wood.

Michelle started to shake — she was so cold and tired.

Where had they taken Bernadette and her mother? To what dreadful place had they taken them?

Madeleine had said, 'They will come back when the war is over...', but they never came back. Only God knew where they had been taken — how they died. She should have died too. Why hadn't she died?

Anne-Marie heated some milk — spooning in generous spoonfuls of honey.

'The poor child's frozen,' she said. 'And so thin...'

They slept in a huge bed with prickly sheets and a faded patchwork quilt, warmed by a stone hot water bottle wrapped in a piece of blanket.

It was wonderful sleeping in a bed after all this time huddled on the floor of the loft — arms crossed on her chest to hold in some warmth.

It had been decided that Madeleine should not return to the village until they had found somewhere for Michelle to go. In the morning Jean Claude would go and see what he could find out.

So she came to travel to Paris under the vegetables in Gilbert's van.

He came to Montrichon three times a week to fetch fresh

vegetables — eggs, sometimes butter and cheese, from Madame Tigny's abundant kitchen garden and brown-eyed cows, taking them to one of the German depots at the Porte de Vincennes.

Gilbert had brought her here after unloading his vegetables. He was well known to the soldiers who were in charge. Michelle hidden under a pile of sacks heard him say, 'That's the lot — they're just a few spare sacks,' and he shut and locked the door. She heard him laughing, and the voice of a soldier in bad French saying he had a bag of coffee for him. He had managed to get some real coffee.

It was Gilbert and Claudette's shop.

It was hard then to get flowers. There was a nursery at Versailles where it was permitted to grow flowers. They had several hectares of carnations and roses and flowering shrubs. There was another at St Denis where they grew lilies and gladioli.

The Germans were particularly fond of roses. They also liked grand centrepieces for their hallways and reception rooms. Claudette's shop was very popular. Like Chantal she had a magic touch with flowers, and she was very charming and attractive. She had sat horror-stricken in the rumpled bed — dishevelled from sleep — the straps of her white satin nightdress slipping off her shoulders, her glossy black hair uncombed.

'Why have you brought her here?' she said. 'Are you mad? A Jewish child — what are we to do with her?'

There was one large, high room with windows overlooking the Boulevard Haussman, and a tiny kitchen overlooking the backyard where Gilbert kept his van. There was a windowless boxroom, and a toilet on the landing. A narrow flight of dusty wooden stairs, cluttered with boxes led down to the shop.

'We can't keep her here,' said Claudette. 'We'll be shot...'

Michelle was trembling with fatigue — her legs aching and weak.

'The poor kid's exhausted,' said Gilbert. 'I had to bring her. Anne-Marie said I had to bring her. There was nowhere she could go. Her mother and sister were taken — her father — they have all been taken.'

'Where are we going to hide her?' said Claudette. 'How long can we hide her? What about the neighbours? What about Madame Fournier? What about the customers? I have so many Germans coming to the shop. Oh my God, Gilbert, this is completely crazy...'

'She can stay in the boxroom,' said Gilbert. 'She will have to be very quiet — make sure she is not seen at the windows. If anyone comes, she can hide in the wardrobe — Madame Fournier is drunk most of the time — she won't hear anything...'

5

The flat was now her office with a comfortable couch, armchairs and a walnut desk.

The tiny kitchen transformed with polished pine and brass — the boxroom a pretty pink bathroom.

She started up the stairs, the dream still beating dark wings in her head. Who was it screaming? Was it herself — or Bernadette — or Maman — or Madeleine — or some anonymous anguished soul?

She would make some coffee, and go through the orders, before she walked to Notre Dame.
She went into the bathroom to wash her hands. Her hands were clean, but she needed to wash them — she had to wash them.

The pink bath was where the wardrobe had been, and the pink basin in the corner where she had slept on a pile of cushions, with a rug of woollen squares knitted from scraps of wool. She had hung a mirror on the wall — a large mirror with a light wood frame carved with flowers. Underneath it was a pretty little table with a round basket of dried flowers — red and pink roses — pale pods and grasses — a china soapdish painted with roses — a pink velvet trinket box.

She washed her hands in the pink basin, and dried them on a pink towel.

She saw herself in the mirror — her fashionable hair — smart black suit — soft white blouse.

She sensed Claudette behind her — her fine-boned face and wide dark eyes — the crimson mouth...

'Don't forget the fresh flowers — fresh flowers for the graves — fresh flowers...'

She turned instinctively to reassure her. There would always be fresh flowers.

In the nursing home when she had become too ill to wander in the gardens gathering wild flowers to fill the hallways and wards with delicate fragrance, she had lain calm and beautiful, murmuring. Michelle had had to lean close over the bed, feeling the cool breath, to hear what she was saying.

It was always the same — 'Don't forget fresh flowers — fresh flowers for the graves — fresh flowers...'

'Always,' she had said. 'There will always be fresh flowers...' Taking Claudette's hand, the thin fingers already cold. Sitting quietly until the darkness came.

But so many had no graves to lay flowers on.
Blood and bones fertilizing the land — ploughed by tanks — furrowed by guns — trodden by marching boots.

Acres of wheat and barley growing high and golden in the enriched soil, stained with scarlet poppies.

Screams gagged with mud and stones wafted into nothingness by the whispering summer breeze — until the winter storms raged — tearing the trees — nudging the ghosts — stirring up a scattering of treasures for the sleek, tail-coated magpies. Misshapen buttons and scraps of jagged shrapnel — the occasional gleam of a spent bullet pricking the slumbering earth.

6

'Excusez-moi, Madame,' said Hélène, 'but Chantal is feeling sick. I thought perhaps she could come up here and lie down for a while. She had curry — she is always sick when she has had curry. Today of all days — when we are so busy...'

She had fallen ill. A tight band encircled her chest, making it difficult to breathe. Through a mist of fever she saw Claudette's anxious face, an indistinct white blob, as she knelt beside her on the floor — her voice rising and falling — rising and falling...

'What are we to do?' she asked Gilbert. 'What in God's name are we to do? We daren't call the doctor. She is burning hot — I can hear her chest rattling when she breathes. This is no place for a sick child — she hasn't even got a proper bed.'
She could not hear Gilbert answer.

She drifted into delirium. Once more in her pretty room in the house in the village. The curtains had little bunches of yellow flowers which matched the eiderdown. Her doll with the yellow plaits and pink and white gingham dress, propped against the pillows with the knitted dog, and brown felt owl.

Her red woollen dressinggown hanging on a peg behind the door, and out of the window she looked straight into the branches of the walnut tree.

Somewhere Bernadette was playing the cello — she leant out of the window to hear better.

Her mother was waving at a truck going past the house. It was full of men in monk's robes — their faces hidden by their hoods. One of them waved back, turning towards them. She knew it was her father — somehow she knew it was her father. He lifted his head and she saw the hood was empty — a black empty hole.

She opened the door to go and find Bernadette — to tell Bernadette what she had seen — but there was no passage — no staircase — just yawning blackness.

She tried to call out, but no sound came.

Claudette put an arm under her shoulders and lifted her up.

'Try and drink this,' she said. 'You must try and drink something. Just a little sip...'

*   *   *

'I will just check the orders, and then I'll come down and help,' she told Hélène. She would go to Notre Dame later when the shop was closed for lunch.
'Tell Chantal to come up. I think I have some Alka Seltzer somewhere...'

7

She had developed a harsh, rasping cough.

Claudette was terrified.
'What if someone hears her coughing..?'

Upstairs Madame Fournier shuffled — drunkenly colliding with her furniture — falling out of bed — cursing and sobbing.

Claudette shut the door of the boxroom and told Michelle to muffle her coughing in the pillow. She had managed to get some cough medicine from the pharmacie. It helped a little.

When she was better, Claudette taught her some ballet exercises.

'It will help you get stronger,' she said. 'It is not good that you have no fresh air, no exercise...'

Michelle held the back of a chair, and swung her legs — arching her arms — bending her knees.

Claudette put down one of Gilbert's old coats for her to stand on, so that she did not make any noise.

They had been lucky with food.

There were always plenty of vegetables. Gilbert brought them fresh from his trips to the countryside. The soldiers at the depot gave him cigarettes, coffee, sometimes a piece of sausage, a knuckle of bacon. Once a box of chocolates.

Claudette said they should eat one a day, and then they would last. She passed the box to Michelle.
The aroma of chocolate filled her with nausea. She shook her head.

Madame Dubois had given Bernadette a box of chocolates for her birthday — dark chocolates in gold pleated cases — chipped with almonds — filled with red, cherry liquid.

*   *   *

They had finished the flowers for the tables at the Étoile Filante.

Philippe always entertained clients and business associates at the Étoile Filante — a superb restaurant, serving superb food.

They had been going there for years — supplying them with flowers for even longer.

Alex had taken Claudette there when food was scarce — the menu restricted.
The Allied armies already trampling the Normandy orchards — the wind of approaching freedom stirring the leaves on the plane trees in the Boulevard.

She had told Michelle they had pink table cloths, and wine glasses engraved with vine leaves.

Nathalie had started sweeping the floor — a green carpet of stalks and leaves, scattered with petals and broken flower-heads.

Michelle helped Hélène finish the buttonholes, and load the van with the wedding flowers.
Hélène was going with Gerard to see to the arrangements and make sure all was as it should be.

'You've done a wonderful job,' she said. 'Everything has gone so smoothly, and the flowers are lovely...'
Hélène reddened with pleasure, taking off her green overall and hanging it on a hook by the door.
'Thank you, Madame,' she said.

'Don't hurry back,' said Michelle. 'We will manage this afternoon. Nathalie and I can finish the orders, and I expect Chantal will recover... You might as well stay and enjoy the wedding...'

Philippe had come to the shop to buy flowers for his mother. It was her birthday. He had not known what to choose.

Michelle had selected the flowers. It had been autumn, so she had made a bouquet of pink and mauve Michaelmas daisies and white chrysanthemums.
After that he had come every day to say 'Bonjour', and then to take her for coffee in the café opposite.

Alex had waited for Claudette in the café opposite, in that spring — so many years ago.

Michelle watched them from behind the curtain. The tall German officer, and Claudette, chic in her little black dress and high heels.

They walked apart up the Boulevard, and though they didn't touch, they seemed to be joined together.

8

Michelle saw the black staff car stop outside the shop — heard the bell as the door was opened.

She went, swift and silent to the boxroom, and got into the wardrobe — choked by her beating heart — pressing herself among the musty seldom-used clothes — an evening dress in a cloth bag — a heavy hairy suit smelling of tobacco — a rubbery raincoat...

The German officer clicked his heels, bending to sniff a vase of roses.
'I understand you have a child living with you,' he said. His French was excellent.
'A child?' said Claudette. 'Why on earth should I have a child living here? I don't have any children.'

'I have already been reliably informed that a child has been seen here.'

'Perhaps the child of one of my customers,' said Claudette. 'Look around if you wish...'

'I'm sure that will not be necessary,' said the officer.

'Oh, but I insist,' said Claudette. 'Then you can tell your informant they were mistaken...'

He lifted his head and looked at her.

He had very grey eyes.

She led the way upstairs — praying that Michelle was safely hidden.

'We only have one room,' she said. 'I'm afraid it is rather untidy.' She avoided looking at him, but was aware of him looking at her.

'Thank you, Madame,' he said. 'That is quite sufficient. I'm sorry to have caused you any inconvenience...'

They stood together in the shop.

He asked the price of the roses — selected a bloom — paid for it and presented it to her.

'Á bientôt,' he said, and left the shop.

'You must keep away from the windows,' she said to Michelle as they ate their vegetable soup. 'Who informed on us? Who can have seen you? Oh my God, what if he comes back?'

She didn't tell Gilbert. There was no point in worrying him.

He came back — several times — leaving the staff car further up the Boulevard with his driver — choosing flowers for her.

Then one morning, when the plane trees were fizzing fresh green, he looked at her with his steady grey eyes, and asked if she would consider having coffee — a glass of wine, an aperitif — with him. 'I am a married woman...' she said, avoiding his eyes.

'I understand you husband is often away,' he said. 'It would give me great pleasure. Just coffee...'

Oh my God! What was she to do?

'That would be delightful,' she said archly, trying to smile. 'One evening perhaps...'

He had taken off his hat. He had dark hair — his face tense and thin. When he smiled his face transformed.

'I will look forward to it,' he said.

'Oh my God!' she said to Michelle. 'What am I to do? I shall have to go. What shall I tell Gilbert? What if he wants to come up here? Oh my God, what shall I do...?

He sent a message. He would be at the Hirondelle at seven, and would wait for her there.

She hugged Michelle.

'You'd better sleep in the wardrobe. Just in case. Don't leave anything lying about. I will do my best to put him off. I have to be very careful not to make him suspicious...'
She had not meant for anything to happen — she was just going to pretend — flirt a little. She had not expected to feel like this.

He had taken her hand across the table — the exciting immediacy of his touch caught her unawares. She didn't look at him — smiling coquettishly — withdrawing her hand.

He asked her about the shop — about Gilbert.

'I know it is not good to be seen with a German,' he said. 'I would not like to feel I am compromising you. I so wanted to be with you...'

She asked if he had always been a soldier.
'Very few of us have always been soldiers,' he said. 'In a war everybody is a soldier...'

In the darkness of the shuttered flower shop, they kissed.

What should have been a repulsive inevitability — an unavoidable acquiescence — was such sweetness.

She found she was holding him tightly against her — overwhelmed by unfamiliar emotions.

It was one thing to allow this German to make love to her to safeguard them all, but to feel this madness — to *want* him to make love to her — to want him to hold her — to kiss her — that was treason — that was collaborating with the enemy with her heart — not just a reluctant body, but with a terrible yearning — a need for this tall grey-eyed man who held her in his arms.

9

'I love him,' she said, the precious food untouched.

Gilbert had brought eggs — six fresh brown eggs. Claudette had used two to make an omelette.

Michelle had finished hers — mopping the plate with the tough grey wartime bread.

'I love him.' She poked the yellow mound of egg with her fork. 'I didn't mean to love him. I can't hurt Gilbert. I don't know what to do.'

Gilbert had been ordered to deliver supplies to depots nearer the fighting, as the Allies made their slow, inexorable progress towards Paris. He brought news of Germans retreating — of waves of Allied bombers — of burning buildings toppling into the broken streets.
Nathalie was speaking to her.

'We still have a few deliveries, Madame,' she said. 'An azalea for the Rue Ampée — these irises for the Hôpital St Agnes — Madame Cortez's roses...'

'You'd better take a taxi,' said Michelle. 'I don't know how long Gerard will be. Take some money from the till...'

She started collecting together the empty flower boxes — taking them out in the little yard.

Gilbert's van had been camouflaged.
If it hadn't been, they probably wouldn't have shot him.

Ambushed by the Maquis — dragged from the van and shot by the roadside. He carried German papers.

Philippe telephoned to remind her that they were going to the Martineau's supper party.
'I'll try and get home early,' he said. 'Are you alright, chérie?'
'Yes,' she said. 'I'm fine...'
'Mother phoned to know if we are going Sunday.'
'As you like,' she said.

Philippe's mother had never approved of her.

A strange, stiff young woman with no family, living in one room over a shop with another strange young woman who wore too much lipstick.

What she really didn't like — that she couldn't say — was that Michelle was a Jew.

She didn't like Jews — she couldn't say she didn't like Jews.

It wasn't 'done' to dislike Jews. But she did.

They were the cause of so much trouble. Greedy and grasping — pushing themselves to the front of queues — getting the best jobs.

She was convinced that they had provoked the war, and then made fortunes on the Black Market.
Good honest people like herself — who couldn't afford the Black

Market — had had to try to concoct meals out of a few potatoes, swedes, bits of tough meat, the odd slice of liver, half a sheep's heart — well, the butcher had told her it was sheep...

Her husband worked as a clerk in the Ministry of Finance, presided over by a team of bullying Germans. Checked and counter-checked — forced to wear an identity disc and submit to being regularly searched.

He developed a twitch on the left side of his face, and his hands had started to shake.

She was not too concerned when Jews were arrested — shoved in the back of police vans. Do them good to have to work hard...

She went out on her balcony to water the geraniums as Madame Godet and her daughter, who was about to be married, were taken away.

So were Monsieur and Madame Schultz, who owned the Boulangerie in the Rue de Belleville.

The shop was closed, the shutters painted with yellow stars. She had never really like Madame Schultz. She always had sugar and butter under the counter — if you could pay for them. She didn't want Philippe to marry a Jew. She did her best to stop it. Refusing to meet her — to invite her to the house. Even now she treated her with unconcealed contempt. Philippe had saddled himself with a neurotic — a misfit — a Jew. Thank goodness they had no children...

She was an old lady now — partially bedridden — heavy and complaining. Her dislike for Michelle — of Jews — undiminished.

Now there were also coloured immigrants.

There was a black nurse who brought her food, and tidied the bed — an Algerian girl who cleaned the room. Coloured men working in the gardens... They disgusted her.

'Taking our food and our jobs,' she said. 'We should send them back where they came from...'

*   *   *

Chantal said she was feeling better.

She came down the stairs, brushing strands of hair away from her face.
'We'll shut the shop early for lunch,' said Michelle. 'I'll go out now, if you think you can manage. Open the shop after lunch, if I'm not back. Are you sure you're alright?'

'Yes thank you, Madame,' said Chantal. 'I'm quite alright now. I will have some tea and maybe a sandwich...'

10

The sun was shining — a lovely June morning.

She walked round the Place de la Concorde — the fountains incandescent plumes, and down to the Seine, its surface sliced with sunlight.
She leaned on the wall, staring at the water.

The creeper of memories thickened and spread — sprouting sharp shoots, leaving lurid scars.

She thought about drowning — wrapped in a blanket of weeds — the water heavy — closing around her — blotting out the light.

A young couple walked past — hand in hand — heads bent together. The girl's hair glossy and curling on her shoulders. Bernadette's hair had been like that — her eyes closed as she drew the bow across her cello's strings.

She could not listen to cello music — rushing to turn off the radio — leaving the room when the Bonnard's daughter played to entertain their guests.

She had knocked over a chair.

Philippe had told them she had been taken ill — which was, in a way, the truth.

She sat in the car retching and shaking whilst Philippe drove her home.

She hoped Cecile did not have any music planned for this evening.

Cecile Martineau was a vain, pretentious woman.
Once she had had a soprano who had sung Schubert.
It had been an uncomfortable evening.

Cecile wanted to show off her new maid, a surly girl from Marseilles, and had had to contain her fury when she dropped a plate of moules marinières on the pale blue carpet.

The soprano's dress was too tight — Michelle wondered how she could breathe at all — cut low on the bosom which quivered as she sang.

Poor Philippe had got a migraine.

She crossed the river at the Hôtel de Ville.

A group of young Americans jostled and laughed in front of her. They wore skimpy vests, their long bare arms swinging, and jeans.

There were Germans too, who had stopped to take photographs — blocking the pavement.
They stood aside politely for her to pass.

Guilt stalked beside her — casting a dark shadow.

Why had she not perished with the others? Why had she not been with them on the last terrifying journey?

What of the workers who had constructed the sinister barracks — the concrete chambers — the furnaces — building the chimneys high? Did they ever wonder what they were to be used for? Did they go home to their wives and children, to eat their pork chops and boiled potatoes, unquestioning? Did the chill dribble of suspicion make them shiver beneath their goosedown quilts?

And after — what about after?

Spreading the hands that had fixed the pipes — the jets — that had made sure the fires would burn well.

'We knew nothing. Our hands are clean...'

And their wives whose washing had been dirtied by the smoke — black, gritty smoke — when the wind showed its displeasure, agitating the shirts and sheets with grey-spotted breath. Scattering their highly polished sideboards with bone-white dust — driving the weeping rain against their gleaming windows.

They knew nothing — nothing.

11

Claudette had never really been the same since those dreadful weeks before Paris was liberated.

The air brittle with suspense — the trees, lush with summer green, shuddering expectantly — a restless, shifting time.

Alex was recalled.

He came to say goodbye.

It was the only time Claudette brought him into the flat.

He said, 'I will come back. When the war is over, I will come back. If I don't come back, you will know I didn't make it...'

Claudette hid her misery — bright and buzzing — rouging her pale cheeks — flirting with the German officers who came to buy flowers for their mistresses.

And then poor Gilbert.

The body was never returned — left to rot in the ditch where he was shot.

Like a shattered glass — still holding its shape — a shattered glass that might collapse at any moment into a heap of sharp fragments — she held herself together.

Michelle cared for her as if she were sick — cutting up her food — coaxing her to eat — brushing her hair — washing her hands and face — sitting by her bedside throughout the weary nights.

Creeping down to the shop after it was closed to clean up — Gilbert's friends brought flowers from the market every morning — counting the money — entering the amount in Claudette's cash book under Gilbert's neat, underlined headings.

She had still to stay hidden in the wardrobe when Claudette's friends came, with sympathy and little gifts — a pot of jam — a few slices of ham — a bag of apples — a bunch of carrots, still with their graceful fernlike tops.

Gilbert's death had cut off their food supply — one of the soldiers from the depot came with a sack of potatoes — removing his helmet and bowing his head to show his sorrow.

The deportations continued unremittingly. It was more dangerous than ever before — a feverish last-minute round up, bundling together the left-overs to appease the insatiable hunger of the Evil, grown fat on flesh and crushed brains.

Pile the ashes high.
The supply of flowers dwindled — bunches of marigolds — blue scabious — dried grasses.

Sometimes Claudette didn't open the shop.
There was nothing to sell.

She would go in search of food — braving the snipers who seemed to be everywhere.

In the last days before the Allies marched into Paris, there was fighting all over the city.

The Resistance emerged from their hiding places — flaunting their red white and blue armbands — defiantly brandishing their meagre supply of weapons — a few rifles — shotguns and revolvers — homemade Molotov cocktails — an occasional captured sub-machine gun.

There was a persistent rattle of gunfire and thud of explosives. German tanks trundled and wheezed in the Place de la Concorde, and among the elegant trees of the Tuillerie Gardens — swivelling blind cyclops barrels up the Champs Elysees.

On the corner of the Place St Augustin a Molotov cocktail blew a German soldier high, like a cloth dummy from a catapult — scattering his motorbike — crumpled lumps of dirty silver paper — his helmet rolling lazily away into the square — in the fractional moment before the spreading petrol — rusty with blood — ignited with a venomous hiss — engulfing the wreckage in flames.

Here round the Ile de la Cité the fighting had been the fiercest

— outside the Préfecture de Police and over on the left bank in the Jardin du Luxembourg and the Panthéon. And then they had come, from all directions — the Free French — the Americans — the British — triumphant over the Pont d'Austerlitz — up the Avenue Victor Hugo to the Arc de Triomphe, to take the German Headquarters in the Avenue Kleiber — down the Rue de Rivoli, the soldiers dodging in and out of the colonnade — to take the German Commandant from his comfortable quarters in the Hôtel Meurice — to sign the surrender at the Préfecture de Police.

And the crowds — exuberant, cheering crowds — laughing and crying — surging up the Champs Elysees — clambering on the tanks and trucks to embrace the soldiers.

They were swept along — Claudette holding her hand tightly so they would not be separated — the tears coursing down her face.

Michelle dazed by the noise — the light and space — so many people — to be in the open air at last — to be able to stand at the window and look into the street.

She was numb and scared, and worried that Claudette might break down — would be unable to go on.

And all the time the unspoken hope that perhaps they would come back — her mother and father, and Bernadette — even Madeleine — and the fear, that was almost a certainty, that they would not.

Claudette received a letter from Germany.

A stiff white card in a stiff white envelope, the writing black and spiky, written with a fine nib.

'My brother asked me to inform you if he was killed. He died in the fighting on the outskirts of Bremen last Spring. He has no known grave. God rest his soul.'

It was signed — Maria Klausmann.

Michelle paused to watch a pleasureboat go under the bridge, tricolours curled by the breeze — a confetti of people in bright summer clothes. Somebody waved.

Gilbert had tried to find out what had happened to Madeleine and her family.

The village had been searched — people had been taken away, including the Bronchards.

Madame Dubois was arrested — but later released.

The search extended to Montrichon.

Anne-Marie and Jean Claude had been questioned, and the farm searched.

Thanks to Madame Tigny's Gestapo connections, nobody was arrested.

The Bronchards were never seen again.

It was rumoured that Monsieur Bronchard and the son, Albert, were executed. Nobody knew what happened to Madeleine and her mother. They could have been released. Madame Bronchard might have decided to make her way to her family. She came from Lyon.

Nobody knew for certain — quite a few people had never returned — it was supposed they had been executed with the others.

12

Michelle decided to have a coffee before entering the Cathedral.

She crossed the square, and went over the Petit Pont to the café on the corner.

She ordered a coffee and a croissant. She had not eaten today. A croissant was soft and easy to swallow.

There were English people at the next table, with short sleeves and beige slacks, studying a map, and behind them a young couple wearing very short shorts, with an unwieldy napsack. The girl had a ponytail, and leather thongs wound round her wrists. They were drinking beer.

She did not know what to wear to Cecile's tonight.

'Do you always have to be in mourning, darling?' she had asked, critical of Michelle wearing black.

Cecile spent a great deal of money on clothes — had dieted to a spidery thinness — frequented beauty parlours — sat in darkened rooms with slices of cucumber on her eyelids — wore ostentatious jewellery and vulgar gold and silver shoes with too-high heels.

Gaston remained indifferent.

Philippe said he had a mistress — a young woman executive in his firm. He had seen them together outside Fauchon. Michelle said that was no proof they were lovers.

She found Gaston pompous and uninteresting — expounding right-wing clichés — the lazy poor — the lazy blacks — burdening the state with their progeny — turning their homes into slums — ineducable...

'I don't want children,' she had said, when Philippe asked her to marry him.

'I am Jewish. Your mother doesn't like me...'

She wanted to say 'I am haunted by ghosts — I am consumed with guilt and shame that I am alive...'

She managed to say 'I find life difficult...'

'I will make it easier for you,' he said.

Claudette had insisted she have a 'proper' wedding.
She paid for everything — the white silk dress and veil — the meal of melon and roast veal — the glistening mountain of profiteroles — the champagne and wines. The flowers.

'You are my daughter,' she had said. 'I think of you as my daughter...'

Michelle watched this girl — this stranger — in the white dress with its full skirt and puffed sleeves — the white satin slippers — somebody fussed with her hair, arranging the coronet of orange blossom — adjusting the veil.

'Where are your gloves...?'

There had been a hunt for the gloves.

The bouquet which Claudette had so lovingly arranged, lying on the table on a bed of fern to keep it fresh...
Fresh flowers for the graves — Don't forget the fresh flowers.

It was after the wedding that Claudette had become really 'strange'. She too was haunted by ghosts.

She suffered with depression — see-sawing moods — preoccupied — falsely gay — her laughter high-pitched.

Sometimes she drank too much wine.

'Gilbert forgive me. Forgive me Gilbert. I loved him — truly I loved him...'

Michelle did her best to comfort her.

There were plenty of admirers — calling with be-ribboned gifts — taking her to dine.
'I don't want any of them,' she told Michelle. 'I do not want them. Sometimes I think if I close my eyes I can pretend — but it is not possible. My heart is dead.'

After Michelle was married — no longer there to walk with in the evening in the Tuillerie Gardens — to window shop in the Fauborg St Honoré — to take coffee in a pavement café, and watch the world go by, she started wandering the streets with baskets of flowers, handing them to passersby — 'For the graves. Fresh flowers for the graves...'

Michelle found her — in the Place de la Concorde — outside the Gare St Lazare — on the steps of the Sacré Coeur.

She would lead her gently back to the shop.

She tried to persuade her to come and live with herself and Philippe. There was plenty of room.

They had an airy spacious flat in the Boulevard Malsherbes, with a balcony where they could plant flowers. She had an orange tree. It had tiny fruit already.

But she refused.
In the end she went to the nursing home near Versailles.

It had a beautiful, if somewhat neglected garden — surrounded by woods.

Outside her window she could see a camellia bush, grown as tall as a tree, and a wild cherry...

Michelle planted white roses on her grave, and snowdrops for the spring — white jasmine for the winter.

And always fresh flowers.

13

The English couple ordered a salad — pointing at the menu — 'S'il vous plaît,' said the woman. Her hair was beige, like her blouse.

'Merci,' said the man. He folded the map and put it to one side.

Michelle broke off a piece of croissant and chewed it slowly.

Her father had talked of Spain — hands clenched, white-knuckled — on the scrubbed wood of the table.

She could not recall his face — she had never been able to recall his face — a blacked-out space — a hole — with a voice — she could remember his voice.

The kitchen was dark — the windows too small.
There was bread and rough paté on the table — a plate of cheese, pungent and runny — red wine, and a bowl of yellow peaches scenting the air.

Her mother had been upset — protesting — and he had said 'We should stand up for what we believe in. One cannot live with shame...'
Bernadette got up — scraping her chair on the rough-tiled floor.

She twirled — snapping her fingers — humming a rhythmic tune.

'Spain!' she said. 'Why are they fighting in Spain?'
She was learning a Spanish piece — spitting bright colours.
She stamped her feet, tossing her hair...

Spain — white horses rearing — haughty men with flat black hats
— the smell of heat and trodden grass.

'Go fetch a salad, chérie,' said their mother, and Bernadette
pirouetted out of the door, where the sun washed the stones —
holding the knife above her head — like castanets.

Better to have died fighting for something he believed in, than to
be herded naked to the slaughter, with less ceremony than beasts
to an abattoir.

Bernadette was never still — like a bright bird — darting —
chattering — singing — still only to play her cello — filling the
little house with rich, sweet sound.

Her mother calm and quiet — safe in her small world — her
husband — her children — baking and sewing — tending her
garden — filling the beds with snapdragons and spicy flox, and
tall lupins with their little green pods — like peas — toy peas.

Michelle would make a plate for her dolls with a wide spinach leaf
— placing on it a few redcurrants — some of the lupin pods — a
tiny yellow tomato — giving them lunch in the long grass at the
end of the garden, among the daisies and the cornflowers.

Flowers — fresh flowers. There will always be fresh flowers. Fresh
flowers for the graves.

Philippe had thought his love would heal her.
She had tried to shut out the demons — they slumbered fitfully
— waking to tear and scratch — holding her with their long nails.

Had they died because of her?

Monsieur Bronchard — sturdy and cheerful — and Albert — big-eared and scrawny — fooling around with his friends on their bikes by the village pump — sharing sticky sweets — letting her join in their football games in the long field by the school — showing her how to fish in the clear stream at the back of the mill.

Madame Bronchard — who had been so frightened — who would not have helped if it had not been for Madeleine.

Madeleine — so full of life — impatient to be grown up — to see the world.

*   *   *

They had gone to Italy for their honeymoon — to Sorrento.

The hotel, bent on the cliff top — its garden tangled and wild — with convolvulus and hibiscus — the fragile pink trumpets twined with coarse, hairy creepers — the paved paths, slippery and broken.

The sea — a green slab layered with blue — spiked with black roots — waved with weeds.

They ate plates of crisp fried calamari, and salads of celeriac and curly, dark-leaved lettuce.

They had been there a few days when the German family arrived.

Blonde and bronzed — father, mother and two teenagers — a boy and a girl — as tall as their father — their long limbs dusted with golden down, their eyes a startling blue.

They wore blue shorts and white shirts — the father had a navy blue cotton jacket with patch pockets — he spoke a little French — the mother a little Italian.

They moved with arrogant assurance — their voices loud, the

gutteral sound making the demons restless — they stirred and shifted sharpening their claws.

Had he been one of their tormentors? Not many Germans spoke French. Had he been one of the grey army who had fouled their land? Had he herded people onto trucks and trains — beating them with rifle butts — burning their houses — shooting men with their arms tied behind their backs?

She felt the father's eyes on her.

He faced her across the dining room — watching her — mocking — suggestive.

She turned her head away quickly, sipping her wine, and looked out of the window — shaded by a hanging vine, the luminous leaves moving gently in the breeze. The sky a square of vibrant blue.

The cannelloni had a rich tomato sauce.

She couldn't eat it.

She had to force herself to stay seated — for Philippe's sake she must not get up and leave the room — for Philippe's sake.

He was so happy holding her in his arms.

'This is such a beautiful place,' he said. 'And you are so beautiful...'

The children clambered over the rocks calling to each other, waving ribbons of seaweed.

The mother sat on the little terrace in a faded striped deckchair, her raffia bag full of sweets and biscuits and bottles of drink — burning her heavy thighs in the fierce glare of the sun.

They passed on the cliff path to the beach.

It was very narrow — the stones cascading in little rivulets down the steep slope — the sharp grass tufted with pink flowers.

She heard him greet Philippe who was ahead of her, and pressed herself against the rock face to let him pass.

He stood in front of her, placing his hands on either side of her head — bringing his face close to hers.

She could smell his sweat — feel his breath.

'Well, little one,' he said. 'You and I could have a good time. Don't you think so?' and he ran a finger down her neck.

Flinching from his touch, anger blinded her.

Under the helmet was a skull — a grinning skull.

The daughter called from above. 'Papa! Schnell Papa!' and some more in German...

He smiled at her — his teeth were very white.

'Later,' he said. 'Later...'

She told Philippe they had to leave.
She said she couldn't stay in a hotel with Germans.
Philippe said they seemed alright. Not all Germans were bad.
He had wanted to go to Pompeii tomorrow — but she was already packing her things.

'We have to leave,' she said. 'We have to leave...'

14

A couple had come in with two small children. They made quite a commotion sitting down. They ordered icecream. The little boy couldn't decide what sort of icecream he wanted.

'Hurry up, chéri,' said the mother.

'He never knows what he wants,' said the little girl. 'I want strawberry and vanilla — strawberry and vanilla — strawberry and vanilla...'
'Sit still, chérie,' said the mother.

She was supposed to go to school — instead she went to the Gare du Nord, or the Gare de l'Est, and waited for the trains which might bring remnants of the deportees — bald, scabbed scarecrows in ill-fitting shoes — barely able to walk — dragging their feet — eyes downcast — men and women, indistinguishable — still contaminated with leprous evil.

The waiting relatives and friends, their welcoming bouquets of soft, sweet-smelling flowers crushed in horrified hands — abandoned, wilting on the grubby stained platforms.

Joyous cries throttled in throats stiff with shock as they tried to recognise a loved one among these stumbling stick-like creatures.

People wept and fainted — collapsing in grief and hopelessness among the drifting petals.

The murmured, 'A child — look, a child!', trailing into the distance.

There were no children... there were no children.

The little boy started to whimper.
'Cry baby,' said the little girl — she had on a tartan skirt, and a

tartan ribbon tying back her hair.

'Sissy. Cry baby...' and she swung her legs, attempting to kick him.

'Hush, chérie,' said the mother. 'Why don't you have chocolate Patrick? You like chocolate...'

'He never knows what he wants,' said the little girl. 'He doesn't know what he likes. He's just a crybaby...'

The father said he would have a pastis, and would they be quiet and behave...

Philippe had thought she would change her mind about having children, but she said 'No — Never — She would never change her mind.'

She walked with Claudette among the sea-murmuring poplars, on springy cushions of grass.

Illness stretched the skin tight on Claudette's face — greenish now, as whey — the dark eyes hollow.

'Let the past go, ma petite,' she said. 'It will cripple you — the burden is too heavy. Let Philippe lead you away...'

She struggled to respond — the demons howling their protest.

'No,' she said. 'I can't...'

The English couple asked for coffee.

'Café au lait,' said the woman.

'Merci,' said the man.

She broke the last of the croissant into small pieces — chewing it with effort, as if it were a tough piece of steak.

15

She would go to the Cathedral now.

In the still, lofty space — the light striking jewelled patterns on the floor — she could ask them to forgive her for being alive — for being smart and comfortable — for having Philippe — for spending her days surrounded by flowers.

She should have been with them.
Her brilliant sister and gentle mother sealed in unspeakable torment. The demons gleefully free — dancing the tarantella — poking the agony with their long sharp nails...

The sun beat iron-hot as she crossed the square.
She took off her black jacket and pushed up the sleeves of her crisp white blouse.

In the surrealistic unreality after the liberation, as the Germans retreated, and the American jeeps took over Paris, she was still afraid to go out into the streets.

Waking — halfway to the wardrobe — hearing noises in the street in the early morning.

The Gestapo coming in the perfumed spring dawn — the rising sun a bloody orb. Hammering on the heavy oak door of the hallway until Madame Didier, her toothless protests unintelligible, dragged back the rusty bolts and unlocked it with her huge bunch of keys.

Gilbert in his pyjamas, hair awry with sleep — hurrying her into the wardrobe — scattering the cushions — Claudette shoving in her few things — scraps of paper — stubs of crayon — her bundle of clothes.

The ordered boots mounting the stone stairs — abrupt commands echoing down the curving stairwell — rifles catching on the wrought iron bannisters — past their door — up past Madame Fournier to the floor above.

Madame Benoit's screams as they took her son away — muffled as they struck her.

The alligator's scaly grey body slithering on the stairs, its greedy head swinging from side to side in triumph — the teeth yellow and pointed.

She fell over and over as the door clanged shut — crying out for her son. 'Mon fils — Bernard — mon fils — mon petit...'

She was dead when the doctor came — pulling off his gloves — fearful of the group of black-uniformed officers in the café opposite.

16

Philippe's mother served boudin blanc in a sauce with onions, and haricot beans with parsley and garlic.

It was Philippe's father's birthday.

The almost insurmountable problem of a gift solved with a book about mountaineering.

Philippe's father was an armchair mountaineer.
He had never climbed a mountain.

She doubted if he had ever seen one — sitting in the dull uncomfortable sitting room, whilst his wife watched game shows on the TV — he imagined himself roped to the man above, driving his pick into the ice wall — snowy peaks towering over him.

It was intensely hot.

The shutters were closed against the midday glare, making the dim room even dimmer.

'Just the beans for me, thank you,' she said.

She couldn't even look at the boudin.

Her mother-in-law made a gesture of annoyance.

'No wonder she has never given you any children,' she said to Philippe. 'Too concerned about keeping her figure...'

The tops of her flabby arms swung as she served the food.

'The same for me,' said Philippe. 'Really mother, it is much to hot for all this eating.'

Philippe's father played with his knife and fork, bending his head over the plate to sniff the contents. His hands shook more than ever now, and he had difficulty getting the food cleanly to his mouth.

Philippe's mother tied a check tablecloth round his neck.
'There,' she said. 'Now you can spill as much as you like.'
And turning to Philippe, 'I think at least you owe me a grandchild. You should put your foot down — not stand for this selfishness...'

Michelle drained her wine, and poured some more.

She knew that her mother-in-law didn't want her to have children — it might be a boy with crinkly hair and a great big nose, or a heavily menstruating girl with dark hair on her upper lip.

She made no attempt to disguise her dislike for her daughter-in-law, her contempt for all things Jewish. It made no difference that Michelle didn't look Jewish, that she did not embrace the Jewish

faith, had been brought up as a Christian. It was in her genes.
That was enough.

The wine made the demons dozy. They jostled sleepily, sheathing
their claws.

Perhaps she should drink more.

If she drank all the time, perhaps they would go away.

A wasp had drowned in the apricot tart.
Her mother-in-law fished it out with a knife before cutting the
tart into portions.

Michelle had more wine — scooping the apricots off the pastry
— pushing it to one side.

'Delicious,' she said.

17

It was cool in the Cathedral.

She breathed the familiar atmosphere with relief — the demons
temporarily stilled.

Crowds filled the aisles.

Groups of Japanese, Americans and Germans, hung with
cameras, clustered round their guides — necks cricked to study
the windows.

Italian families, the women clothed in black — the little boys in
T-shirts striped pistachio and white — their hair slicked shiny.
The little girls with little crosses hanging from their ears, and
white shoes — dutifully crossing themselves. Bold-kneed hikers
with shorts and brown leather sandals.

She lit two candles at the little altar, where the Virgin Mary bowed her head — her arms full of lilies.
The massed candles glowed — wicks sooty in the melting wax — sending shoots of vaporish light high — high up — to vanish in the soaring pillared arches of the roof.

She closed her eyes.

Bernadette and Madeleine sang 'J'attendrai — Le jour et la nuit j'attendrai toujours...'
They had new cotton frocks with tight waists and full skirts.
They were going to a party.

Michelle wanted to go too.

'When you are older, chérie,' said their mother. 'There will be plenty of parties...'

Bernadette said they would bring her some cake. 'I hope there'll be dancing.'

'Not at the Guignot's,' said Madeleine. 'We'll be lucky if there is any cake. Fernand's mother is a real misery...'

They went together up the street — their skirts swinging against their tanned legs. They were laughing.

Bernadette's dark glossy curls tumbling on her shoulders — Madeleine's short blonde bob catching the sunlight.

She should not be long.

Chantal was rather scatty, she shouldn't leave her alone too long. Claudette would have liked Chantal. They had the same feel for flowers — could turn a few left-over blooms into something wonderful.
She would have to shut the shop on time this evening, to go home and change for Cecile and Gaston's soirée.

She didn't want to go. She hated these occasions, but she had to do it for Philippe.

She would wear her black silk.

She would sit a minute where she could see the wondrous rose windows.

18

Cecile said, 'You should go and see Georges. He is so sympathetic — so sensitive...'

She served tea in glass cups — pale scented water with thin slices of lemon.

'Tannin is terribly bad for the nerves. Georges says you should never drink tea or coffee — especially coffee...'

Michelle, uncomfortable on the silk-buttoned sofa, took the proffered cup.

The room was oppressively stuffy and smelt of stale face cream.

Cecile never opened the windows. She was afraid of draughts.

'I just can't risk it with my neck,' she said. 'Gaston doesn't care for Georges. He thinks all psychiatrists are a waste of time. He says Georges doesn't pay his taxes. "Cushions stuffed with bank notes." How else could he afford that magnificent house at Chantilly?'

She pushed the sugar bowl towards Michelle with pale freckled fingers — the nails frosty orange.

'You shouldn't take sugar,' she said. 'Georges says it is terribly bad for you. If you have to have a sweetener, you should use honey...'

Michelle took two lumps — refusing the plate of biscuits.
'They're special biscuits,' said Cecile. 'There's a new shop in the Rue des Halles — date and almond — all natural ingredients... Georges says you should eat nothing but natural ingredients — eating the right things nourishes the mind as well as the body...'

Georges was a young man — thirty-four, perhaps thirty-five. He had dandruff — his belly soft under the expensive shirts.

How could anyone confide their innermost secrets to Georges?

Cecile didn't need a psychiatrist. She needed attention. Her life was a succession of beauty parlours — little lunches — charity functions. She had a boring husband who took no notice of her. Her son Hervé, a stooping long-necked young man with his mother's pale freckled skin and sandy hair, had gone to work in Canada. Her bad-tempered little dog, Zaza, who had shed hair on the furniture and dribbled saliva on the carpet, had died. No doubt she was lonely, despite the frequent trips to health spas to be massaged and pummelled, steamed and immersed in healing mud, cosseted by glowing young people in white uniforms.

They went to Nice in the winter — Paris was too cold — it gave her such a pain in her shoulders — and in summer they went to Canada to visit Hervé. There it was too hot. The heat made her feet and legs swell and upset her stomach and her sinuses.

Michelle tried to avoid these tête-à-têtes.

Gaston was one of Philippe's most influential clients. It was important for her to make an effort.

So she came and listened to Cecile's endless moaning — her inept and rigid opinions — sitting in her stiflingly vulgar salon, drinking her disgusting tea.

She had brought her gladioli — scarlet and cream — they fanned their brilliance against her vulgar wallpaper.

'Georges says absolutely no animal fats — a little lean meat — plenty of fish — fish is full of minerals, very good for the nerves — but absolutely no animal fat...'

*   *   *

As the winter approached, she went with Claudette to get a ration card.

Since Gilbert's death, there had been only one ration card.

Claudette had had to barter some of Gilbert's clothes to get a little extra food.

The butcher, who had been a friend of Gilbert's, sometimes gave her bones to make soup, and fatty trimmings from Black Market roasts.

There was no fish — at least there was no fish for ordinary people.

She wore an old coat of Claudette's and a pair of beach shoes stained and shrunken by the sea. All her clothes were Claudette's, but her other shoes didn't fit her.
They both wore Gilbert's socks to keep their feet warm.

The woman behind the grill — harassed — uncertain.
'But she has no papers. I can't issue a ration card if she has no papers. If she has no papers she doesn't exist...' and she burst into tears.

The cold seared them. Paris froze to a shuffling stillness.

The shops displaying dummy goods — cardboard cakes and jars of coloured stones.

They couldn't open the shop. There were no flowers.

Uprooted rails and cratered roads, ice and blizzards had brought transport to a halt. Harbours and factories, reduced to heaps of rubble, could produce nothing.

The rich had their flowers flown from the south of France — on VIP flights with visiting Generals and Embassy staff who entertained lavishly despite the chronic shortages — fed and fuelled by the Black Market entrepreneurs, who were everywhere.

Lobster and venison for the rich, whilst the ordinary people fought over a few loaves of bread.

The fuel crisis was so bad that even the street lights were turned off. There were continual power cuts.

They were down to the last few ends of a bundle of candles the Germans at the depot had given Gilbert.

It was impossible to get candles.

*　　*　　*

A lonely time for souls.

She went round the other side, and lit candles beneath the tall bronze cross.

A girl with a shaven head sat cross-legged on the pavement by the railings, a tin lid between her feet.

A little fountain played in the centre of the square.

There were round beds of red and pink geraniums.

Michelle halted — dizzy.

The young women with their shaven heads stamped with swastikas, running the gauntlet between the hissing, spitting crowd.

Haughty, defiant, weeping, cowering — pelted with fruit and stones.

Collaborators.

But they had all been collaborators.

To live was to collaborate. To work, to eat and bring up children was to collaborate.

Defeated and occupied, there was no choice.

Claudette said, 'What if someone saw me with Alex..?'

And she had said, 'You were risking your life for me. You and Gilbert were both risking your lives for me...'

The girl said, 'Can you spare some change..?'

She looked up at Michelle — her face pale, with the translucent pallor of a plant which has grown under a stone, deprived of light and air.

Michelle fumbled in her bag and gave her a fifty franc note.

'Oh, thanks,' said the girl. 'Thanks a lot...'

19

Chantal was making up a bouquet.

The work table strewn with flowers.

Her overall was wrongly buttoned — underneath she wore a lime green singlet. Lime green didn't suit her, her skin was too sallow.

She spread the flowers deftly with her short, stubby fingers.

Michelle was always amazed at the speed she worked. Her clumsy-looking hands swift and sure.

'It's for a 25th,' she said.

Somehow she had made the flowers shimmer, mixing whites and pale blues, with a touch of lilac, and pale, pale fern — almost grey.

Gerard was sitting in the yard reading the paper and smoking.

He said the flowers for the wedding had been a great success, and he had left Hélène dancing with a very handsome chap from Air France.

Michelle was pleased. She was fond of Hélène. She would give her a day off.

She went up the stairs to her office.

She sat at the desk, where the table had stood, where she had sat so many times with Claudette. Gilbert had taught her to play cards and set her sums, so that she would not fall behind too much with her education.

'To be educated is to be free,' he used to say, which was the sort of thing her father would have said.

She pulled the order book towards her.

She didn't open it.

Stealthily the freight cars shunted into the siding — gasping in the clear night air — weary with their load. The sightless engine — hungry for coal — cursing its way to nowhere.

The faceless drivers, rendered deaf and mute by the knowledge of their destination — where rivers of Death overflowed their banks, polluting the earth.

Monsieur Cadet was an engine driver.

He bought his wife violets every morning.

She got up quickly, knocking over the crystal vase of pink roses. Water spread on the carpet with the broken glass — the torn petals.

Chantal said, 'Are you alright, Madame?'

She appeared in the doorway, her hands full of leaves. There were bits of stalk in her hair.

'Yes, thank you,' she said. 'I must have caught it with my arm. Don't worry, I'll see to it...'

She went into the bathroom. Her hands were shaking. The demons jeered, jabbing her with their sharp elbows.

She drank some water, and sat on the edge of the bath.

The black eagle swooped — its beak eager for flesh — the yellow eyes pitiless.

Philippe phoned to say he was on his way home.

'Have you eaten today?' he asked.
'A little,' she said.
'I'll bring you a sandwich from Antoine's,' he said. Antoine sold delicious sandwiches. 'You sound tired chérie. Shut the shop early and come home. You will have time to have a bath and a rest...'

20

'I understand you are bothered by recurring nightmares...'

Gaston and Cecile's drawing room had French windows which opened onto a terrace patterned with leafy shadows.

Gaston did the arrangements when they entertained.
He considered Cecile incompetent.

She would serve rubbery cocktail snacks and vegetarian bites and
she had no knowledge of wine.

She would have kept the windows shut in case she caught a chill.

'Good God, woman,' said Gaston. 'Don't be so absurd. It's
summer...'
She had said that summer chills were the most treacherous.
'Rubbish, woman,' said Gaston. 'You could do with some fresh
air.'

The side tables were spread with attractive foods — appetizing
morsels — a formal garden of salmon and shrimp — cubed
chicken and quails' eggs — fenced with lettuce and asparagus.

There were buckets of ice balancing the champagne — trays of
whisky and vodka.

Inscrutable Vietnamese dispensed the food and drink.
Michelle sipped her champagne.

As usual the sight of so much food took away any appetite she
might have had.

Georges' plate was piled high — he poked at it with his fork.
Who had told Georges about her dreams?

Only Philippe knew about her dreams.

They no longer shared a room because of her dreams.

They no longer shared a bed because of her dreams.

She had to be alone to struggle with the demons.

Philippe had tried to banish them with his love, but it was no use. She had seen the pain darken his face as she turned away.

How could he have told this odious person about her dreams?

She saw him across the room listening attentively to a gesticulating redhead.

He looked thin, and there were streaks of grey in his dark hair.

The column of ghosts wound past her into the distance — limping and crawling — their faces hidden by shrouds — crowding round — tugging — beseeching her to go with them — the demons snapping at their cracked and broken feet.

'I would be most happy to help,' said Georges, popping a piece of smoked salmon into his sloppy mouth. 'A lot of these things go back to some incident in childhood...'

'If you'll excuse me,' she said. 'It's rather hot in here.'

She stood on the terrace — grouped with chairs and bright sun umbrellas. Coy statues held basins of fruit aloft. There was a gentle evening scent of roses and lavender — the grass whiskered brown by the sun.

The demons had lost none of their vigour over the years. They were vicious and wakeful — gorged and bloated on suffering.

Tearing the wounds so they could never heal — and somewhere, in the darkness, the most dreadful demon — wheezing and snuffling — so monstrous — so satiated — he waited for the tormented to come to him — slipping on the slime as the path pitched downwards — down — down to where he crouched with black-webbed claws to tear them apart.

He was waiting for her.

'Don't forget the flowers,' said Claudette. 'Don't forget the fresh flowers. Fresh flowers for the graves...'

'No,' she said. 'I won't forget.'

She finished her champagne and put the glass down on one of the round white tables.

Somebody said, 'Michelle! How are you? You look wonderful...'
She was aware of a peroxide head and sparkling necklace — a wrist of bracelets.

Claudette stood beside her — chic in black.
'I have to go,' she said. 'I'm late. Have you met Claudette?'
The peroxide head yawned red lips.
'Why don't you sit down a minute? It's nice and cool out here...'
'I can't stay,' said Michelle. 'I have to catch a train...'
She took Claudette's arm.
'Come along,' she said. 'We must hurry.'

She caught a glimpse of Philippe's white face — anxious — startled — turned towards her.

Cecile said, 'Darling, where are you off to? The evening is just beginning.'
Michelle didn't answer her.
'We must hurry,' she said to Claudette. 'We mustn't miss the train. We have to go and get the flowers...'

They managed to get a taxi at the corner of the Boulevard.

Claudette said, 'It's lovely to be back. I shouldn't have stayed away so long...'
She sat on a stool whilst Michelle filled a basket with flowers.

The shop smelt wonderful — summer encapsulated in the shuttered coolness.
There were a lot of carnations — white, red and pink —

delphiniums in all shades of blue and mauve. A green bucket of deep purple-red roses.

'I shouldn't take the peonies,' said Claudette. 'The petals drop so quickly, and the gladioli are too stiff...'

Michelle said they should go straight to the Gare du Nord, and get the Metro to Drancy.

But Claudette wanted to go first to the Place de la Concorde.

'It will be floodlit,' she said. 'I do so love to see the fountains floodlit...'

Outside Printemps Michelle gave some carnations to a couple waiting for the lights to change.

'For the graves,' she said. 'Fresh flowers for the graves...'

The woman looked away. The man bowed, taking the flowers. 'Merci Madame,' he said.

They walked quickly, Claudette's heels clicking on the pavement.

'Paris is so beautiful at night,' she said.

Outside the Crillon, Michelle tried to give some dark blue delphiniums to a woman in a grey satin dress.

'I don't want any flowers,' she said. 'Edouard!' calling to her escort who was paying off the taxi. 'Tell this woman I don't want any flowers.'

'They're for the graves,' said Michelle. 'There must always be fresh flowers...'

'Please go away,' said the woman. 'Edouard, tell her to go away. I think she's mad.'

Michelle stood by the fountains, the horses rearing in the glittering water.

A young couple walked past, hand in hand.

'Oh, what lovely flowers,' said the girl.
'How much are the roses?' asked the young man.
'They're not for sale,' she said, and handed them a dark red velvet-petalled rose — velvet as the butterfly wings on the buddleia where the demons lurked.
'Oh, thank you!' said the girl. 'It's lovely...'

Michelle didn't mention the graves. The girl was too young to think of graves.

Claudette had crossed the road and was standing at the entrance to the Tuilleries. She was talking to a tall thin girl, with short blonde hair and skinny arms.

It was Madeleine.
She cried out. 'Madeleine! How wonderful! I am so glad...'

She started towards them.
Somebody lurched into her.

'Sorry, darling.' The man was drunk. 'How about a little stroll? Have a little drink..?'

She saw two gendarmes approaching.

The man staggered away, catching the basket with an unsteady arm, spilling the flowers onto the road.

She went down on her knees trying to pick them up before the cars crushed them under their wheels.

'Wait, Madeleine!' she called. 'Please wait! I'm coming...'

One of the gendarmes said, 'Let me help you, Madame.' He bent to pick up some of the flowers. 'Are you alright?'

'Thank you,' she said. 'I'm quite alright. My friends are waiting...' But when she looked at the entrance to the Tuilleries, Claudette and Madeleine had gone.

'Oh,' she said. 'Oh they've gone without me. I must catch them up...'

'Perhaps we could take you home,' said the taller gendarme.

'There have to be fresh flowers for the graves,' she said. 'I'm taking fresh flowers for the graves.'

She picked up the basket.

'It's very kind of you, but I'm late...'

He put a restraining hand on her arm.

'I think you should come with us,' he said.

'Perhaps you could take me to Drancy?' she said. 'I have to catch a train. I'm meeting my mother and sister. I'm bringing the flowers. The flowers for the graves... If you could hurry — I'm late already. My friends have gone without me...'

The gendarmes were nonplussed.

'Isn't it a bit late for catching trains?' said the shorter one.

'They go at night — so they cannot be seen — so that no one will know the corpses are on the move.'

The demons had gone wild with delight — screeching — stamping — punching the air.

'Be quiet!' she said. 'It's the demons. They think they've won...'

The shorter gendarme took her arm.

'Come along,' he said gently. 'We will see what we can do.'

The other one took her basket with the remaining flowers. The roses dark as congealed blood among the innocent whiteness of the carnations.

'That's very kind,' she said. 'I don't want to miss the train. There must always be fresh flowers. Fresh flowers for the graves.'

A Wedding Has Been Arranged

America, 1954.

The long white satin sleeve of her dress was fastened at the cuff with a single small round satin button.
She held the bouquet of sweet-smelling white lilac and trailing greenery in her lap.

She could always get a divorce if it didn't work out.
Divorce wasn't such a dreadful thing nowadays.
She could just get a divorce.

*   *   *

She sat with Linda on the perfectly mown spring-green grass of the lawn, which sloped and spread soft pathways between the floppy beds of shrubs and flowers — jasmine and mimosa — tulips and narcissi — widening out as it met and blended imperceptibly with the expanse of white beach and distant violet-shaded ocean.

Between them baby Lottie, in a faded cotton frock and matching hat, tried to stick her chubby fingers into the springy turf.

Behind her the house, with its wide paved terrace, sat comfortably in the afternoon sun, and the old twisted cherry tree foamed with whipped cream blossom — the breeze blowing flurries of confetti petals on the green softness of the grass.

'Jeez,' said Linda. 'I wish I was getting married.' She leant over and tickled the back of her daughter's neck with a piece of grass. 'It would be just grand to be married...'

Maddie said, 'Of course you'll get married — there's plenty of time...'
Maddie had decided a long time ago that she must get married.

It was very necessary to be married.
To be a Mrs rather than a Miss was very important.

She was going to be a lawyer.
It was tough being a lawyer if you were a woman.
There were not many women lawyers, although things were getting better.

To have any freedom at all one had to be married.
Being a wife gave you immediate status.
You were treated with more respect.
No longer judged by your bust size, or dismissed as some foolish little thing who should be in the typing pool — or making the coffee — who might be promoted if they were 'nice' to the boss.

There were other advantages to being married.
No more worries about having a date — for the dance — party — dinner — theatre — whatever...
Someone always there — to book restaurant tables and airline tickets — to order taxis and deal with the landlord — plumber — neighbours — garbage problems — who could fix the car, and be responsible for understanding the small print in insurance documents —and, best of all, when in a tight corner and pressed to make an immediate decision — the classic get out — 'I'll have to ask my husband...'

Until there was complete equality between men and women a husband was essential.

Of course you had to find the right husband.
She was pretty sure she had found the right husband.

Matt was very nice.
He was tall and nice looking in a straightforward sort of way.
He was already a lawyer — reasonably ambitious — hard working — honest — and absolutely devoted to her.

His family were nice.

His mother and father were nice.
His brother and sister were nice.
All very wholesome — and pretty rich too.

She thought she had chosen well.

Of course there were some disadvantages.
She would be expected to get meals.
No more crawling home after a hard day and having a sandwich
— or beans out of the can in front of the TV.
Matt was fussy about vegetables and liked a proper breakfast with
flapjacks and syrup and scrambled eggs, whilst all she could face
in the morning was orange juice and toast.

Also he was very sporting — into long walks, tennis and golf.
Maddie didn't like sports, but she could easily get out of that.
She just wouldn't do any. She would encourage him to go with
friends.
It would give her time on her own.

And she would not be able to come home so often to this lovely
house where she had grown up — putting on her old sand shoes
and dirndl skirt, and running along the beach to the little
harbour to find Jerry varnishing his boat or mending the lobster
pots.

No more sitting and talking about this and that, and that and
this, as she had been doing for years and years and years.

But that was just foolish, and she knew that it was foolish.
There would never be any place in her life for him.
Not the life she had chosen.
A life of smart city lawyers and clever talk — people who drove
new cars and took planes to anywhere they wanted to go — just
for lunch — or tea — or cocktails.

And there was no place for her in his life.
Living from day to day on how many fish he caught, and what he

could sell them for — dependent on the weather and the season, and the whims of the chefs in the restaurants he supplied.

It was a foolish dream, and she would have to pack away her sand shoes for ever.

'Jeez,' said Linda, lying back on the grass with her unruly reddish brown curls spread behind her. 'Jeez, I just love this place...'
She was very thin — the collar-bones showing under her white blouse.
She was working mornings in the general store at the harbour.
She could take Lottie.
Everybody loved Lottie.
She was such a contented, friendly baby.

Annie came across the lawn carrying a tray.
She had made small sandwiches with chopped chicken, and little cakes with different coloured icing.
She knelt down and hugged Lottie.
'I thought you girls might be getting hungry,' she said, giving Lottie a kiss. 'Hungry work discussing weddings...' and she got up and went back up to the house.

Linda was Maddie's oldest friend.
They had played together on the beach since they were not much older than Lottie was now.
Linda's mother — too young really — abandoned by Linda's father when she was a baby, had a hard struggle.

Maddie was in the charge of Annie — darling Annie — Maddie thought she loved Annie more than her mother.
Annie was young then too.
She was sorry for Linda's mother — managing to bring picnic food for them all, and making enough so there would be 'leftovers' for Linda's mother to take home with her.

Maddie's parents were rich.
They would never miss a few slices of bread.

When they had a glut of fruit or vegetables, Annie would ask Maddie's mother if she could give some to Linda's mother — apples — cherries — tomatoes and fresh green peas.

When they were older and played by themselves, Annie still gave Maddie packages for Linda's mother.

'Give Linda these peaches — they're rotting on the ground — and some of these cakes I made when your mother had that Mrs Sachs to tea. They didn't eat them — Mrs Sachs is on one of her diets. If she got up and got busy doing something she mightn't need to diet all the time...'

They had stayed close friends — despite the difference in their background — the difference in their schooling... Maddie was sent away to a very select boarding school. A square grey building — unsmiling winter or summer — severely clad in grey uniforms and black patent shoes — their days strictly regimented — work hard — play hard — work hard.

Maddie accepted school.

She had already decided that she was going to have a career — not just be a society wife — worrying about her figure and her husband's possible infidelities.

Her mother was just a society wife — a life full of vacuous nothing with people she didn't really like.

The first thing she did when she came home for the holidays was to put on her old sand shoes and run down the beach to find Linda and Jerry.
When she was due to go to college, she went to her father's study and asked him if he would do something for her.

'I want you to do something for Linda,' she said.
'And what would you like me to do?' he said, swivelling round on his brown leather chair.

Maddie loved her father.

He was always fair — never fussed about class and doing the 'right thing', like her mother.

She was sure he had been responsible for insisting she should play with who she liked when her mother had objected to her playing with the ordinary kids.

'They might lead her astray,' she would say. 'They're not like us...'

'Nonsense,' he would say. 'Do you really think Maddie is going to be led astray by anybody? She can play with who she likes. It's good for her to mix...'

When she was eight Hornby was born, and her mother had him to worry about, although he had a nanny, and she spent little time in the nursery. Still, it stopped her fussing so much over her.

'I want you to pay for Linda to go to secretarial college and do a proper secretarial course so that she can get a proper job, and get paid a proper wage...'

Her father drew some Snoopy-like figures on his blotting paper. He was very fond of Snoopy.

'Alright,' he said. 'You find out about it and arrange it — and I'll sign the cheque...'

'That,' she said, 'is the most super thing you've ever done in your whole life, Dad...' and she gave him a terrific hug that knocked his glasses off.

Linda was a bit reluctant at first.

'What'll Mum say?' she said.

'She'll be pleased,' said Maddie. 'It'll give you a chance. You'll be able to get a decent job...'

When Maddie graduated, she decided to go straight to law school.

'What do you want to got to law school for?' said her mother. 'What a ridiculous idea. You should be thinking about getting married. What will people say? Women don't do law... it's not feminine... it's just not done. You don't need to be a lawyer. How

many women lawyers are there anyway?'
'Not many,' said Maddie.
'Not enough,' said her father.

Her mother teetered perpetually on a social seesaw.
As the wife of one of the most prominent members of society, from one of the wealthiest and most influential families, she should have been able to do and say what she liked. Instead she worried constantly about doing the 'right thing', saying the 'right thing', vulnerable to any form of criticism — embarrassed by the extreme tolerance of her husband, and her avidly feminist daughter.

Thank goodness Hornby was still too young to start having radical opinions.
At least she hoped he hadn't.

He was away at school a lot, and when he was home he was always out on his boat, or at his friends' houses listening to dreadfully loud music and playing pool.

She knew all the ladies at the club would want to know why on earth Maddie wanted to be a lawyer.
It wasn't the sort of thing their sort did.
'Strange profession for a girl...'
Barbs behind the smiles.
She'd never find a husband — men don't like clever women — they made them nervous...
'Penny's getting married in the Spring — such a nice young man she met at college — very nice family...'
'Sarah's going to Europe — nothing like travel to broaden the mind...'
'Mary-Anne's going to do a course in interior design — she's very artistic...'

Maddie's mother flushed and flustered rushed home, telling Annie she was going to lie down till suppertime.
'I have such a headache...'

'I'll bring you some tea,' said Annie.
'Oh, thank you, Annie...'

What would she do without Annie?
What would any of them do without Annie?
And then she started worrying whether they had always treated
her right — paid her enough — expressed their gratitude enough
— had not offended her in any way...
And she got more flushed and flustered and miserable, and her
headache got worse.
She had not been sure about Annie at first either.
A homeless waif Greg had found on a park bench.
Other people got their servants from proper agencies.

They had not been married long and only had a daily woman
who came to clean and do a little laundry and prepare vegetables.
Greg said she should have a cook, but she had been determined
to be a 'proper' wife and cook delicious meals for him when he
came home from work.

She had been a complete failure.
She had spent six months before her marriage at a very superior
domestic science college learning the art of cooking and home
maintenance, where she had made rubbery soufflés and disastrous
duck à l'orange, and learnt the importance of making laundry
lists and labelling storage jars.

She couldn't even organise the 'daily', who spent most of her time
in the kitchen drinking coffee, eating cookies, and complaining
about her back.

Greg had brought Annie home with him one day.

She had been brought up in an orphanage — nothing much
seemed to be known about her parents and, as was customary,
when you reached sixteen, they gave you a few dollars, a bag
for your belongings, some addresses of hostels and possible
employers, and waved you goodbye.

Greg had noticed her outside his offices, sitting on a bench.
She had sat there all day, huddled in her coat.
He sent the doorman Freddie to ask if she was alright.
'Give her a few dollars,' he said.

Next day she was there again, so he sent his secretary down to find out what she was doing there.

Miss Carson had been rather huffy.
It was cold.
She didn't like having to put on her coat and hat and gloves, and go out and speak to some young layabout.

'She's one of those orphan girls,' she said.
'What orphan girls?' said Greg.
'She's sixteen,' said Miss Carson. 'When they're sixteen they have to leave the orphanage and find a job. She's supposed to be looking for a job, not sitting around on benches in the cold…'

There was a long pause.
'What were you doing when you were sixteen?' said Greg, and before she could answer, 'Tell Freddie to go and ask her to come and see me. Tell him to bring her up himself, and go and get some coffee and biscuits — chocolate biscuits…'

So he had brought her home.

'Here you are sweetheart,' he had said, kissing the top of his wife's head. 'This is Annie. She is going to live with us and help us, and you won't have to worry about anything any more.'

She pulled the cashmere rug up to her chin.
She heard Annie's soft steps on the landing.
'I brought you a few plain cookies,' she said, putting the tray down on the bedside table. 'Eating a little will help your headache…'
'Oh, thank you, Annie,' she said.

In the fall of her first year at law school, Linda's mother died.

Linda wrote, 'Ma died last Wednesday. She was so ill. Annie was a great help...'

Annie wrote, 'The poor little thing was so weak — she just gave up the struggle. I've done my best to help Linda sort things out...'

Linda had been working for some time as a secretary to the proprietor of a big gas station on the main highway, and going out with Brad, one of the mechanics. A swaggering blond muscular young man, with an impressive tan and very white teeth, who rode a motorbike very noisily and very fast.

Linda had spent all the summer evenings with him — roaring off into the dusk — riding pillion — her arms round his waist.

She hardly came to the beach at all that summer.

That Christmas there was a fine dusting of snow on everything.

Maddie took the car to drive round the beach road to find Jerry, but he was not there.

The boats shrouded white humps on the frosted shingle — the sea flat and smooth and shiny like a skating rink.

He wasn't in the café either.

She looked up the hill to the white clapboard house where he lived with his older sister Mona and her husband, Sol.

Sol was a fisherman too.

There were lights in the windows, and smoke coming from the chimney, but that was strictly out of bounds.

They had all played together on the beach when they were kids — herself and Linda — Jerry and Mona and Sol, and any other kids that were hanging around.

Swimming and fishing. They ran races and played ball games and had picnics.

Her mother had never been happy about it.
They were not 'our type'.
What would people say?

She would rather Maddie had played with the rich kids, doing careful breaststroke in the clear blue water of their designer pools, monitored by reliable domestic servants.

When they got older, they had barbecues, and played music and danced.

Mona always kept an eye on her.
Mona was no fool.
She knew as well as Maddie knew, that she must never step over the line with Jerry.
That it could go nowhere.
That it would be disastrous.

Maddie had never been up to the white clapboard house overlooking the bay.

Once Mona had come by whilst they were talking — the summer graduated, and she had stood uncertainly.

'Haven't seen you for a while,' she had said.
'I've only just got home from the college,' said Maddie, suddenly comfortable.
'You all finished now then?' said Mona, watching her brother.
'Not really,' said Maddie. 'I'm going to law school in the autumn...'
'Law school,' said Mona. 'You going to be a lawyer?' She was astonished.
'Thought you'd be off to Europe...' She was going to say more, but stopped.
Maddie knew what she had been about to say. 'Thought you'd be looking for a husband...'
'No,' said Maddie. 'I'm going to be a lawyer...'

She drove the car up to the highway to fetch Linda and take her home, that is, if she wasn't going on the back of Brad's bike.

Linda was very pleased to see her.
'Jeez,' she said, getting into the car. 'This is great — thought I'd have to freeze to death waiting for a bus...'

Her house was just the same, except, of course, her mother wasn't there.
It was very cold in the shabby little kitchen.
The sitting room was very cold too.
'Shall I light the fire?' said Maddie.

So many times they had collected driftwood together for the fire — dragging it along on a makeshift trolley they had concocted with a bit of hardwood and some old pram wheels.

'Please,' said Linda. 'I'll make some coffee,' and put some water on to boil.

Maddie knelt on the floor and arranged the twigs carefully on the crumpled up newspaper, before lighting it.
There was a basket of logs.

Linda came and stood behind her.
'I'm pregnant,' she said, and sat down suddenly on the sagging sofa.

Maddie felt she had been punched in the stomach.
She didn't know what to say.
She remained on her knees in front of the newly lit fire, and put on a few more pieces of wood.

'Are you sure?' she said.
'Yes,' said Linda. 'I'm quite sure.'
'Are you going to get married? Is it Brad?' She felt foolish.
'No,' said Linda. 'I shan't be getting married. And yes, Brad is the father — and — well — oh God, it's so stupid... Jeez, it's so stupid...'

She got up slowly and went out into the kitchen, and poured the boiling water into the coffee jug.

'Annie sent some honey cake and apple pie,' said Maddie in an attempt to sound normal. 'She's doing so much baking for Christmas. Oh, and some sausage rolls...'

She took them out of her bag, and put them on the table.

She remembered how Linda's mother had always been so pleased when she had brought something from Annie — strawberry jam — there are so many strawberries this year — or, 'There was so much leek and potato soup over from dinner Annie thought it would be a shame to waste it...'

Linda's mother had always seemed old — old and tired — although she was probably as young as Annie, and definitely younger than her own mother — and now she was dead — and Linda was pregnant.

'Annie was a great help,' said Linda. 'She came and helped sort things out. She even bought me a new mattress so I could use the bed...' Her voice trailed away.

There was only one bedroom which she had shared with her mother, sleeping on a divan by the window.
'I've made my bed into a sofa — with cushions,' she said. 'It looks very nice...'

They took their coffee by the fire.
'So what will you do?' said Maddie.

'I'll work as long as I can,' said Linda. 'And then — well — I suppose I'll have to go on welfare for a bit...'

'What about Brad?' said Maddie, trying to sound casual — what about Brad the contemptible swanky creep...

'He's gone,' said Linda. 'As soon as I told him, he quit his job, and rode off into the sunset on his precious bike, and I haven't heard from him since...'

'Will you keep the baby?' said Maddie.
'Of course I'll keep the baby,' said Linda. 'I'll manage — I'll be able to get jobs — I'll manage...'

That Christmas she met Matt.
He came to their Christmas party with some of her friends.
A New York lawyer.
Personable — charming — very good family — the ideal candidate for a potential husband.

During the next few months she saved as much of her allowance as she could, and in the spring holidays, before Linda's baby was born, they went on a shopping spree, herself, Linda and Annie, and she bought Linda a cot and all the bedding, and a bath and towels, and Annie bought little clothes and nappies, and they had a special tea at the luxurious Meridian Hotel, in a lounge full of luscious plants, and a fountain with goldfish, and chairs with deep, soft cushions.

'I think you should give Linda a pram for the baby,' she said.

They were having supper on the terrace.
The evening was very warm, and the garden smelt wonderful, with just a gentle breeze coming from the sea.
They were eating dressed crab, and little homemade rolls and butter.
Dressed crab was her father's favourite.

'What do you mean?' said her mother. 'A little gift perhaps, but a pram...'
'She needs a pram,' said Maddie.
'Don't be silly dear,' said her mother. 'Prams are much too expensive...'
'Not as expensive as a plate at one of your stupid charity lunches,'

said Maddie.

'They raise a lot of money for very good causes,' said her mother. 'A new outfit to wear at one of your "charity" lunches would probably buy several prams,' said Maddie. 'Anyway, Linda is a good cause...'

'I hardly think so,' said her mother. 'It's her own fault she's in this predicament.'

'Oh, mother,' said Maddie. 'Don't be such a prig. I wonder how many daughters of your precious ladies club have ever got themselves into a "predicament". Of course it's more discreetly handled by those with money. A quick stay in a private nursing home for a sudden, urgent gynaecological problem, and all is forgotten...'

Her father said, 'OK Maddie — I think you'd made your point. Your mother and I will be delighted to provide Linda's baby with a pram. Choose one and I'll let you have the money. It's the least we can do...'

'But Greg...' said her mother.

'I think Annie said something about strawberry ice cream,' said her father. 'Go and see, Maddie love, will you...?'

Matt proposed as she knew he would, and she accepted.

It was the autumn term of her final year at law school. He came in a brand new dark blue convertible to spend the weekend, staying in the best hotel in town, and asked her to marry him.

She had spent quite a while during the summer staying with his family in their house on Long Island. A sprawling white mansion with extensive grounds.

She liked his family, particularly his young sister Emily, who had a mass of unruly dark curls, rather like Linda's reddish-brown ones, and she giggled a lot.

Matt bought her a beautiful ring. A square emerald surrounded by little diamonds.

She was going to refuse it, but she knew he wouldn't understand, and that he would be upset.
His family would be upset.
Her family would be upset.
So she just said 'It's beautiful', which it was, and allowed him to slip it on her finger.

They decided to marry the following May, to give her time to revise for her finals, and then they would move to New York, where she had already secured a place with a law firm — Hart, Schwartz, and Burroughs — to do her articles.

Matt already had an apartment in New York, but they would look for something larger, on the East Side, near Central Park.

She waited to tell the family until she came home for Christmas.

Her mother was thrilled — overcome with relief.
The horrors of having to explain away a spinster daughter — pursuing a legal career — so little time for a social life — so many exams — really doing terribly well — all vanished.

Instead of having to listen to everybody else talking about their daughters' forthcoming weddings — or worse, last year's weddings — or worse still, the arrival, or imminent arrival, of grandchildren — instead of listening with feigned interest to everyone else's children's success stories, she now had her own wedding to boast about — a successful, wealthy prospective son-in-law to boast about.

'It would be nicer in June,' she said. 'Why have it in May? The weather isn't so reliable...'
'Because of my finals in July,' said Maddie. 'I need time to revise.'
'You're not going on with this law thing after you're married?' said her mother in alarm. 'Really Maddie...'
'Of course I'm going on with my 'law thing',' said Maddie.

Her mother was speechless. How was she going to explain that?

No girl of her class worked after she was married. It just wasn't done.

'What if you have a baby?' she said lamely. 'You can't carry on working if you have a baby...'
'I'm not going to have a baby,' said Maddie. 'I don't want any children...'
'Don't be silly darling,' said her mother. 'Of course you want children...'
'No,' said Maddie. 'I don't want children. I am going to be a lawyer. I won't have time for children...'
'But what does Matt say?' said her mother. 'He can't want his wife to work, and not have any children...'

Maddie shrugged. 'I don't care what he says,' she said. 'He knows how I feel. He doesn't have to marry me...'
'But what will people say?' said her mother.
'I don't care what people say, for God's sake,' said Maddie.
'Oh dear,' said her mother. 'I'm getting one of my headaches — I'll have to go and lie down...'

What would people say? Carrying on with a legal career after she was married. How was she going to explain that?

It was too cold for sand shoes, so she put on her fur-lined boots, took off her engagement ring, put it in the trinket box on the dressing table, and crunched her way along the icy beach to tell Jerry she was going to get married.
The winter sun streaked the surface of the sea with gold.

He was with a group of fishermen by the little jetty.
Her heart gave its customary little leap, seeing him tall and easy in the thick navy sweater.

They went into the café by the water's edge and sat opposite each other by the window, and he said 'Well, it's all going the way you wanted,' and he didn't look at her, putting more sugar in his coffee.

'It couldn't have been different,' she said. 'I wish it could, but it can't — so I'm going to do the best I can — the very best I can...' Maddie sat with her mother in the drawing room, working out the seating plan.

Her mother was getting all fussed about protocol — who should take precedence over whom — which relative, friend or VIP was more important..

'Start with the top table,' said Maddie. 'That's easy. Then the second table for the closest friends and relatives. So. Hornby — Matt's brother and his girlfriend — his mother's sister and her husband and Annie...'

'Annie isn't on the guest list,' said her mother.
'Why not?' said Maddie. 'Of course she's on the guest list...'
'Well dear — I mean, well, we all love Annie, but she is only the cook...'
Oh mother, you're impossible,' said Maddie. 'Annie runs the house, and looks after all of us. She is more important than any of these people...' and she waved her hand at the long typed list of names that lay between them on the table.
'I just don't think it's appropriate,' said her mother.

'It's my wedding,' said Maddie, 'and I say Annie is to go on the family table. Because she is family.'
'But she'll just feel awkward,' said her mother. 'It's not her place...'

'I would be quite happy to have a quiet wedding in a registry office,' said Maddie. 'I would rather have a quiet wedding in a registry office...'

'Oh, Maddie please,' said her mother.

'No mother,' said Maddie. 'You can put all the others where you like, but Annie goes on the family table...'

There was more trouble over the bridesmaids.

Her mother didn't want Linda to be a bridesmaid.
'Do you have to have Linda as a bridesmaid?' she said.

They had chosen the dresses — very simple purple lilac silk — with head-dresses of lilac flowers and ribbons.

'I mean — well — she is a mother, and Lottie is very sweet — but she is rather young — not quite two…'

'What you mean,' said Maddie, 'is that she is a little bastard, and that Linda is a fallen woman, and you are worried what people will say. I can never understand why you care so much about what people will say. You are right at the top of the social hierarchy. Your husband is wealthy, successful and respected, and all you worry about is what people might say. People will find something nasty to say whatever you do. If you wore white shoes, there would be whispers, "Fancy wearing white shoes…", and if you wore brown shoes, there would be whispers, "Fancy wearing brown shoes…". You have always worried about what they must have said about you allowing me to play with Linda — of having her to the house, and at my birthday parties and at Christmas. Even after she'd had Lottie. "Fancy letting her daughter mix with people like that…". Linda's mother worked hard and had a decent, miserable life. It wasn't her fault her husband deserted her. She did her best for Linda…'

'Please dear,' said her mother. 'You're giving me another headache…'

'Well I think it's pathetic,' said Maddie. 'Of course Linda is going to be a bridesmaid, and Lottie will be adorable.'

'What about your cousins Elspeth and Cynthia?' said her mother. 'Aunt Enid will think it rather strange they have not been asked…'
'Mother,' said Maddie, 'I hardly know Elspeth and Cynthia. I don't want them to be my bridesmaids. I don't care what Aunt Enid thinks. I am having Linda and Emily, and darling baby Lottie…'

The spring sun was warm on her face.

Lottie ran across the soft spring greenness of the lawn, scooping chubby handfuls of frothy cherry blossom — a snowstorm of petals blown by the wind, and throwing them joyfully in the air.

Linda sat up. The grass had striped the back of her white blouse with green.

'You've always known what you wanted to do,' she said. 'It must be great to know what you want to do. I never knew what I wanted to do...'

'I was just lucky,' said Maddie.

She kept her eyes on the glittering surface of the sea — changed now from violet to aquamarine, ruffled white by the breeze.

'But you chose such a tough thing to want to do,' said Linda. 'Jeez, there must be only about two women lawyers to every hundred men. Aren't you scared?'

Her father had said the same. 'It'll be very tough sweetheart. It's a man's world. They don't exactly welcome women...'

She had had to choose something really tough — something tough enough to substitute for what she really wanted.

She thought of her old sand shoes and skirt in the wardrobe in her bedroom — Jerry's familiar lean figure coming to meet her along the beach...

'Things are changing,' she said. 'In a few years time there'll be lots of women lawyers — lots of women everything. Anyway, I've had lots of support...'

Linda giggled. 'I don't remember your mother being very supportive...'

'She doesn't think women should have careers,' said Maddie. 'She thinks it's unladylike, and all that rubbish...'

'Jeez,' said Linda. 'She must be relieved you're getting married...'

Maddie didn't answer.
She was tired of it all.
Perhaps getting married was a mistake.
Perhaps she should have just thrown everything up and put on her sand shoes and gone...
Gone to tread uncertain stardust — diamond flecks in the fine white sand — a moonlit pathway to the sea — leading who knows where...

'I hope Lottie behaves,' said Linda. 'Jeez, it would be just awful if she spoilt your wedding...'

'Of course she'll behave,' said Maddie, watching her heaping the fragile creamy blossom into little mounds. 'She's just gorgeous...'

Maddie descended the stairs.
Behind her on the landing Madame Roberta, who had done their hair, Sophie, who had done their makeup, and Marcia, who had done their nails, stood in a hushed admiring group.

Outside in the garden, people bustled up and down the hessian path leading to the pink and white striped marquee, carrying dishes and glassware.

The others waited in the hall.
Linda and Emily, their unruly curls uncustomarily neat and tidy, with their ribboned head-dresses of purple lilac, looked really stunning.

Baby Lottie sat in the big armchair in her lilac dress and little matching shoes, holding her teddy bear.

Her father and Hornby solemn in dark suits and silver-grey ties.
Her mother in a powder blue two-piece — always powder blue.

'I feel comfortable in blue,' she had insisted, when Maddie had suggested a change.

She had quite a spectacular hat, though, with a lot of tulle and blue silk flowers.

In the middle of the hall by the round table, laden with bowls of yellow roses, stood Annie in her 'sensible' apron.

'Why aren't you ready, Annie?' she said.

'She's not coming to the church dear,' said her mother. 'There's so much to see to here…'
'If Annie doesn't come, I'm not going,' said Maddie. She felt sick. The people round her blurred into a jumble of colours. Behind her the little group drew in their breath with an audible hiss.

Her mother started to speak, but her father stepped forward and untied Annie's apron.
'Better get your coat and hat Annie,' he said. 'We can't upset the bride.'

The car swept majestically down the beach road.
She had wanted to ask the chauffeur to take the top road, but thought her father would think it odd.
He knew how she loved the sea.

It was a lovely day, and the water was a pale harebell blue, reflecting the sky.

She didn't look towards the harbour, or the jetty, or up at the white clapboard house overlooking the bay.

She kept her eyes on the sprays of white lilac on her lap.

She prayed that Jerry would be well out to sea on his boat — that he would not have seen the cavalcade of be-ribboned cars on their way to the church.

If it didn't work out, she could get a divorce.
If she really couldn't bear it, she could get a divorce.

Her father said, 'I'm really proud of you, sweetheart — really proud,' and he patted her hand.

She had planned for this day.
This is what she had wanted.
This is what she had chosen.
Now she had to do her best to make it work.

And then she was getting out of the car, and Emily was fussing with her veil, and Linda was arranging her train, and she was entering the church on the arm of her father as the organ thundered out the first chords of the Wedding March.

And so be it...

Scorn

1

Stefan said, 'I only do beards — and moustaches. I am an expert on facial hair...'

He had suggested they meet in the Russian Café near the Piazza del Duomo.
Dimly panelled, with green glass-shaded Art Deco lights on dark brown polished tables.
The bar worn and scratched — etched and chiselled — layered echoes of the past.
Viva il duce — Viva zio Joe — 'fascisti porci' scribbled over black swastikas — Russian lettering — Happy New Year 1946 — the outline of a Lamborghini, 'the best car in the world' — an unsteady drawing of a gondola — signatures — dates — hearts entwined — lists of footballer's names...

The shelves behind the bar had jars of dessicated herbs, and odd-shaped bottles of yellow liquid.

'They serve wonderful beetroot soup...'
A thick deep purple, swirled with sour cream — bitter black bread spread with mascherone — little glasses of vodka...
Peter would have preferred a comforting bowl of minestrone, with lots of vegetables, and a glass of chianti. He did not care for vodka, and the coffee was gritty and bilious.

'Facial hair is frightfully important,' said Stefan. He licked his fingers and wiped them on a paper serviette.

'It tells you so much about a person. You have to get it absolutely right. One could hardly give Jesus a bushy red beard, or a waxed moustache. In this production of Boris Godunov the whole cast, apart from a few women of course, have beards — not a hairless face in sight.'

Stefan was clean shaven — his skin smooth and pale as uncooked sausage meat — pale-eyed, his hands bonelessly flexible, with closely bitten nails.

Peter's hands were thin and bony — the knuckles lumpy and raw, the skin rough and blueish with cold.
The bones of his wrists protruding from the sleeves of his worn jacket.
Stefan noticed Peter's discomfiture, the imperceptible reluctance to swallow the rich dark liquid.

It was diverting to speculate on the discovery that these rock-hard unattractive knobbly globes, unearthed by chance, could be transformed into a juicy vegetable — delicious in all sorts of ways... Cavemen perhaps, playing football, kicked one into the fire...

The café was not very full.
An expensive overweight couple sat at a corner table eating blinis and sour cream.
The man wore a yellow brocade waistcoat.
The woman had a black suit with a nipped-in waist, and a lot of diamonds — a sparkling black pincushion.
She had thrown her blonde mink stole onto the chair beside her — a glossy breathing mound — waiting to throttle her — the soft-skinned ferocious little animals waiting to take their revenge...

'Very good isn't it?' said Stefan. 'Excellent soup...'
He raised his glass. 'Na starovya!' he said.
Peter took a small sip of his vodka. 'Salute!' he said.
He was beginning to feel rather ill.

2

Peter had met Stefan at the party.

A party organised by Signora Fratelli, one of the Governors of the Scuala d'Arte, for all those who had finished their course and received their diplomas.

The Board of Governors had visited the Art School to see the students at work. They were a bizarre group — a mixture of Business and Bohemia. The business contingent with razor sharp creases and sober silk ties — discreet flashes of gold cuff links and watch straps. The bohemian divided between the eccentric in circus performer's scarlet satin jump suit or surrealistically patterned overalls, and the scruffy with cord trousers held up by string and long hair tied back with bootlaces.

There were three women — a tall thin grey-haired business woman in a navy blue suit and white blouse, an exotic older woman, her fusty blonde hair wound with a vivid scarf, wearing a fake leopard-skin jacket and knee-length red boots, and Signora Fratelli, impeccable in a Valentino suit, her voluptuousness expertly restrained with expensive undergarments.

They stood in a group at the door of the studio, shuffling their feet, and the folders of papers they held, whilst Professor Ciano explained the purpose of the class — the purpose of the Course — the importance of Art in Society...

Suddenly becoming bored with his speech, he motioned them to inspect the work of the students, intently painting the objects on the table. Fruit and flowers arranged in Terracotta jugs and bowls.

Signora Fratelli had stopped to speak to him. She had liked his painting.
'I feel I could eat that melon,' she said.
Later he had received a letter on pale blue notepaper with crinkled edges, to ask if he would paint her portrait... Perhaps he would get in touch and they could discuss terms...
And then a thick white envelope containing a gold-edged invitation to the 'Leavers' Party'.

He had to have a black suit.

Daniel had a black suit.

Daniel was a violinist. He had to wear a black suit whenever he had a job. He played anything, anywhere. In the orchestra at the Scala — for the ballet — for symphony concerts, or musicals — anything.

He lived on the top floor, the ceiling sloping sharply, so there was not much room to stand up.
He practised sitting on the bed — the music propped against the pillow.
He had bought the suit secondhand in the market.
He would lend him the suit.

'Do you have a studio?' asked Stefan.
Peter almost choked on a piece of black bread — it stuck somewhere between his mouth and his stomach.
A studio — what a thought! — a high-ceilinged attic with white walls and a roof of glass — smelling of wet oil paint and turpentine — a studio...
'No,' he said. 'No — I don't have a studio.'

He had been lucky to find a cheap room in the centre of the city, not far from the Art School.
The rooms were cheap in Dora's rundown mess of a house. The peeling plaster and wooden-treaded stairs steeped with lingering smells.
The smells of deprivation and poverty.
Cheap scent — stale clothes — sour milk — boiled washing — rotten cabbage — floury pasta — rancid fat...
The airless landing choked with dust. The broken seat in the cupboard of a toilet — windowless — a piece of coarse string doubled and knotted for a chain — buzzing with flies.

Dora lived on the ground floor.
Her carrot red hair, inexpertly dyed — wiry with age, a lopsided

bundle on the top of her head, held in place with plastic 'jewelled' combs.

She wore long gypsy satin skirts and a long-fringed shawl, which got caught on door knobs and in the backs of chairs, dipping into cups, gathering dust and crumbs.

Her sitting room, gaspingly hot, filled with tasteless ornaments and dying plants — shrivelled cacti and drooping rubber plants. Curling photographs of faded sepia people and postcards of bright sunny beaches, propped on the mantlepiece beneath a picture of the Virgin Mary in her obligatory blue dress, holding a lily, her eyes raised to a starry Heaven.

The sofa and armchairs sagged hopelessly, the covers soiled and unpleasantly greasy.

The net curtains, stiff and yellow, spotted by flies as they hurled themselves at the light, clusters of dried bodies on the grimy sill.

Avaricious — greedily stuffing her mouth with macaroons, and struggling with the latch of the window to shout at Signora Capetti to clear off.

Signora Capetti accosted the young men, vainly searching for her son, vanished in the war — in the black rocks at Trento — splintered stones to impale your heart.

Now she wandered the streets in her rusty black clothes — clutching at the young men's arms... 'Have you seen my son? Just a boy — have you seen my son? Tall like his father — only a boy...', sitting, swaying and moaning in doorways.

'Clear off — mad old woman. You should be locked up...' she would shout, spitting crumbs into the street. 'Va via — stupido...'

She expected the rent to be paid on time — not a day late. Climbing heavily up the stairs — wheezing — clutching her chest, banging on their doors. 'What day do you think this is? I'm not a charity — I shouldn't have to climb the stairs with my heart...'

Bridget was scared of her.

She had the room opposite Peter on the first floor. She was also an art student.

A nice girl. She wore round glasses, her undernourished hair scraped back into a bunch held with an elastic band.

She was thin. Her shoulder blades sharp under her overwashed jumper.

'No funny business,' Dora had said.

It was hard to imagine any 'funny business' with Bridget. She blended with the colourless room, overlooking next doors' drainpipes, the stench of overflowing dustbins wafting upwards in the warm Spring air. It was better in the winter when cold and rain inhibited the rotting process.

She had made a cover for the bed with knitted squares.

She had bought some wool in a sale — odds and ends from a basket outside the wool shop — discontinued shades — dull colours that nobody wanted — beige, sludgy green, a few balls of bright orange and a blue, somewhere between royal and navy — predominantly beige.

'Anyway, it's warm,' she said. 'Even if it is a bit dull....'

Sometimes she made soup, going to the Market at the end of the day, filling a bag with the discarded leaves of cabbage and cauliflower, wilted spinach — overripe tomatoes, split and squashy — the coarse outer stalks of celery, a few black-eyed potatoes. Peter would buy broken pasta — bits from the bottom of jars and bins — 250 grammes for just a few lira.

Daniel would bring bread — occasionally a piece of cheese.

Lucia had made soup from discarded vegetables from the market. Early in the morning to the bakers for yesterday's leftover bread, and as darkness fell to the market for the vegetables. Sometimes there was fruit as well, bruised pears and peaches, split plums, blackened bananas.

Their mother had become too ill to leave the brass-knobbed bed in the alcove behind the curtain — too weak to sit in the broken armchair in the cramped room where Peter slept on a mattress between the heavy-legged table and the ornate sideboard, wedding presents from her family.

Anna slept on a trestle bed against the wall where the crucifix hung — a single candle on the shelf below, with a vase of powdery dried flowers.
Lucia had a sleeping bag, laid on the floor across the door, the only place where there was room.
In the corner was a heavy old sink with a cold tap, and a tin bath in which they washed themselves and did the laundry.

There was always washing — there were always sheets to wash — for years there had been sheets to wash — the indignities of illness.
First their father, and now their mother.
Peter could hardly remember his father — a shape between the blankets — the continual rasping cough — the bowls of yellow phlegm — the awful smell of vomit — and the washing, always the washing, always wet sheets hanging from the makeshift clothes horse by the window. Their mother scrubbing them in the tin bath with a bar of brown soap, Lucia or Anna turning the handle of the wringer — the damp making the walls grey with mould.

Lucia had slicked his hair with water and held his hand as they trudged behind their father's coffin in the driving rain. The black-clothed women huddled under black umbrellas, like so many black-winged crows. The boy in a white surplice holding a black umbrella over the priest, mumbling the Latin words as the coffin was lowered into the earth.

Until their mother became ill, she worked as an office cleaner. It was Lucia who fetched him from school and fed him hunks of bread and jam, and pale milky coffee, the grounds re-used until all the colour had gone.
Then it was Lucia who did the washing, the blue veins in her skinny arms standing out with the effort of lifting and rinsing the sodden linen — sheets — so many sheets...

She made wonderful soup, mashing the vegetables to a pulp for their mother — coaxing her to swallow a few mouthfuls.
She had to give up going to school.
She went to see the Mother Superior, a liberal and understanding woman, who had spent a lifetime working among the poor and disadvantaged. She agreed that Lucia could take work home with her, and bring it once a week to be corrected. Sometimes Anna would miss an afternoon's school and take Lucia's place at their mother's bedside, where she lay, her body distorted by the parasitic tumour flourishing unseen — twisting her bones, stretching the papery skin, so that Lucia could go out a little — walk a little — breathe a little.

It was Lucia who had slicked his hair with water, and found him a black tie, and held his arm as their mother's coffin was lowered into the ground, the cheap plywood already splintered.

Anna had gathered wild anemones from the slopes above the town, tying them with a piece of white ribbon, to lay on the coffin, but they came undone, the fragile petals scattered in the mud — trampled by the pallbearer's boots.

*   *   *

Two young men, arms linked, walked past the window of the café.
One was wearing a purple velvet suit with a matching hat, as if he had had a large bowl of beetroot soup poured over him...

Guido had wanted to come to the party with him.
'I could wear my new white suit,' he said. 'I've got some absolutely marvellous white suede shoes, and a fabulous pale pink silk shirt...'
'I'm sorry, caro mio,' said Stefan. 'There is only one invitation...'

Guido was very demanding — very spoilt — it could be very trying... but, he was very beautiful — one couldn't have everything.

'It was quite a party,' he said.

Peter, putting more sugar in his coffee to offset the bitterness, agreed...

3

The party was at the Contessa Marciapiani's Palazzo.

Flaming torches guttered on wrought iron stands either side of the pillared doorway, spirals of sooty smoke, cindered with golden sparks bending against the breeze. The Italian flag rippled next to her family's coat of arms on white flag poles.

A wide stretch of soft, carefully raked gravel crowded with cars — Mercedes — BMWs — Aston Martins — a Maserati — a silver Bentley. A group of uniformed chauffeurs standing together smoking.

There were beds of azaleas — the flowers milky flurries in the semi-darkness, and the tall pointed shapes of Roman cypress black against the sky.

A footman with white gloves took his coat, and examined his invitation.

The hall had a marble floor, and a wide marble staircase.
There were little gold chairs, and marble tables with gold legs, and gold urns of tall fluffy grass and palm fronds.

In the middle was a square pool with goldfish zigzagging among white stones, and a marble fountain with water spouting from the mouth of a fat gilded carp standing on its curvy tail.

There were huge portraits of the Contessa's hook-nosed ancestors in arrogant postures against dramatic landscapes, mountains, stormy skies — Vesuvius erupting — with various dead animals — a wild boar stuck with a spear — a bunch of pheasants swinging by their necks, casually, like a bunch of carrots — a torn stag cornered by hounds...

To the right of the stairs, double doors led into a long reception room lit by glittering chandeliers.

The Contessa, a widow of middle years — patron of the Arts, and dedicated Egyptophile, wore black velvet with an Egyptian collar of multi-coloured stones, a golden headdress studded with diamonds, and a gold snake curled round one arm.
She mingled regally — offering a jewelled hand — red stones glistening like fresh blood.

The tall windows had curtains of blue and gold striped satin, which matched the covers on the tightly upholstered sofas and chairs, pushed back against the walls to make more room.

A tiger skin rug with snarling head crouched in front of the marble fireplace, above which Bacchus lounged in an olive grove eating grapes, waited on by scantily clad nymphs and fat pink cherubs with sprouting wings.

Further along a man in a steel helmet and red and blue tunic sat unmoved on a rearing horse among pine trees — Spring flowers at the horse's feet.

A string quartet on a round platform festooned with gold vine leaves, and flanked by snooty gold cats with long necks, played operatic excerpts — a selection of well-known arias from La Boheme, Traviata, Tosca, the Barber of Seville...

Daniel's suit was too small for him.
Bridget had told him to stand casually with the arm holding his glass bent across his chest, so that the jacket would not look so obviously short in the sleeve...
'If you wear black shoes and socks,' she said, 'the trousers will hardly notice... It's bound to be crowded, so nobody will be looking at the bottom of your trouser legs...'

It was very crowded.

Bridget had been right — nobody was going to notice that his trouser legs were too short — nobody would be able to see the bottom of his trouser legs. Nobody would notice him at all.

He looked round hopefully for some familiar faces — other students from the course.

He glimpsed Margharita — a skinny figure in a white mini dress, talking to one of the 'business-type' Governors. They were standing by a glass pyramid lit from within. A tall girl, she had to lean down to hear what he was saying, blonde hair falling across her face.

Gold sphinxes guarded the French windows, closed now against the chilly Spring night.

Outside, a lighted fountain sprayed sparkling drops onto the terrace, and onto the glossy dark green leaves of orange and lemon trees in pots of carved grey stone, their fruit glowing like the baubles on a Christmas tree.

He did not know any of his fellow students very well, and now they had all graduated, he would probably never see them again. Apart from meeting in the canteen to drink coffee and complain, they had had little to do with each other.
He had never attended the sporadic social events — the Discos — Poetry readings — Experimental plays — Coffee and Cola evenings...

He saw Dino with his mouth full of food, partially hidden by a golden vase of bullrushes, and Gina in a red and purple toga and beaded turban, in a group near the table where the food was laid out on a white damask cloth reaching to the floor.

Even the food had an Egyptian theme.
Pyramids of prawns in aspic decorated with lobster claws, and

chicken layered with smoked turkey mousse and spinach purée among golden candelabra and gold dishes of baked aubergine and sweet peppers in oil — salmon mousse striped with tomato and celeriac coulis shaped into sarcophagi, gold tureens of jellied consommé, and mounds of quails eggs in a creamy sauce.

There were cakes and fruit in brandy, strawberries in wine, and all kinds of bread in cradle-shaped rush baskets...

Peter was very hungry.
He had had some champagne. Waiters were going round with trays of drinks — whisky, wine, champagne, fruit juices — but he couldn't face the scrum round the table.
A tall thin young man with short fair hair approached him with a plate of flaky pastry stars and crescents.
'I'm Stefan,' he said, offering the plate to Peter.
'Do try one of these, they're really delicious. Cheese and ham. Very tasty.'
Peter thanked him, and took one from the proffered dish.
'Take more than that,' said Stefan. 'Most of the people here have no need for food — no need at all. They should be made to fast — or sent to a remote island of rock and stone... rid them of their impurities. I think these round ones are prawn...'
They were delicious — Peter made an effort not to gulp them down. He really was very hungry.

'I'll get some more in a minute,' said Stefan. 'One needs a certain technique on these occasions... I understand you are to paint the magnificent Signora Fratelli. A fine figure of a woman — as they say...'

Peter could see her talking to the cellist. The musicians were having a break, and a glass of champagne.
She was resplendent in red — very low cut — exposing a large amount of swelling flesh.

'Her husband is Assisente Commissario. You better watch your step... He's over there helping himself to food.'

Signor Fratelli was a bull of a man — not tall, but broad, with a neck the same width as his head. He looked as if he was about to burst out of his dinner jacket — the shoulder seams straining as he lifted a forkful of food to his mouth. His eyes were small — sunken into his flesh, his chin dark with tomorrow's beard.

Very jealous man,' said Stefan. 'Very quick tempered...'

He seemed perfectly at ease.

'That young man with the frilly shirt and ridiculous tie is the Contessa's latest toy boy. She has a son somewhere — he collects butterflies — always trekking off to remote places with his pith helmet and butterfly net...'

The Contessa mounted the platform, and there was a general 'shushing'.

'She's going to make a speech,' said Stefan. 'I've got to go — have to be back at La Scala before the end of the performance. Give me your phone number, and I'll give you a ring...'
He took an envelope from his pocket, scribbled it down, and made his way through the crowd, turning to wave as he reached the doorway.

They didn't get many phone calls, which was fortunate as Dora didn't like them getting phone calls.
The phone was in the hallway, and she would shout angrily up the stairs for them to hurry up, and not to spend all day in idle talk, and then retire to her room, leaving the door ajar so she could listen to their conversations.

It was most unlikely that he would phone anyway, and he shouldn't allow himself to be intimidated by Dora.

He turned his attention to the Contessa, who was saying how honoured she felt to be involved, if only in a very small way, helping young artists, and was delighted to announce the creation of the Marciapiani Award, in memory of her dear husband, which would fund a gifted student during his — or her — studies...

There was much clapping and cries of 'Bravo', and the waiters came round with more champagne to drink a toast to this generous benefactress.

*　　*　　*

'The Contessa has enough Egyptian bric-a-brac to kit out her own personal pyramid,' said Stefan.

The Russian people were eating chocolates and drinking brandy.

The woman took a lipstick from her black satin handbag — it had a gold chain — and applied a smear of red scarlet to her small fat mouth — a red splodge in her flat sallow face.
Dreadful people — unspeakably vulgar... How had they escaped the Gulags? — the Siberian hordes?
Savages in rough sheepskins would happily skewer them to the floor.
A little blood would go unnoticed in the beetroot soup...

'Did you get home alright?' he said.
'Yes,' said Peter. Perhaps Stefan wouldn't notice if he didn't finish the vodka. 'Yes, thanks...'

4

His head still fizzing with lights and champagne, he stumbled slightly on the rough pavement.

They had had to file past the Contessa to shake her hand, a cold metallic gauntlet of gold and flashing stones, and smile grateful 'Thank yous'.

Her smile stretched unmoving — fixed at a sufficiently friendly width to display interest and sympathetic encouragement.

The night was dark.
At first he did not see Signora Capetti.
She emerged from the shadows, a crooked black shape, and grasped his arm with hooked fingers.
'My son,' she said. 'Mio figlio — Have you seen my son? Only a boy — tall like his father.'

Distant feet marching — high black boots in perfect step — relentlessly marching — the grating swish of shingle being dragged by the sea — shouted commands — splintering wood — screams — the staccato rattle of machine guns — and then the silence — the haunted silence.

He took her arm.
'Come,' he said. 'I will take you home — It is late...'

Bridget had taken her home once — coaxing her out of the rain — leading her gently.

She had come back shaken and upset.

'It's disgraceful,' she said. 'Not fit for an animal. No wonder she prefers the streets. There must be somewhere she could go where she could be looked after. Nobody should have to live like that — poor old thing. It's not right...'

It was not far — down a narrow alley — slimy steps — a hovel.
The door, already ajar, rotten and creaking...
The light from the street lamp made it just possible to see the interior of the room.
A bare earth floor scrapped with bits of cardboard — an indescribably filthy mattress strewn with rags, a chair with a broken rush seat — a blackened paraffin heater balanced precariously on broken bricks, and a round metal table, like the ones at pavement cafés — scratched green paint with a hole in the middle for the sun umbrella, with a crippled candle in a saucer

amid mounds of spent matches.

Peter found the box, which had fallen among the cardboard, and lit the candle, the flame wavering in a pool of wax, jumpily illuminating the dirt-streaked walls and heavy wood crucifix over the bed.

The stench in the room caught his throat in a stranglehold — he dared not breathe.
Signora Capetti sank down on the mattress — still moaning.
He left her sitting there — still as death — her hands twisted in her rosary.

Dora came out of her room, a slatternly figure in her grubby robe patterned with black dragons, a pink nylon hairnet over her bushy red hair, to admonish him for disturbing the household. She must have been waiting for him, because he had been as quiet as possible. She regarded him suspiciously, noting the dark suit under his old raincoat — the black shoes — the tie...

'What time do you think this is?' she demanded. 'Waking decent people in the middle of the night. I won't have this sort of thing in my house... It better not happen again...'
Really she was dying to know where he had been, why it had been necessary to dress up. Her curiosity unsatisfied, she returned to her room slamming the door so hard that the wonky letter rack fell off the wall.

'Of course it's a sham,' said Stefan, finishing his beetroot soup.
It had stained his lips a sickly mauve, giving him a sinister ghostly appearance. 'A colossal sham. The Contessa wouldn't know a work of art if it came up and introduced itself — and the way she dolls herself up like a reincarnation of Nefertiti — grotesque — totally grotesque...'

A man at the next table was smoking a cigar — the smoke sweet and pungent.
Peter coughed. He had almost finished his soup.

It floated uneasily in his empty stomach — sloshing gently from side to side. He quickly swallowed another piece of black bread. Stefan looked at his watch and said he would have to go soon. 'I have things to do before I go to the Theatre,' he said.

Peter would have to go too.
He had a meeting with Signora Fratelli to discuss the portrait.

Stefan tipped his chair back and gazed at the smoke-blackened ceiling. It would spoil the atmosphere of the place to clean it up — repaint it...
'Make sure she doesn't cheat you,' he said. 'One million liras — at least. You must not do it for less than a million...'

Peter agreed, only too aware that he would be incapable of asking for anything...
He was intensely nervous.
Such an opportunity. He was so lucky to have been chosen. She could have chosen Dino or Carolyn, whose work was reliably representational and held no surprises.

He did not aspire to be a portrait painter, although it could be a useful way to earn a living.
His pictures, swirls and squares of colour — so much colour — canvasses overflowing with colour. He was intoxicated by colour...

In the sad dark street where he grew up, the gagging mist wrapped a wet, suffocating cloak around the houses — leaning conspiratorially — shutting out the light. Only the rain could seep between the sloping roofs — turning gutters into torrents — sweeping the debris on little crested waves. There was no colour — only the grey of the stones — grey tiles — grey washing hanging on strings from the windows.

Somewhere else the burnished globe of the sun slid down behind the edge of the glowing pink-rimmed earth.
The opaque blue of the sky reflected in the clear still waters of

lakes, where graceful floating plants spread green fronds on the soft white sand.

He would take his pad and pencil, and tin of broken crayons to the market square, where shiny bright fruit tumbled on the stalls, and glinting silver fish — striped and spotted with greens and blues, coral pink bream, orange whiskered prawns, and shiny black eels — lay among blocks of ice.

The perfumed soft shapes of flowers — starry love-in-the-mist — spicy sweet williams, purple and red as crushed currants — clove scented carnations, pink and white and yellow dipped in red — elegant roses, their long stems stripped of thorns — massed in green buckets shaded by a wide blue and white striped awning.

In the dark room smelling of fetid bandages and linament, among wet sheets and nightclothes, where no saffron sunlight or silver moonlight, the warm scents of Spring or sharp crackle of Autumn penetrated, he would sit at the wide-legged table and draw — sketching his sisters — Lucia kneeling by the wash tub — stirring soup in the dented cooking pot, the wooden spoon worn flat — draining pasta in the chipped sink — Anna, head bent over her school books — her curly black hair curtaining her face. He would draw on any piece of available paper — used envelopes, the edge of newspapers, the back of shopping receipts, every inch of his drawing pad — hands and feet, noses, ships in full sail, rowing boats, lake steamers, trees and birds, tall-spired churches and churches with round domes...

Stefan paid the bill, waving away Peter's attempt to contribute.

He could afford to be magnanimous.

There was so much overtime with this production — lots and lots of overtime — and the Dress Rehearsal would go on for hours and hours and hours — probably all night.

5

Stefan sauntered through the Galleria.

He swayed his hips slightly, a sufficient signal of availability, his hands in the pockets of his brown leather blouson jacket. He wore dark glasses — black 'shades' like in a gangster movie. He always wore dark glasses in all weathers — they added a certain mystique to his appearance.

Today he did not linger, or take any interest in the people sitting at the tables with their espressos and cappuccinos, plates of small pastries and glasses of tea. He was in a hurry to get to the Teatro Massimo in the Via Broletto, conveniently near the Scala, to see Guido finish rehearsing.

He found Modern Ballet a frightful bore — well, perhaps not more of a frightful bore than he found Classical Ballet — and quite incomprehensible — watching the skinny figures in their white all-in-one garments doing knee jerks — stalking around one another with their elbows stuck out — the stage adorned with giant fruit — a green apple, a pear and something orange with a long brown stalk, which he thought was probably an apricot.

He arrived as they reached the Finale.

Guido, wearing thick striped socks over his black leggings, pirouetted across the stage dodging between the fruit, with two girls bent double, arms swinging, behind him.

The music swelling to a climax of crashing cymbals and wildly high notes on the flute.

He took his accustomed seat on the left side of the stage, at the end of the third row of the stalls, stretching his legs into the aisle. He hoped they would not be too long. He would be late at the Scala.

He glanced round to see the reaction of the director, producer and choreographer, who always sat in the centre — a huddle of overworked sweaters, from where they would suddenly erupt with explosions of displeasure, to see if they were looking satisfied.

He became aware of a man sitting at the back of the theatre. He had an aura of wealth.

A hand with two gold rings lay on the back of the seat in front of him. His hair was impeccably groomed — not just neat and tidy, but groomed. His eyes were fixed on the stage, where Guido, appearing from behind the apple, fell on his knees and flattened his body in a single movement.

'Who was that?' he said, as they stood outside the stage door smoking.

'Who?' asked Guido. 'I really hurt my shoulder...'

'The man in the stalls — the old queen.' He said it with menace, envisaging the man's pleas as he whirled the spiked ball round his head, ready to rip him apart — the soft flesh punctured and torn...

'He sends me flowers,' said Guido casually. 'Roses by the dozen — gardenias...' He puffed on his cigarette. The spiked ball spun, catching the man's face — a pulpy mess.

'Well,' said Stefan. 'Isn't that nice — very nice — how flattering to have such an ardent admirer.'

Anger shook him.

Inside the red cave of his body the veins swelled and twisted with rage.

He was the one who ended relationships.

He was the one who controlled relationships.

No silk-shirted poof from a soft-piled penthouse could intrude on his territory — until he was finished — until he said it was over — until he was bored with this preening boy...

Guido giggled. 'He sends me notes — saying he can't live without me...'

'How very nice,' said Stefan, his voice calm and smooth as double cream pouring from a jug. 'And what do you reply...?'

'Oh, I never reply,' said Guido. 'We share the flowers, and I stick all the notes round the mirror in my dressing room. Caro mio Stefan, don't be annoyed — It's just a joke...'

6

'Where the hell have you been...?'
Erica wore a man's waistcoat — a chainmail of pins — a tape measure round her neck, pencils and sticks of grease paint in her thick curly black hair, bunched untidily on top of her head.
'There are eighty-five beards to check — the dressing rooms are knee deep in hair, and most of them have no idea how to make up at all... Absolutely no idea...'
'I'm here darling,' said Stefan. 'I'm here...'
'You better see to Sergei first,' said Erica. 'He's making a fearful din...'

Stefan went up the narrow dusty passage to their room to fetch his case of combs, skeins of hair and spirit gum, his special haircutting scissors and trimmer.
The room was a mess — Erica was incredibly messy.
There was a half-eaten salami sandwich and an open bottle of mineral water on the table with today's paper and a pile of scores.
Erica's blouse hung over the back of the chair, a pair of tights rolled into a ball on the floor, and bits of cotton wool stained with nail varnish.
She was a slut.
All women were sluts.
Still, she knew her job — never shirked — was competent, reliable and punctual.
He could tolerate her — better than he could tolerate most people.
She was OK.

He bent to pick up the case which he had put in the corner for safety behind a selection of dusty riding boots left from a production of William Tell, and stopped with arm outstretched.

The Man at the back of the Theatre smiled at him from the front page of the newspaper — a dazzling white smile — arms around two showgirls, plumed like performing horses — collared with diamonds — pressing their near-nakedness against him...

Stefan sat down on a chair, and pulled the paper towards him. 'Paul Santini celebrating the opening of his new night club, the 'Stella d'Oro' with two of the glamorous artistes who will be appearing nightly in the spectacular floor show. Earlier this year Paul Santini was cleared of any involvement in attempting to smuggle 20 kilos of heroin found on his yacht, 'Il Ucello Bianco', when it docked at Naples after a trip to Morocco. Two of his crewmen were subsequently arrested...'

A drug dealer — the man who sent Guido roses was a drug dealer... His wealth came from the shivering creatures who lurked in doorways, in the parks, at the railway station — limbs scabbed and punctured, whining for money to perpetuate a self-inflicted hell.

Contempt burnt a sulphuric lattice in his chest.
Contempt for those furtive ragged obscenities — he trampled them with hob-nailed boots — boneless bundles of clothes — rag dolls spewing sawdust...
Contempt for Santini — decked in gold and silk — massaged and manicured — daring to send Guido roses.
Contempt for his wealth — accumulated from filthy coins — cleaned and counted and changed into freshly 'laundered' lira bills.
Contempt for bowing bank managers and corrupt policemen...
The burning spread, the spiralling fumes making him dizzy. He grasped the edge of the table, gasping for breath.

'For Christ's sake, are you still here?' Erica was in the doorway. 'There's pandemonium out there. Ferranti has called a lighting check, and there's not a single electrician to be found. Sergei is threatening to go back to Russia. He's sent his dresser to find out the times of flights to Moscow — and the 'Prince' has been sick on the velvet footstool...'

'Sorry sweetie,' said Stefan. He took a swig from the bottle of water. 'I'm on my way. Better go and see what I can do with the great Tsar Boris... Ya idyot — I go, I go...'

Sergei was too big for the small dressing room. He filled the space with his huge bulk. He wore a collarless shirt and blue jeans, fur-trimmed velvet robes heaped round him on the floor.
'What is this wisp of a beard?' he boomed. He intoned his words as if singing a recitative. 'This is no beard for a King... I am not an ancient prophet or a wizard from a fairy tale — I am a King — King of all the Russias — I have to have a beard of Royalty...'

Stefan moved some of the robe from around Sergei's feet, pushing the voluminous folds to one side.
Sergei wore brown woollen check slippers.

'I have sent Constantin to buy tickets for Moscow.' Sergei lowered his voice to a subterranean rumble. 'I have not come all this way to sit in a dog kennel. It is an insult — I am the King of all the Russias — where are my jewels, my crown?' He kicked the robe. 'Where is the gold? This is brown — BROWN! It is unthinkable.'

Stefan made soothing noises. That stupid bitch Isotta. Why hadn't she used the second dressing room for the women's chorus? There were hardly any women in this opera.

'This is a casual robe,' he said. 'Something comfortable for when you remove your ceremonial robes — which are quite magnificent — and this room is only temporary. It should have been explained. Your dressing room was not quite ready...'

Isotta was in her pokey office.
She had one leg shorter than the other, and wore a built-up shoe to compensate. She had bad teeth and a problem with body odour. She wore 'little black suits' with long scarves — very long scarves, which almost brushed the floor.
She was old — too old for this job.
Granted she knew where everything was kept down to the last safety-pin, but she made mistakes. She got tired and made mistakes. She was drinking a cup of milky coffee, dipping in a biscuit and sucking the soggy crumbs.

'The women's dressing room,' she said. 'It is full of rocks from the Valkyrie...'
'Well get rid of the rocks,' said Stefan.
Stupid old woman. He grasped the ends of the long scarf and twisted them round and round her neck — pulling them tight...
'Fill the bloody room with flowers — find some easy chairs — for Christ's sake, do you want the fat Slav to go home...?'

7

Peter was late too.

The street where the Fratellis lived was longer than he had thought, and their house was at the far end. It was a rich street of haughty grey houses with fretted windows ornamented with carvings of leaves and fruit, and high grey walls with wrought iron gates enclosing paved forecourts — some with fountains and potted shrubs.

The Fratellis did not have fountains or potted shrubs. Hostile stone griffins perched on stone columns either side of the gate, and the doorstep was black-veined marble.
The door was opened by a squat young woman in shiny black. She had a faint moustache and the swarthy skin of the South. Her eyebrows met across the top of her nose in a fierce black line.

She led him, walking uncomfortably in flat laced-up black shoes, across the tiled hall. Bronze statues postured in discreetly-lit niches.
There were a lot of mirrors.

The drawing room was very large.
There were black leather sofas, and chairs and tables of curved perspex, and strange steel lights, corkscrewing up to the moulded ceiling. There was a heavily framed painting of snowcapped mountains against a puce sky streaked with orange, and more mirrors...

In one corner was a black grand piano with the lid ostentatiously open...

Signora Fratelli rose to greet him.
She wore black tailored trousers with a gold chain belt threaded with a red and white scarf, and a cream silk blouse with a bow at the neck.
She was, as Stefan said, 'a handsome woman'.
Her features were large, but she had very nice hair — thick and black and glossy, and large dark eyes...
She overdid the makeup — the eyeliner and mascara, the brows exaggeratedly arched — too much lipstick, and too much powder caked in the lines around her mouth.
She overdid the jewellery — too many bangles, too many rings, too many chains round her neck...

He apologised for being late, but she did not seem concerned, and told him to sit down, imperiously ordering the girl, who was standing awkwardly by the door, to bring coffee — and the panetonne...

'I thought you could paint me by the piano,' she said. 'I sing, you know — I am a singer — I study with Signora Peshkova at the Scala...'

She got up and went to the piano. Striking a note, she took a deep breath, and with one be-ringed hand on her diaphragm sang 'Me-me-me-me-me...ma-ma-ma-ma-ma'... rapidly ascending a scale with dramatic crescendo, finishing with three short shrieks.
She had a big voice which wobbled round the notes.
She sang the last high note again. It was very off key.
Peter, embarrassed, stared at her feet...
She was wearing very high heels.
He did not know how he was supposed to respond to this display of truly terrible singing...

The girl hovered with a tray.
'Put it down Tina, for goodness' sake.' Signora Fratelli was

flushed from her exertions. A pink stain spreading on her neck. 'Put it down here.' She indicated a table by the sofa. 'You should have sliced the panetonne... I told you to slice the panetonne...'

*   *   *

Lucia had brought a round spicy panetonne and a bunch of black grapes, and they had climbed the slopes behind the town, feathery with Summer grass, and she had told him she had decided to go to London.
She was going with Teresa.

'We shall be together,' she said. 'So we will be alright. Teresa has already been to London. She says it is easy to get work...'

She had been studying English. Teresa had lent her some tapes and a booklet.
'I have to go,' she said. 'I cannot stay here. Every time I go into the room I see father or mother dying — in the same chair... The smells and sounds of dying — I have to get away — and Anna wants to get married.'
They had quarrelled over Anna's wish to get married.
Lucia said she was too young. 'You will throw away your life. Do you want to live in a slum forever — trying to keep your children clean — watching them play in the drains...?'

Roberto was good looking, strong and swanky. He wore red neckerchiefs and belts with brass studs.

'He will have his own garage one day,' said Anna. 'We will build our own house — with a shower — a shower with blue tiles and a blue shower curtain...'

'And until then,' said Lucia, 'where will you live until then...?'

*   *   *

'She is more accustomed to going barefoot among the chickens...'

Signora Fratelli passed him the plate of panetonne that she had sliced with a silver cake knife.

'Of course I have had to give up my career... My husband... it would not do for me to have a career... I just do the occasional recital or variety performance for Charity... that sort of thing...'

She was childless.
She had seen many eminent specialists, and undergone numerous tests and examinations.
There was nothing to prevent her having children — nothing whatsoever. Perhaps her husband might like to come for a few tests?
To suggest that Benito was unable to father children — to father sons — was unthinkable.
To cast the slightest suspicion of doubt on his virility was unthinkable...

'I have picked out a dress I think will be suitable,' she said, 'and I thought a tall vase of lilies...'

Peter said he thought that would be very nice. It was always nice to have flowers... He was eating his slice of panetonne very slowly — he still felt queasy from the beetroot soup and sour black bread. He was suddenly overwhelmingly tired, and wished he was in his room and could lie down — just lie down and close his eyes...

'I am quite happy if you want to take photographs,' said the Signora. 'Next time you come bring a camera...'

Peter hadn't thought about taking photographs.
He didn't have a camera.
Perhaps he could borrow a camera.
Perhaps Stefan would have a camera, or know someone with a camera. Stefan would surely know someone who would lend him

a camera. Oh God. He felt sick...

'That would be most helpful,' he said. 'Most helpful.'

8

Stefan had invited him to the Theatre later in the afternoon.
'When you have finished with the Signora, wander over and I'll
show you around — I can always get you into the auditorium to
do some sketching whenever you like...'
Peter thought he would go home and lie down a bit first. He was
still feeling unwell.

He mounted the stairs slowly, trying to breathe as little as
possible.
Dora had been cooking with garlic — the smell battled with the
thick wad of other gagging smells.
He was used to smelly houses — used to holding his breath.

Bridget's door was open — she always kept her door open — it
was too claustrophobic with the door shut.
She was sitting at her little table by the window, painting.
There were leaves spread out on the table on sheets of wet blotting
paper.
She loved painting leaves — the different shapes — the different
shades of green.
She was painting greetings cards, hoping to make a little money.
Her watercolours were delicate and immediately pleasing. She
painted directly onto the paper — the edges of the leaves soft,
undefined.
The card shop in the Via dell'Orso had said they would take some
on a sale and return basis, taking a small percentage if she sold
any.
There had been a problem getting the card.
The heavy white card necessary was expensive — and then there
were the envelopes...

The man in the Art Shop was reluctant to let her have the paper on credit, but relented when she showed him an example of her work, becoming quite enthusiastic, even suggesting she should have dark green envelopes. He agreed she could pay in instalments, and wrote it all down in his ledger in black curly script with a wide-nibbed pen.

She looked up and smiled, and asked how he had got on with the Signora.
Peter said he thought everything was fine, but that he wasn't feeling too well, and was going to lie down for a little while...
'I'm going out soon,' he said. 'You can use my room if you like — the light is much better...'

He took his shoes off and lay down on the bed.
He wished he could talk to Lucia.
It was such a long time now since she had gone to London.
At first she sent cards — the Tower of London, Big Ben, Buckingham Palace — sometimes a letter.
She was doing fine — she was working in an Italian restaurant in Soho — they were all Italians working there. The hours were long, but she got proper meals and plenty of tips...
She shared a room with Teresa in Camden Town.
She was comfortable.

But somehow — gradually — the letters became less frequent.
Now, occasionally, a few lines — 'I am fine — How are you?', 'I am well — We have had a lot of rain.' No real news.
Once she sent some photographs of herself and Teresa in one of the lovely parks they have in London.
She looked just the same — just as thin — but she was laughing.
They were both laughing.
Peter was glad — glad that she was happy.
Hoped she was really happy.
And Anna — he hardly ever heard from Anna. She was expecting her third child, and they were still living in the tiny messy flat over Roberto's father's garage.

Roberto's mother had come to tea — sitting stiff and disapproving in her black cloth coat and dress of dizzy grey and white stripes. She accepted a cup of coffee, wiping the spoon on her handkerchief, and nibbled an almond biscuit.

There was a special offer on almond biscuits at the Standa where Anna was working — stacking shelves and arranging displays of tins decorated with sprays of plastic flowers.

'I had hoped for a better marriage,' she said. 'A good family — at least *some* sort of family — They are much too young...'
Lucia said, 'Yes — I agree — much too young...'

Roberto's mother ignored her — her eyes assessing the room — the furniture — calculating its worth — if it had any...

They had piled the bedding on the bed in the alcove, and drawn the curtain.
None of them wished to use the bed.
Without discussion they had continued to sleep on the floor.
The thought of the bed where their parents had lain with feverish limbs and pulpy sores was too awful to contemplate.

Roberto's mother left without finishing her coffee, or the almond biscuit.
She commented on Anna's bare legs — 'Nice girls wear stockings — and she has no education... and who is going to pay for the wedding?'

Lucia had tried to dissuade Anna.
'We have no money for a wedding,' she said. 'No money — Why don't you wait a little...?'
'We will never have any money,' said Anna. 'When are we going to have any money — where will we get any money from? I can't wait until we have enough money — I shall be old — old...'
She had put her curly head down on the table and wept.

Lucia made her a dress from an old linen tablecloth with a lace border which she found in the old sideboard. It was yellowed with age. She washed it and bleached it — and washed it and bleached it, and cut it cleverly so that the lace made a pretty trim, and took it to the cleaners in the dark side street that tipped towards the square, to ask Signora Grevi who sat in the window patching and mending — adjusting seams and hems with her old treadle sewing machine, whilst Signor Grevi in shirtsleeves and braces, enveloped in steam, worked the press at the back of the shop, a soggy cigarette stuck to his bottom lip — coughing — always coughing — to ask Signora Grevi if she would machine it. It would take too long for her to sew it by hand — she had so little time — now she did two jobs. She worked as a clerk during the day, and as a waitress in the evening.

It had been a makeshift wedding.
People were kind. The lady on the flower stall had given Anna a bouquet. The bakers had made a small cake and kept left-overs from the day before.
Anna's workmates had bought her some towels, and the laundry where their mother had once worked gave her a pair of embroidered pillowcases.
There were a few bottles of wine.
They had stood in Roberto's parents' shiny modern flat, among cheap plywood furniture with a crowd of Roberto's disagreeable relations and noisy friends, eating stale cake and sipping acid wine.
It was not a happy day.
Lucia had done her best, but she had not wanted it. She wanted better things for her sister — a better life.

She didn't like Roberto or his family.
His father was particularly unpleasant — more unpleasant than his mother.
She wanted Anna to have a nice home with nice things, to have someone to care for her — to look after her. She didn't want her sister to be a drudge, and live in a miserable little flat filled with petrol fumes from the garage below...

She had sat and cried — not attempting to wipe away the tears that dripped off her chin down the front of her old cotton frock. Peter had made coffee, and tried to comfort her — but she had not stopped crying — she couldn't stop crying. She had nursed their dying father and mother with few tears, had stood by their gravestones with few tears — but now she could not stop crying...

It seemed such a long time ago.
It was a long time ago.

He must write and tell her about the portrait.
He hoped it would please her.
She had been so pleased when he won the scholarship to the Scuala d'Arte.
She had sent him a chocolate coin wrapped in gold.
He had it somewhere among his drawings.
Perhaps he would make enough money to go and visit her in London.
He would very much like to go to London.
He must not forget to ask Stefan about a camera.

In the street below Dora was shouting. 'I will call the police — you should be locked up — mad old woman — clear off — imbecile...'

He stood again in the dank dreadful cellar — fungoid — stinking — Signora Capetti grasping her rosary — moaning — black boots marching — the sooty wick of the candle sinking in a pool of melted wax...

9

'Who the hell are you?' said Erica. 'And what the hell do you want?'
She had knocked over a box of pins and was on her knees picking them from the cracks in the rough wood floor boards, and between the folds of the pile of heavy robes.

Peter stood awkwardly in the doorway.
The man at the Stage Door had directed him here.
This girl had hair like Anna's — thick and black and curly. 'Stefan said this would be a good time to come,' he said. He carried his pad and pencils in a cloth bag over his shoulder.

He had never been backstage before — never been in the Scala — never been to an opera. There had been a lot of church music when he was young — most of it not very good church music.

Bridget loved the opera. She said Puccini's music was particularly beautiful, bending her head as she spoke so he would not see the sudden tears.

Erica looked up at him.
Not Stefan's usual type — a bit different from that sylph-like dancer with his hair cut close — a curly blond fleece, and rouge on his cheek bones.

She was not sure about Stefan.
He made her feel uncomfortable.
He had a menacing stillness.
The anaemic skin — his eyes cold milky moonstones — expressionless when he smiled.
He smiled a lot.

He never raised his voice, or lost his temper, coping calmly with the temperamental behaviour, the bitchiness and tantrums, the confusion among all connected with the 'Theatre' — from the 'Stars' to the cleaners, especially in a big production — especially with opera, where everyone considered they had divine rights.
But the cooler and calmer he became, the more dangerous he seemed.

She would not like to meet him in a dark alley.
She was not afraid of a sexual attack — Stefan did not like women.
She had a feeling he would enjoy inflicting pain and humiliation.
She had watched him watching others with a shiver of unease.

Peter said, 'Let me help you.'
He knelt down beside her.
Her arms were brown and strong, and she had a square watch with a moon on the face.

'Cosy — cosy — cosy!'
Stefan had arrived soundlessly.
'It's pandemonium back there. Sergei refuses to wear the robes. He says they are too heavy. He says he can't stand up — let alone sing... First they were not grand enough — now they are too heavy! And there are not enough boots for the Chorus. That stupid cow Isotta didn't order enough boots — incompetent old hag...'

He made a strange gurgling sound which Peter supposed was laughter.

Stefan looked down at Peter on his knees, picking up pins and putting them into an old tobacco tin. He felt kindly towards him — which was an unfamiliar feeling. He never felt kindly towards anybody — he didn't like people. There was nothing sexual about it, he just liked him.
He was an innocent — a sheep among wolves — unaware of the duplicity of those around him — quietly tolerant — expecting nothing — pleased with whatever was offered.
He was poor, but not pathetic.
Stefan loathed pathetic people — twisting their arms until they cried for mercy — pulping their faces with 'a blunt instrument' — it was always 'a blunt instrument' in newspaper reports — until the blood soaked their shirts — careful not to touch them. He couldn't touch anybody with his bare hands.

'I have to phone around for more boots,' he said. 'I shouldn't be too long — Erica can show you around...'

'I don't have time to conduct Guided Tours,' said Erica sharply.

'Well, darling, I expect you'll still be picking up pins when I get back — Ciao...'

He would phone Guido from the telephone near the Stage Door. He didn't want that old bitch Isotta listening to his phone calls. It was unlikely that Guido would be there. He would probably still be at rehearsals, but he would try anyway.
These bloody boots were going to make him late.

The phone, battered, the mouthpiece grey with old spittle, hung unsafely on the wall by the stagedoorman's glass box. The wall round it scrawled with names and telephone numbers. A pencil hung from a nail by a piece of worn string beneath a dog-eared notice which read: 'Please do not write on these walls', and another larger one which said 'NO SMOKING'.

The fire bucket in the corner was full of cigarette butts, and balls of fluff, blown by the draught from the Stage Door, moved along the skirting tangled with dead matches.

It was pretty disgusting, and normally to be avoided, but he was in a hurry, and had no time to go out and use the public kiosk across the street.
It wasn't exactly very savoury either, smelling of urine and aged tobacco smoke, and liberally decorated with obscene messages.

Guido's phone rang — the sound ping-ponging in the empty rooms — dropping hollow celluloid balls on the shaggy white rugs.
He was not there — He knew he was not there — How could he be there — ? He would still be at the Theatre — It was too early for him to be there...

Stefan's hand tightened on the receiver until the veins stood out like coiled blue snakes.

He would be late.

Santini smiled his shark white smile, and preened his immaculately groomed hair with an immaculately manicured hand, revealing a discreet flash of diamond-studded cufflink.

Stefan pushed in the mocking smile with all his strength, his hands safe in black leather buttoned gloves, pushed until he heard the bones cracking, and felt the head loll sideways — the neck snapped like a twig...

Damn the bloody boots — Tonight he didn't want to be late.

It wasn't his job to see to the bloody boots, but as he was expecting to take Isotta's place — when she finally retired, or passed out — he had to appear obliging and conscientious. It was a pity he could not dispose of her now, swiftly and silently.

He could throw her down the lift shaft. She was always complaining that the gates were faulty — trip her up by her crippled leg — a fading shriek among the black wires and paraphernalia which worked the lift...

That would have been a good way to dispose of his parents — shove them down a lift shaft.

Unfortunately they hadn't had a lift.

Stefan disliked and despised his parents — the balls of their feet teetering on the bourgeois line.

He disliked his mother more than his father, and despised them both.

His father a sales rep for a fertilizer manufacturer, travelling all over Italy, prematurely balding, his digestion ruined by meals in cheap hotels, stiff from hours behind the wheel in the searing heat of summer — the wet chill of winter — arriving home weary and crushed, he would leave his sample case in the hall.

'Take that thing out of here...'

His mother in her too-tight dress — her dresses were always too tight — standing in the doorway of the over-stuffed sitting room.

'Take it out of the house — Porta via quell' odioso cosa...'

'They're poisonous,' said his father in his creased suit — his suits were always creased.

'So?' said his mother. 'So — it is alright for us to have poisons in the house — It doesn't matter if we get poisoned...'

At mealtimes, when his father was there, the silence bristled with antagonism.
The food only edible when his mother bought pizzas from the bakers.
Stefan arranged his into a face, curling the anchovy into a mouth — the olives two black eyes — devouring it slowly — methodically dissecting it — leaving the eyes until last to spear with his fork.
When his father was not there there were no mealtimes, which was a relief — the less time he had to spend with his mother the better.
She was a slut — slopping about in her dressing-gown smeared with face cream — smoking.

Once a week a skinny girl from the convent — her hands chapped red — her legs lumpy and bowed — came to clean the house.
Stefan disliked and despised her too — not in the same way as he disliked and despised his parents. She wasn't worth feeling that strongly about.
She was pathetic and servile — allowing his mother to revile her constantly as she scrubbed and polished — cooking large quantities of spaghetti to last the week.
It was put in a bowl in the fridge — so that it was easy to ladle some into a saucepan to heat up when it was time to eat something — lugging the heavy boiling pot to the sink to drain — crouched by the weight...
The good nuns had taught her well.

His mother had a liaison with their bank manager — a dapper little man in pinstriped suits and pinstriped shirts.
If, when he came home from school, the house smelt of aftershave

and cigar smoke, he knew the bank manager had had an extended lunch hour.

He was married, of course, but was able to get away quite frequently with the excuse of important financial meetings and formal dinners...

When she went on these assignations she transformed herself from the everyday slut into a spangled travesty of a sophisticated lady — her high heels making dents in the acrylic carpet — which she had insisted on — even upstairs.

'Everybody has carpet upstairs now,' she said when his father had protested at the expense. 'You'd just better get out there and sell some more of your poisonous fertilizers...'

Stefan had contemplated spiking her coffee, or the Cinzano she was so fond of, with a sprinkling of fertilizer.

It would probably only make her sick.

He had thought of trying it out on next door's cat, which was always fouling their rosebed, so that the roots of the bushes were rotten — the blooms sparse and puny.

At fifteen he had taken the housekeeping money from the tin behind the coffee grinder, put all his mother's tarty clothes into the washing machine on 'Boil', and left.

He told everybody his parents were dead — killed in a car crash — a multiple pile-up — on the road from Naples to Rome, returning from a holiday in Sorrento — his voice choked with emotion as he recounted this tragic story...

He retraced his steps back down the corridor.

The whole place could do with a coat of paint — and some new lighting.

He had never seen such small lightbulbs.

He would use Isotta's office to phone round for the stupid boots. He would open the window — unless it was hermetically sealed — Isotta was terrified of catching cold — and let out some of the smell of dry hair, stale face powder and throat lozenges.

10

The auditorium muffled in red velvet, slumbered fitfully, irritated by the discordant buzzing from the stage.

Peter moved along the rows, and took a seat in the centre of the stalls.
Around him a ghostly audience yawned and rustled their programmes — jewels glinted in the dimness of the gold-fronted boxes — opera glasses raised by long pale gloves.

Erica had said it was pointless waiting for Stefan to come back, and had shown him where to come.

The orchestra pit was deserted except for a solitary musician drinking a can of Coca Cola and reading a newspaper.
The double basses lay on their sides — bows on seats.
The timpani's pom-pom sticks crossed on the stretched skin.
The harp shrouded in a silk cloth.

On the stage the gold domes of a Russian cathedral soared into unlit space — massive ornate doors flung open.
A flight of white marble steps (at least it looked like marble) faced the auditorium.

At the foot of the steps a group of people were arguing.
A small man in a brown striped suit with wide lapels, a yellow bow tie and highly polished brown shoes, his hair 'en brosse', was listening with arms crossed to a tall thin man with long dark hair, a white shirt with the sleeves rolled up, and a blue-spotted cravat, who was gesticulating violently.

A young man in jeans and T-shirt carrying a steel tape measure and a folder of papers, stuck a cigarette behind his ear, and an elderly woman with a brace on one leg, also carrying a folder of papers, leant on a stick.

'Has anybody tried it — ? Did anybody try it?' The tall man threw his arm out in the direction of the staircase. 'The treads are too narrow — too narrow — Has anybody measured them — ? Has anybody seen the size of the Chorus — ? Has anybody measured their feet — ?'
His voice rose.

The man in the brown suit stepped forward and struck one of the steps with the flat of his hand.
'They seem solid enough,' he said.
'I have not said they are not solid — No one had said they are not solid — their solidity is not in dispute. It is the width — the width. They are too narrow — This is an Imperial staircase — not a stepladder...'

The man in the brown suit spread his hand out on the step.
'Seems reasonable,' he said.
'They might be reasonable for a group of Italian maidens,' said the tall man, his voice rising still further. 'This is a production of Boris Godunov — It is full of Russians — Russian Barbarians. They are very large. They have very large feet — very large feet — has nobody noticed they have very large feet...?'
'Perhaps we could use the steps for the Ballroom scene in the first act of Traviata,' said the elderly woman. 'Or Don Giovanni. Steps are always useful in Don Giovanni...'

'I don't care what you do with them,' said the tall man. 'Make them into a garden shed — a henhouse — a jetty — just get rid of them...'

'But the expense,' said the man in the brown suit. 'We are over budget as it is. Is there nothing we can do...?'

The young man with the tape measure stepped forward and measured the steps. 'They will have to be rebuilt,' he said.

'Exactly,' said the tall man. 'They have to be rebuilt — quickly — as quickly as possible.'

They left the stage, still arguing.

The musician took a sandwich from his music case, spread a napkin on his lap, and began to eat.

Peter took his notebook out of the cloth bag, and started to sketch.

He roughed in the outline of the cathedral.

There was another cathedral painted on a backcloth, slightly to one side of the offending 'marble' staircase.

It was very effective — very Russian.

The physical pleasure that drawing always gave him made him feel better.

He had to remember to ask Stefan about a camera.

He roughed in the golden domes with a soft-leaded pencil.

The sole musician sneezed — folded his newspaper — and disappeared through a door under the stage.

11

Gypsy children danced ahead of him on the pavement, their chatter turning to a miserable whine as he approached.

'A few lira Signor...', 'For the Grace of God Signor, a few lira for food...'

He strung them up like the pheasants in Contessa Marciapiani's picture — a strap round their necks — strung them up together on the branch of a moulting fir tree — watching until their skinny limbs ceased to twitch... He ignored them — avoiding their dirty grasping hands.

He did not demean himself to quicken his pace — nor demean himself to quicken his pace to see Guido.

He took the long way round, through the dishevelled public gardens, past the disused tennis court with its rusty netting, encroached by sombre laurel trees which strew the paths and cracked surface of the court with browning leaves and dark berries — the size of small cherries — which lay rotting. They were poisonous — even the birds wouldn't touch them. They knew they were poisonous.

Perhaps he should gather some.
He could make a liqueur — invite Santini for cocktails.
'You must try this Paul — it is splendid — very special...'

Watching the cruel lines in the pampered face twist as he clawed the air. The smooth-shaven skin turning the colour of the berries — the careful tan darkening to purple...
Perhaps he would give Guido a little to punish him — just a little — enough to give him stomach cramps...

He slowed his steps to a halt by the worn statue — faceless and limbless, except for one broken foot in a sandal.

It stood in a circle of gravel between defeated palms which had long ago lost any suggestion of their Egyptian origin — shading desert pools — hung with glossy dates.
He always halted here.
There was something very satisfying to think that someone considered important enough to be commemorated with a statue should end up an anonymous lump of stone identified only by one broken foot, where lizards slithered and beetles scurried.

He turned and left the park, crossing the road to buy a bottle of white wine from the shop on the corner.
The man behind the counter wrapped it in several sheets of tissue paper before putting it into a plastic carrier bag.
'Nice evening,' he said. 'Thought there was going to be a storm...'
'Tomorrow,' said Stefan. 'Tomorrow there will be a storm...'

12

Signora Fratelli stood in dramatic pose, head thrown back, one hand on the piano lid — the gorgon nails too long for useful activity — the fat white fingers ringed with gold and multicoloured stones, the fat white wrists jangling with jewelled bangles and gold chains hung with horseshoes and hearts, scarab beetles and gold cats and birds with ruby eyes.
She wore a ballgown of wide green and silver stripes with a fanning silver bow on one fat white shoulder. Her black boot-polish hair smooth in the front, swept up the back in a cascade of curls scattered with silver leaves.
Dwarfed by the folds of her ballgown stood a tall Chinese vase of lilies. The vase painted with gilded dragons puffing gilded smoke.

Signor Fratelli glowered down on her from the wall above. He was in full dress uniform. The bull neck encased in gold braid — gold braid looped on his shoulders and over his thickly medalled chest.
He held his gold-braided hat in a Napoleonic gesture, clutched to his heart.

Tina entered pigeon-toed, nervously carrying a tray with coffee and a plate of small cakes — some with fruit and candied peel — some dipped in chocolate.

'Put it down girl, for Heaven's sake,' said the Signora. 'On the table — here — beside the sofa...'

Tina put the tray down gingerly on the glass-topped table.

'Where are the serviettes?' said the Signora. 'I told you not to forget the serviettes. Go and get them — the flowered ones — the flowered ones I bought this morning...' She turned to Peter. 'What do you think?' she said. 'Should I stand here?'

'The flowers are rather low,' said Peter. 'Perhaps we could put them on something — make them a bit higher...' He paused. 'Did you want the portrait of Signor Fratelli included...?'

She looked up in surprise and giggled.
'I had forgotten he was there,' she said. 'That picture has been there so long I don't notice it any more...' and she giggled even more.

She was quite good-looking when she smiled. She was probably quite a nice person really — under the affectations and self importance — the ridiculous clothes and vulgar jewellery.

'Pretend it's not there,' she said. 'Just ignore it — just don't paint it...'

Tina had come back with the serviettes.
She put the packet on the table by the tray of coffee and cakes.
'Not the whole packet you silly girl,' said the Signora. 'Oh never mind. Leave them. Go and get the small table from the hall — the one we put the letters on — the one by the front door — Hurry up...'

They managed to lift the vase onto the table, and Peter pulled the flowers out a bit so that they spread and looked as if the Signora was standing amid a mass of lilies.

She had put a velvet cloth on a table by the window, and laid out a dazzling display of necklaces — pendants and pearls — sharp spikes of colour in the sunlight.

'I can't decide what to wear,' she said. 'Perhaps you can help me choose...' She dipped her fat ringed hands into the gleaming heap. 'Benito doesn't like me wearing them — it makes him nervous,' she giggled again. 'It shouldn't make him nervous in his position — I tell him there is no point in having lovely jewellery if it has to stay locked in a safe...'

She let the necklaces slide back onto the velvet cloth and went over to the sofa.
She moved gracefully for such a large woman.
'We'd better have some coffee before it gets cold,' she said. 'And you must try one of these delicious little cakes — the chocolatey ones are my favourites...'

Perhaps he should take some photographs.
Erica had lent him her camera.
He liked Erica very much — clean and wholesome.
The girls at Art School had not appealed to him — the 'Arty' with bedraggled hair who smoked cheroots, made sculptures out of bits of wire, and talked nonsensically about conceptual areas — the mousey quietly painting drab landscapes and figures with bad hands, and the strident with cropped hair and thigh-length boots that they wore winter and summer, slapping the paint on with palette knives and swearing.

Erica was confident in a completely natural way.
She had the ability to make decisions without hesitation. She was positive when she said 'That is the wrong colour — This should be over here not over there — He should stand further to the left — that hat is not right — there should be more flowers...'.

There was never any doubt — she did not ask anyone else's opinion — No 'perhaps' or 'do you think it should be this way or that way...?'
She was very good at her job — she had an artist's eye, and an instinctive feel for what was right.

She said the camera was very simple to operate. 'It's very basic — but it takes good pictures...'

Peter didn't like the idea of taking photographs.
He thought photographs were pretty useless.
The colours and textures would be all wrong.
He was sure he would take dreadful photographs.
They probably wouldn't come out at all.

He hoped the Signora would give him plenty of time to make sketches. He could really only work from sketches.

*   *   *

It had started to rain and they had to run. She ran easily — long-legged in jeans and denim jacket. She had removed the pin-studded waistcoat and hung it in her locker. 'Come and get a coffee,' she had said. 'I'll buy you something to eat. You can pay me back when the Signora pays you...'

The café was in a side street behind the theatre.
It was thick with smoke and noise. A jumble of talk and laughter — people called to each other across the room.

Erica was greeted with pleasure. 'Hi there.' 'How's it going?'
A young man in a velvet jacket came over and sat down with them.
'There should be a samovar in the monastery — There has to be a samovar...'
'We don't have a samovar,' said Erica. 'There is nothing in the Stage Directions about a samovar.'
The young man hit the table with his fist. 'Stage Directions! — Why should it be in the Stage Directions? All Russians have a samovar — There has to be a samovar...'
He got up abruptly and went back across the room and sat down at another table.

'He's probably right,' said Erica. 'But we don't have a samovar — and Isotta is too useless to have thought of getting one. Have the cannelloni — it is very good here.'

The rain had made her hair even curlier — some strands escaped from the untidy bun, falling damply round her face, making her look less severe — softer and prettier. When she smiled, she smiled with her whole face, her teeth white and even.

A young man in a sheepskin jerkin and baseball hat called over to her.

'Hi, Erica — where's the "Phantom"? I've been looking for him all day...'

'Busy,' Erica called back. 'Very busy. It's been pandemonium all day...'

'That's what they call Stefan,' she said. 'He comes and goes so silently — appearing from nowhere and disappearing again — like the "Phantom of the Opera"...'

'Ask Stefan to get a samovar,' shouted the young man in the velvet jacket. 'He seems to know what he's doing...'

'He's weighed down with boots at the moment,' said Erica, and hummed 'These Boots Are Made For Walking'...

The waitress, a bony girl with frizzy orange hair in a red check dress with a white collar, arrived with the cannelloni. It smelt very appetising.

She put a basket of bread and a bowl of parmesan on the table, and asked if they wanted any wine.

'Oh yes please Serena,' said Erica. 'Why not? A carafe of red... That would be very nice...'

And to Peter, 'is that OK for you?'

Signora Fratelli dabbed her thick red mouth delicately with one of the flowered serviettes.

'He forgets the combination,' she said. 'He writes it down on pieces of paper and hides it, and then he can't find it. He won't let me know what it is in case someone breaks in and threatens me — He sees crime everywhere — everybody is a potential criminal...'

13

Guido lit pink candles.

He was fond of pink.

He had spread the table with a white cloth, and folded white napkins into peaks on white plates. He moved the candles infinitesimally so that they were exactly equidistant from the

single red rose in the centre of the table in a slim tube of glass.
He loved setting the table — lining up the cutlery — angling the
basket of bread — the glass bowl of salad — the leaves curling
crispy — shiny with oil.

He hadn't closed the blinds.
The darkness leant on the windows — dribbling rain against the
glass.

Stefan sat on one of the big armchairs, upholstered in a creamy
fabric faintly patterned with pink, his eyes half-closed, watching
Guido fiddle with the table. He was very skittish tonight —
darting in and out of the kitchenette, his feet bare and supple on
the white rug, a white teatowel printed with pineapples tucked
into the belt of his white trousers.
He was making his 'special' sauce for the spaghetti.

Stefan watched him, half-listening to his prattle, aware of the
velvet petals of the red rose, shadowy in the light from the
candles.
The passage from the Stage Door to Guido's dressing room
webbed with expensive cologne — expensive liquor — a bowl
of white peonies among the mess of powder puffs and sticks of
greasepaint — red roses...

He prattled because he was lying.
Stefan knew he was lying.
He knew that Stefan knew he was lying.

He had said, 'Of course he has not been in my dressing room —
don't be silly, Stefan — you are just being silly...', and he prattled
on about this and that — inconsequential rubbish — and Stefan
knew he was lying.
Green cactus spines pierced his chest — sour green liquid — sour
green flesh...

The car, a sleek grey bullet, lurked predatorially in the street by
the Theatre.

Paul Santini in grey Brioni suit and grey silk shirt, his well-groomed black hair winged with grey, his eyes blank grey pebbles, coldly stalked his prey.
Sometimes a chauffeur in black livery waited for him, sometimes he came alone.

'Is he still sending you flowers?' said Stefan, his eyes fixed on the red rose.
Guido appeared briefly in the door of the kitchenette holding a wooden spoon.
'He's very rich,' he said. 'Oodles of money...'
He had had several glasses of wine, and was getting rather tipsy.
'He has a fabulous place...'

'Really,' said Stefan. 'And how do you know that?'
'Everybody knows that,' said Guido.

He carried the steaming dish of spaghetti to the table. 'Phew, this is hot — Come and eat, caro mio — I'm starving...'

Stefan sat down with his back to the black square of night, and poured himself more wine. The bottle was almost empty. The sight and smell of the food nauseated him.

'He has a fantastic collection of paintings, and lots of servants — servants for everything...'
'Really,' said Stefan. 'I suppose everyone knows that too...?'
'Of course,' said Guido. 'His chauffeur often waits outside in his car...' He helped himself to spaghetti sprinkling it liberally with parmesan. 'I can't stop him coming, caro mio... He is a very important person...'

He ate his spaghetti hungrily, expertly twirling it round his fork. There was meat sauce round his mouth.
He wiped it off carefully with his white napkin.
'It's a fantastic car,' he said. 'Just like flying — incredible...' He made a swooping motion with his hand. 'You are not eating — what is the matter? — This is your favourite...'

Stefan said it was late — he was tired — the spaghetti was delicious, but he had no appetite...

He would like to sabotage Santini's 'fantastic' car — but he didn't know how to sabotage cars — he didn't know anything about cars...
Perhaps he could set it on fire.
He wasn't keen on setting things on fire.
You couldn't control fires — they tended to spread — to burn things you didn't want to burn...

He was too tired to think how he could destroy Santini's cars — to destroy Santini.

He drank more wine and nibbled a piece of bread, stirring the spaghetti absently with his fork — the prongs reflecting in the candlelight. The candles had burnt low, dropping globs of pink wax on the white cloth.

He dragged the fork down the side of Santini's face, leaving tramlines beaded with blood — rammed the prongs through the back of the expensively manicured, expensively ringed hand — impaling it to the starched white linen...
He had drunk too much — Guido's head a misshapen blur...

'Do you want some cassatta?' Guido put a ball of icecream on the table, and a plate of fan-shaped wafers.
'OK,' said Stefan. 'Just a little...'

They would play out the game — with Guido precariously walking the tightrope of deception.
They would play the game.
He would wait until Guido became careless in his subterfuge — complacent with the success of his duplicity.
Then he would unleash black hounds to drag him down — to savage this pretty boy, until he was no longer pretty...

The icecream was melting — the sandy white vanilla crumbling

214

away from the sticky red glacé cherries — sticky as drying blood — before it turns black — black as hounds — black as an abattoir floor...

'Yum, yum,' said Guido, licking his spoon. 'I love cassatta — caro mio, you haven't eaten your cherries — I love the cherries — You mustn't waste the cherries...'
And he leant over and spooned some of them off Stefan's plate...

14

Daniel and Bridget had brought their own plates, knives, forks and glasses.

Peter cut the pizza in the box, and poured the wine.

He had bought the pizza in the Pizza Valentino, the best pizzeria in Milan.

He had passed it often — all glass and soft lighting — smart people sitting on high stools at the bar — girls with silky legs and silky hair — men in dark business suits with designer ties — glass-topped tables by wide-paned windows — plants as large as small trees fanning the ceiling with greenery — groups of chic girls in high pointed shoes of soft leather, waiting at the 'take away' end of the counter to choose their favourite pizza — the young men nonchalantly possessive.

In the winter wafts of warmth and stomach-aching smells as the doors swung open.

In summer people sitting out on the pavement under dark blue Valentino umbrellas, with little dishes of olives, drinking cocktails — pink, orange, red, even blue — spiked with fruit and green mint leaves, and little pleated paper parasols.

Now he stood at the 'take away' counter and waited for the

white-hatted chef, who slapped and rolled the dough expertly into shape, his hands white with flour, slamming one black oven door on the raw rounds of dough and pale cheese, and opening another to take out the freshly cooked pizza, bubbling in a golden case. Waited for it to be brought to the counter and placed in its square white waxed box, and deftly tied with flat pink string.

He had already bought the wine, a red Bardolino, and a bunch of lilies of the valley for Bridget. They would make a really nice card — she had sold all her first batch of cards.

Signora Fratelli had given him the first payment for the portrait. She had handed it to him in a thick white envelope with her initials embossed on the flap.
She had been pleased with the first sketches.
He had spent the morning drawing her hands, and her neck and shoulders, and the lilies in the Chinese vase.
He had done a great many sketches.

Tina had remembered the serviettes this time, and the cake knife. There was a lemon cake with lemon icing — she put the tray down — flat-footed in the painful shoes.

'Forks, Tina,' said the Signora. 'Little forks to eat the cake — in the drawer in the dining room — with the fruit knives — and don't forget you have to get the fish for dinner. It is ordered, so you just have to pick it up...'

The pizza was still hot — it had marked the waxed box with a circle of grease.
Daniel and Bridget sat on the bed, and he sat on the chair.

Bridget had been quite overwhelmed with the lilies of the valley.
'They're so lovely,' she said. 'So lovely — and the scent!' She put them carefully in a jar of water.
'I'll have to paint them as soon as possible — whilst they're still fresh...'
The thin pale face flushed — her collar-bone prominent under

the thin cotton of her much-washed blouse.
She was too thin.
Daniel was too thin — the joints of his jaw visible when he ate.

He was too thin.
They were all too thin.

Bridget took a slice of pizza downstairs and across the street where Signora Capetti sat, a black bundle in the doorway of No. 10, shuttered and empty.

Dora opened her window to shout.
'Don't feed the old hag, for Heaven's sake! She should be shut up — she's mad — crazy — she'll keep coming back if you feed her — like some mangy old cat...'

Daniel and Peter leant out of Peter's window to watch as Bridget knelt beside the old woman and gave her the pizza. She had put a sheet of white paper on a piece of cardboard, and made an improvised plate — they had none to spare.
The yellow claws took it shakily from her.
Signora Capetti whispered her thanks. 'My son loves pizza,' she said. 'He is so late today — I don't know where he can be. Have you seen him? Have you seen him anywhere? Please tell him to hurry...'

'You eat that up,' said Bridget. 'It will do you good...'
'Why waste good food on that filthy creature?' shouted Dora. 'She should be locked up — put in an asylum...'

'She's a vicious cow,' said Daniel. 'The old woman does no harm. She should be looked after. She certainly can't look after herself. There is no need for Dora to be so abusive.'

'She has no heart,' said Peter. 'She is without feeling. Perhaps she was unlucky in love — jilted — left at the altar...'
'You wait until I leave,' said Daniel. 'She'll be up in my room scavenging like a carrion crow.'

Daniel was going to Rimini for the season.

He had got a job playing in a dance orchestra in one of the luxury hotels.

He was very thrilled.

He was to start at Easter, which was much earlier than usual. 'Rich people come at Easter,' said Daniel. 'It's not so hot or crowded as in the summer — anyhow they can come when they like...'

The pay wasn't very good, but he would have free board and lodging which was worth a lot, and the food would probably be very good — even the leftovers in a place like that would be very good. 'Lobster salad — profiterolles... It's going to be great.'

The orchestra was small. They would play from early evening as long as they were required — for the 'cocktail hour' and then for dancing. 'We will be able to swim and sunbathe on the beach...'

Peter had worked in Rimini last summer — as a waiter.

They were very poorly paid, relying on tips to keep them going.

He had shared an unpleasant room with Mark, a Chemistry student, who poured over his text books most of the night.

There was no bed linen. They slept on disgusting mattresses on iron bedsteads with broken springs.

Mark had lent him a beach towel to sleep on, and another to cover himself. He had bought half a dozen cheaply in the market.

They worked very long hours, from early morning until well past midnight, with a couple of hours off during the day.

Peter had walked along that wonderful beach, his bare feet sinking luxuriously in the soft fine sand.

The sea shimmering in the sunlight, an expanse of blue glass, barely shifting, stretching into the distance, mingling with the sky, the line of the horizon barely distinguishable — a slightly lighter shade of blue — white-sailed boats motionless on the still water.

Sometimes they would swim, and then have their meal, a plateful of stale food left from the day before. The owner of the restaurant didn't believe in wasting anything, however unsavoury.

'It is all good food,' he said, when Mark complained that the meat was like cold rubber. 'What do you expect — that I give you salmon and caviar...?'

The restaurant was right on the beach.
People would sit under the umbrellas and eat icecream and drink beer, and the children ate plates of chips, and drank violently coloured fizzy drinks.

In front of the restaurant the sand was hardly visible beneath the sprawled bodies of sunbathers — the sea a heaving mass of arms and legs — brightly coloured beach balls, and strangely shaped inflated animals, garish and noisy.

There were a lot of Germans.
They ate steak and chips and veal and chips, and cakes toppled with cream.
The women ordering iced pastries with their coffee in the middle of the morning.
Large quantities of reddened flesh exposed to the tireless rays of the sun, barely covered by brief bikinis — the men's bellies sagging over their shorts and swimming trunks.

The English were not quite so brazen.
They were fussy about their food, picking at it and poking it round the plate — spaghetti bolognaise and chips — pallid burgers for the children — drowned in ketchup — choosing the cheapest wine — assiduously applying the suntan oil — the sand adhering to their sticky bodies.

He would have had to work there again this year if it had not been for the portrait.
Daniel would have to give up the room — he could not afford to pay rent during the summer when he was not there. Peter and Bridget would look after the bits and pieces he couldn't take with him.

Bridget was coming back up the stairs.
Dora in the hall continued to harangue her.
'It gives the city a bad name,' she shouted. 'What will visitors think — smelly old people and drunken layabouts in every doorway.'

They drank toasts to each other.
To Daniel's successful summer.
To Bridget's continuing success with her greeting cards.
To Peter for a successful outcome to the portrait — many more
to come.

Bridget lit the candles, and Daniel played a tape of Glen Miller's
band on his portable tape recorder — satisfying sounds —
swinging familiar tunes.

Peter thought of Lucia far away in London.
Perhaps he would be able to afford to go to London one day.
London — an image of close heavy grey buildings and spacious
green parks — a turmoil of people and traffic, black taxis and
red doubledecker buses — pigeons and Nelson, one-eyed, high
on his column.
Lucia had sent so many cheerful postcards.
He hoped things were really alright, that she didn't work in a
restaurant with an unspeakably filthy kitchen.

The kitchen in Rimini had been unspeakably filthy — thick
with grease — solidified — hard as rock — the floor littered
with bits of brittle bread and trodden cheese, broken ravioli and
slimy potato peelings — black plastic bins overflowing with
phosphorescent fish heads and grey chicken's feet — gluey pasta
scrapings — swarming with flies...

They reeked of rancid fat.
At the end of the season they had thrown away their impregnated
clothes.
Mark had said 'You'll never get rid of the smell — just chuck
them...'
He had given him two T-shirts, a black one and a white one. He
had bought half a dozen cheap in the market. Another good buy.
He was good at spotting bargains.
'You can invite me to your first Private View,' he said. 'I expect
you'll be famous one day...'

The wine and music were making him sleepy.
He thought of Erica, battling with braided robes, her dark curly
hair falling round her face.

Downstairs they could hear raucous laughter from Dora's
television.

Across the street Signora Capetti's black form was swallowed up
in the darkening doorway.

15

Stefan went up the dusty stairs quickly to Isotta's office —
soundless in his soft-soled shoes.

She was eating caramels, making a disagreeable squelching noise.
Today she wore a black blouse of some airless man-made fibre,
the collar speckled with dandruff, a turquoise scarf draped round
her shoulders.
Her glasses hung round her neck on a much-fingered black cord.

'I know I sent the order,' she said. 'I remember distinctly...'
A brass ring of keys lay on the desk in front of her, the sort of
ring of keys that prison warders hang from their belts — keys of
all sizes, from twisted dungeon keys to tiny flat suitcase keys with
tatty labels, the writing indistinct and illegible.

She picked them up, her nails, filed to sharp points, scraping
the top of the desk, selected a very small key, opened the centre
drawer of the desk and took out a file.
'We are always ordering spirit gum,' she said. 'I can't think what
you do with it all...'

Stefan made deprecatory noises.
What did the stupid cow think he did with it? Drink it?

He garrotted her with the turquoise scarf. She looked like a turquoise tortoise — lidless eyes popping — her tongue forced out between the thin saliva-bubbled lips.

'Have you looked in the cupboard in the stockroom?' she said.
'There is none in the cupboard in the stockroom,' said Stefan pleasantly. 'None at all...'
'Well I don't know,' she said testily. 'I can't find it here...'
She ran a sharp nail down the line of figures.
'Perhaps you forgot to order it,' suggested Stefan silkily.
She never remembered to order anything.

The stockroom cupboard was a joke — full of balls of string and half-finished rolls of sellotape.
There were several boxes of coloured chalk and a pile of glass ashtrays, all of which had probably been there for many years, and for which there seemed to be no obvious use, unless you smoked heavily and sent a great many parcels.

'Shall I order some?' he said.
'I suppose so,' she said. 'But you will have to try and be more economical with it, we have to keep the expenses down...'
'I don't think anybody would be very pleased if all the beards started falling off half way through the performance,' said Stefan.
'There are a great many beards in this opera...'
'There seems to be a great many of everything in this opera,' said Isotta. 'The whole thing is going to be much too expensive. Nobody did any proper costing.'

Stefan picked up the telephone receiver and wiped the mouthpiece with his clean white handkerchief.
Wiping away the horror of her wet belching breath.
He didn't wish to carry on conversing with this ignorant cow squelching her caramels.
He tied the scarf tighter.

They lowered her into the polluted earth wrapped in the turquoise scarf — her leg brace laid on her chest with her false teeth...

She got up and hung the ring of keys over her arm.

'I'd better check the women's dressing room,' she said. 'Make sure they have enough soap — that's another thing that keeps disappearing. I expect they're filling their suitcases with soap to take back to Russia.'

*   *   *

The Chorus were packed together on the reconstructed Palatial Staircase like football supporters in tracksuits and trainers, jeans and check shirts with rolled-up sleeves.

Little groups, including a few sturdy women, stood uncomfortably about on the stage.

Sergei stood on the red carpet outside the Cathedral, his massive bulk clothed in a pale grey tracksuit with Viva AC Milan in large white letters across his thick chest.
He was talking to the thin man who today wore a black polo-necked sweater and black trousers.

He did not seem very happy.

The orchestra sat in bored rows.
The strings plucking their instruments quietly, and poking the music with their bows.

Peter had been there for some time in a seat in the sixth row of the stalls — sketching.

Sergei's voice boomed out into the empty auditorium.
'The music it shivers — many shivers — the persons walks on the graves — the bones shivers — the persons they feel these deads... It is not an operetta — no fans, no fine ladies. Many deads — the deads they not live — You not dead many times — you dead forever...'

The man in black raised his arm as if to interrupt, and then let it drop.

He went to the front of the stage and spoke to the conductor, who stood in the orchestra pit, leaning morosely against the stage, with a copy of the score laid out in front of him.

'I really do feel the tempo is a little slow, Sergei...' he said with forced cheerfulness.

'Pah,' boomed Sergei. 'You know nothing — You think nothing — You are stuffed with spaghetti and tomato sauce — What do you know? You know nothing...'

'I think we are getting a little confused here,' said the man in black, spreading his hands soothingly. 'Perhaps we could compromise a little on the tempo...'

'Compromise?' boomed Sergei. 'What is compromise? I sing as I sing — the orchestra follow. Signor Spaghetti will follow — all will follow...'

Erica slid into the seat next to him.

'Dear oh dear,' she said. 'The great Sergei Mikhailovsky doesn't seem very happy... Stefan said he would join us as soon as he has sorted out Isotta — She is really completely useless...'

*   *   *

Stefan descended the stairs slowly, flaming wheels of rage spinning in his head.

Guido pirouetted and swooped across the white rug.
He had drunk too many Campari and sodas.
They had eaten in a small restaurant in the Via Bigli.
Guido had been late — apologising profusely.
'Cedric wanted us all back on stage for a pep talk — It took ages...'

Santini cracked his knuckles displaying the heavy gold rings — the air thick with his expensive cologne.

'I'll have a veal cutlet with spinach,' said Guido.
'Two portions of spinach per favori...' He ate a bread stick very fast. 'I'm starving...'

Santini's shadow spread across the table — a black creeping stain on the pale pink cloth.

Stefan had made a detour to pass the Theatre.
The grey bullet shape of Santini's car crouched further down the street.
Tonight there was no chauffeur.

Guido stank of Santini — the white shirt open to display the golden chest — a fine gold chain round his golden neck — a fine gold chain on the golden wrist. He chattered incessantly, avoiding Stefan's eyes — a long stream of puerile nonsense.

Stefan leant across the table and fingered the gold bracelet. He had reduced his bread to a pile of crumbs.
'That's nice,' he said. 'I haven't seen that before...'

'Oh I've had it for ages,' said Guido casually, eating another bread stick. 'Thought it was about time I wore it... I wish they'd hurry up with the food, my stomach is positively cavernous...'

At the next table two women argued.
'It's a lie,' said one of the women. She wore a scarlet suit and clashing lipstick. 'A downright lie — do you take me for a fool...?'

The stain had completely covered the table — it dripped — slow drop after slow drop on the blue fleur-de-lys patterned carpet.
Stefan gagged on the overpowering scent.
He drank his wine in one gulp.
His fury like a caged beast — tearing at the bars of its cage — snarling — tail lashing...
If he let it loose it would tear Guido limb from limb — chuck the headless torso into the gutter — savage those stupid people at the next table...

Carnage and broken glass — the candles setting the fleur-de-lys patterned curtains alight — In minutes an inferno — a dose of hell — a small dose of hell...

'You'll get indigestion if you eat so fast,' he said.

Guido clung and said he would never love anyone else — and the cold shell that encased Stefan's heart turned to icy ragged splinters preventing him from breathing...

He saw Peter and Erica sitting together, and noiselessly joined them.

Sergei had left the stage accompanied by the thin man in black, and the orchestra was playing the Prologue.
Sergei was right. The music shivered — a portent of doom — of distant bells and horsemen — discontent and treachery.

'The Russians are always so gloomy,' said Erica. 'Let's go and get some coffee before we all become manic depressives...'

16

Erica suggested they should go to Lake Como one Sunday, 'On the bus — We could take a picnic.'

Peter thought that was a great idea.
He would love to go to Lake Como.

He wanted to ask if it would be alright for Bridget to come as well, but decided it would not really be appropriate, that Erica would not be very pleased.
He felt unreasonably guilty about going without Bridget. She would say something nice, like 'How lovely — That would be really good...'

He knew how much she would enjoy it — looking for wild flowers and grasses — picking up pebbles and stones from the lake shore — paddling in the gently lapping water. A day of breathing fresh clear air, instead of being cramped up in her stale little room, the windows closed to keep out the smell of decomposing rubbish from the dustbins below, and the whining screech of fighting cats — soaking yesterday's bread in a little watered-down milk and a scattering of sugar — to eat with a spoon.

It would be so unkind to go without her to this magical lake — where oranges and lemons hang their perfumed fruit among the glossy dark green leaves of the citrus trees, beneath the climbing forest of blue/black pine and lettuce-green oak and birch, reaching up to the hazy mountains — snow-capped — craggy pyramids streaked with mauve shadows.

Erica said she would bring bread and ham, cheese and fruit, and a bottle of wine, and they could take a boat trip round the lake.
'The azaleas and magnolia should be in bloom,' she said. 'It's a wonderful sight — the gardens of some of the villas come right down to the water...'

Bridget said, 'How lovely — I hope the weather stays fine...'
She bent her head.
She had not tied her hair back, and it hung loose and limp, obscuring her face.
She was painting a pink tulip.
Peter said, 'I'm sorry — I mean, I'm sorry you are not coming with us — Do use my room — at least you can have the window open in there...'
He felt mean and miserable.
'I'll bring back some wild flowers...' he said.

'A day at Como,' said Stefan. 'That's an excellent idea...' They were in the Russian Café drinking little cups of the bitter coffee, and eating hard oat biscuits.
'We could all do with a break — a change of air — a change of scene — We are all developing Russian melancholia...'

Guido didn't want to go.
He said he was exhausted and needed a rest.
'I'm terrifically tired — that beast Cedric is a positive slave driver...'
He said he was planning to spend Sunday in a darkened room.
'Just to rest — eat a little fruit — drink a lot of mineral water...'

Behind his golden brow Santini's sleek white yacht rocked seductively on its moorings, the sapphire waters of the Adriatic curling frothily against its sides, a tantalising invitation to extravagant luxury and vicarious excitement.

'We'll take a boat trip on the lake,' said Stefan. 'Very restful — chill out — no aggro...'
'Those boats smell dreadfully of diesel oil,' said Guido. 'Toxic fumes... darling Stefan, must I..? Why don't you go without me? I will take the phone off the hook and sleep...'

Guido's golden head resting on the high-backed white-cushioned lounger — deeply tanned young men in short white jackets serving drinks — rattling with ice cubes — bowls of salted cashew nuts — deep fried calamari and giant prawns with a garlic mayonnaise dip...

A stateroom comfortable with deep soft seating and deep soft carpets — white glass and polished brass fittings...

An inscrutable Chinese butler supervising the serving of the black-beaded caviar and grilled trout with melted butter and tiny fresh peas — filling the glasses with champagne — invisibly discreet...

Santini a toad with darting forked tongue — expertly targeting and devouring the foolish tempted to come within range...

How do you kill a toad? With a shovel — with your boots — stamp on it — squash it flat — splayed out — grey blood and pink-tubed innards...

'I get dreadfully sick on buses,' said Guido.
'Don't make such a fuss,' said Stefan. 'You'll enjoy it...' and he locked his hands together to keep them still — to keep them from slapping Guido across the mouth — to restrain himself from twisting the golden arms until he cried out...
'You can take a travel pill,' he said. 'Modern buses are very comfortable...'

Erica said, 'Shit... Stefan gives me the creeps, and have you met "wonderboy", the golden-haired Prince of the Fairies?'

*   *   *

A thick vapid mist shrouded the lake — veiling the villas — the groves of citrus trees — the sloping pines and snowy peaks.

They shivered on the deck of the pleasure boat, their hair and clothes coated with moisture — their faces masked with fine wetness.

The lounge below the deck was very crowded, steaming with wet waterproofs.

They squeezed themselves into a corner.
There were wooden benches and tables ringed by seasons of the bottoms of wet glasses and cans — the benches narrow and hard.
Guido sulked — his pale blue denim jacket wet across the shoulders.
His 'outfit' was all pale blue — jacket — shirt — jeans.
His shoes a darker blue suede — fashionably pointed.
He had complained since they had left Milan.
The bus was overheated — his seat didn't adjust — he knew it was going to rain — look at the sky — anybody could see it was going to rain — why were they determined to go to Como when it was certain to rain?
Now he had ceased to complain — remaining stiffly silent — expressionless behind his dark glasses.

Peter was slightly taken aback by the 'golden boy', as Erica called him.

He made no attempt to hide his effeminacy, crossing his legs and pouting. The pale blue shirt open at the neck to reveal two gold chains, one thick and one thin, a gold bracelet round his wrist — a gold ring with an amber stone on his right hand.

Peter thought he was probably right.

It wasn't the right sort of day to come to the lake.

It wasn't the right sort of day for a picnic.

Perhaps the mist would lift later, but it didn't look very promising. There wasn't much room on the bench, and he was squashed between Stefan and Erica...

There were groups of Americans with waterproof covers over their hats and shoes — studying guidebooks and maps — trying to work out the money — talking loudly amongst themselves.

Germans who had spread the table with paper napkins and were eating bread and gorgonzola and drinking German beer out of cans.

Japanese businessmen in dark suits lined up at the observation window — adjusting their light meters — waiting for an opportunity to take photographs.

'Well, we could have something to eat,' said Erica.

She put her bag on the table.

'I'm not hungry,' said Guido. 'I feel sick...'

'You don't have to eat anything,' snapped Erica. 'There is no obligation to eat anything.'

She started taking things out of her bag — pannini — slices of ham — slices of cheese — a plastic box of salad — a bag of peaches...

Peter did not feel hungry either.

He felt awkward and disappointed — let down — the expectations of a luminous happy day smothered in drizzle and acrimony. He was glad now that Bridget had not come — she would have been so disappointed too.

Erica put out bottles of wine — red and white.

'No champagne?!' said Guido.

Stefan picked up the red wine and peeled the foil off the top of the bottle.

'His admirers bring him champagne,' he said.

It was the first time he had spoken — inscrutable behind his dark glasses — still as a waxen image — his voice fluid as melting wax.

'Oh dear — silly me,' said Erica. 'I didn't realise we had a celebrity among us...'

'I didn't want to come,' said Guido. 'I told Stefan I didn't want to come...'

'Is there a corkscew?' said Stefan.

He would never be able to kill Santini.

He would never be able to get at him.

He was not an experienced assassin.

He didn't have a gun — even if he had a gun he wouldn't know how to use it — to kill someone with a single shot — to kill someone at all with any number of shots.

He would never be alone long enough with him to beat him to death. You can't beat someone to death quickly — a knife? — but if he didn't have time — he might not die — and he had to die.

But to kill Guido — that was another thing — to kill Guido he could take his time — stab him many times — make sure he was dead — come and go without suspicion — he had a key — the concierge was always asleep or watching television — it would be easy...

He would wear his black leather jacket — black leather gloves — black trousers and boots.

Black wouldn't show the blood.

It would mean sacrificing his new black leather jacket which was a pity...

He would keep his clean clothes in a locker at the station where he could pick them up afterwards, and shower and change in the Albergo Diurni which provided soap and proper bath-sized towels...

'You'll have to put up with wine today,' he said. 'Do you want red or white?'

'That Guido is an objectionable little creep,' said Erica.
They stood side by side on the deck.

The mist had lifted enough to see the villas — the stone steps coming down to the water, where little boats bobbed on the breeze-ruffled surface — tied to rings in green-slimed jetties — the walls covered with vines tangled with roses and bougainvillea. Banks of azaleas in every shade from cream to crimson spreading across the lawns.

'I hoped Stefan wouldn't come,' she said. 'He just presumed he was invited...'

The sun came out briefly — touching the snowy peaks of the mountains with a glossy wand, before the clouds closed again.
They had icecream at a café by the lakeside.

Stefan talking now — talking about South America — riddled with ageing Nazis in panama hats — drinking flowery drinks at the pavement cafés — ogling the honey-limbed girls in itsy bitsy white bikinis...

'Gives one quite a frisson — sitting among torturers and murderers, paying for the tequilas and tortillas and sex with money minted from melted gold teeth — and the sun ripens the fruit in their gardens...'

He finished his icecream — licking the last remnants off the spoon. 'I love peppermint icecream...'

'You are gruesome,' said Guido with a shudder. 'Absolutely gruesome...'
'Much better to cavort with drug barons on their vulgar yachts,' said Stefan lazily. 'No hands-on involvement — No pleasure to be derived from inflicting distant torment — *and* their victims

have a choice... The sun shines on them as well — gives them wonderful tans...'

'It's a pity it doesn't shine on us,' said Erica. 'We could all do with a nice tan...'

17

Erica had a flat.
A really nice flat — light and airy, with high ceilings and high windows overlooking a garden with accacia trees and conifers — beds of fat salmon-pink and yellow begonias — bushes of small blue and white flowers and all kinds of shrubs.
There was a paved circle in the middle with a mossy stone birdbath and a wooden bench.
It was very untidy — artistically untidy.

There were long dark blue dusty velvet curtains hanging on brass rings from thick dark wood poles, and a carved oak chest with bowls of coloured glass balls, dried flowers and grasses — notebooks — a bronze of a running man and a bowl of blackening bananas.

There was a table piled with papers and pencils and coloured felt tip pens — jars of buckles and buttons — baskets of ribbons, bits of braid, silk tassles — boxes of sequins and beads.
There were unfinished mugs of coffee — bits of torn bread on a plate — an open packet of biscuits.

Fashion drawings — front covers and pages torn from Vogue — photographs of fashion shows — photographs of models — of hats and shoes — jewellery — the pyramids — palm trees — Alain Delon — Anna Magnani — pinned higgledy piggledy on the walls.
The polished parquet floor scattered with rugs — piles of books and swatches of cloth — tall white altar candles in heavy black candlesticks.

A half-finished jacket marked with chalk and long tacking stitches spread over the back of a comfortable-looking sofa with a lot of cushions — velvet — patchwork — tapestry fruit and flowers — plain and striped...

Erica picked up the jacket and draped it on a chair.
'It's a bit of a mess,' she said. 'Do sit down. I'll make some coffee...'
She collected a couple of mugs from the table and went into the kitchen which could be seen through the doorway of stripped pine — dirty dishes and saucepans — jars of pasta — a cheese grater — jumbled together on a pine table.

The sofa was very comfortable.
Almost as comfortable as Signora Fratelli's — but more homely.
She had become quite chatty.
At the last session she had talked about holidays.

The maid had brought in crescent-shaped pastries glazed with flaked almonds — still uncomfortable in her black lace-up shoes — her work-rough hands clumsy with the elegant handle of the silver coffee pot.

'Go and get my cardigan from my bedroom, Tina,' said the Signora.
She was dressed in the green and silver ballgown. 'I feel a bit ridiculous sitting here like this at eleven o'clock in the morning — the brown one — it is on the chair by the window...'

She poured the coffee, and gestured towards a pile of travel brochures on the table. 'Benito wants to go on safari — I said absolutely not — sleeping in a tent with wild animals prowling around outside is not my idea of a holiday. I want to go to Greece — or Turkey — but Benito says he doesn't want to go and look at a lot of old stones — he can see enough here — or America — I'd love to go to America — but he is very insistent. I told him he would have to have lots of injections to go to Africa. He is terrified of injections....'

He sat back against the cushions.
He was very tired. It had been a very tiring day.

He wondered what Erica would think of Signora Fratelli.
She had a low opinion of the bourgeois, and Signora Fratelli was definitely bourgeois.
She had a low opinion of the police too — lazy and corrupt...
Commissario Fratelli had an awesome reputation as a hard man.
Not someone, as depicted by the Signora, who was frightened of burglars and injections.

Erica had come in with the coffee. She had to clear a space on the table to put it on.
Peter got up to help her, gingerly moving a dress pattern and a bunch of dried flowers — yellow roses — fragile — papery — evoking another age — the rustle of silk dresses — pointed velvet shoes — the flick of a lace cuff...

Erica put down the tray of coffee, took his head in her hands and kissed him on the lips.

There was no tingling excitement — no bells rang — no surge of swoon-making ardour.
Her mouth was just a mouth unexpectedly touching his.
He was acutely embarrassed.

He put his hand awkwardly on her shoulders, and wondered what he should do next.

They stood for several moments — immobile — clasped in silent embrace — then she disengaged herself and moved away.
'Sorry,' she said. 'I didn't mean to jump on you...'
He wanted to say he thought she was wonderful — that he had desperately wanted to kiss her — that he didn't know what was the matter with him — but all he could manage was a stuttered 'sorry'.

They sat down at the table.

'This has been rather a gruelling day,' she said. 'A leisurely picnic gone astray...'

As he reached the street he heard the urgent sound of fire engines — sirens wailing in the gathering dusk.

The rain-filled clouds split with streaks of crimson — uneasy as if the sky too was on fire.

He walked quickly, an increasing feeling of dread — of something horribly wrong, making him hurry.

There were a lot of people at the end of the street.
A brigade of black clad women — couples shoulder to shoulder — men in caps — and smoke.
Dark swirls of smoke rising into the crimson sky — choking black smoke flecked with crimson flakes of fire dancing against the black rain clouds — demon's wings flying...

Dora wrapped in her long-fringed shawl jostling for a better view — and Bridget and Daniel...

Daniel had an arm round Bridget's shoulders, her white face streaked with smoke and tears.

She couldn't speak.
'It's Signora Capetti,' said Daniel. 'She's dead — a terrible fire — the house went up like a torch — there was nothing anyone could do...'

He saw the rickety paraffin stove balanced on the bricks — the matches on the table — the lop-sided candle — the cardboard on the floor — the awful bed — all engulfed in flames.
Signora Capetti a charred heap of rags — indistinguishable from the rest of the charred rags.
Wordlessly he took Bridget's hand.
'Oh my God,' he said. 'Oh my God...'

'Now she will be with her son,' whispered Bridget, tears running unchecked down her thin grimy face. 'At last she will be with her son...'

They stood together in the inky water running down the street from the firemen's hoses as they continued to douse down the blackened heap of rubble, the frame of the house a ragged skeleton — gaunt against the livid sky.
They could hear Dora's voice strident among the small shocked crowd. 'She should have been put away — I always said she should be put away...'

The rest of the house had been boarded up for years.
Drunks and derelicts had broken in to sleep on the rotting floorboards, leaving bottles and cans and mounds of accumulated filth — the staircase unsafe — the roof leaking.

Once it had had flowered balconies and freshly painted shutters.
Signora Capetti had had window boxes of geraniums and petunias outside her basement windows and a camellia in a wooden tub outside her door — long ago — before the black boots had taken away Signor and Signora Stein from the house — before the black boots had trampled her heart.

Dora had spoken of the Steins — 'Jews,' she said. 'They came for all the jews — They took all the jews — '
She could even remember Signora Capetti when she was not crazed.
Her husband was in the army.
He never came back either.

Now she raised her voice in condemnation.
'She should have been put away — I always said she should be put away...'

Bridget swayed — she was deadly pale.
They linked arms to support her.
'Come,' said Peter. 'Let's go — there is nothing we can do for her

now — nothing at all — let's go somewhere warm and have a hot drink...'

He could not face going back to the dismal smelly house to listen to Dora's 'I told you so...' tirade, and sit in the meanly furnished room drinking watery coffee. He had a little money now — they could afford to go to a café.

They went to the Café Florida.
It was clean and comfortable — homely — with scrubbed pine tables and chairs with woven rush seats.
Peter ordered hot chocolate and pannini with prosciutto and cheese.
Daniel said, 'Oh thanks — this is great — ', and started to eat his pannini hungrily.
'It was awful — I was upstairs listening to Oistrakh playing Beethoven when I heard the fire engines — and then I heard Dora shouting in the street 'It's the old woman — old woman Capetti' — so we rushed out — there was black smoke and flames pouring out of her basement, and people shouting and screaming — and then there was a huge explosion and the whole house just caved in... and then you arrived...'

Bridget wasn't eating.
She was crying again, making no attempt to wipe away the tears.
Peter took some paper serviettes from the glass in the middle of the table and gave them to her.
'Please don't cry,' he said. 'She is at peace now...'
He cut her pannini into bite-size pieces and pushed the plate in front of her.
'Try and eat a little — just a little...'
'It's very good,' said Daniel. 'Very good — You'll feel better if you eat something — Peter's right — she's at peace now — she won't be cold or hungry or sad anymore...'
Peter put sugar in her hot chocolate.
'And drink some of this — you're shivering...'

It had been a really bad day.

18

'How the hell are we going to find cushions here?' said Erica.

She stood with Stefan amid bulging laundry baskets and overflowing tea chests.
They had tried 'Props' and had retreated, defeated by upturned chairs and tables — all kinds of tableware — boxes of swords and pistols and artificial flowers — sofas, lamps — rolled carpets — plaster statues, busts and balustrades...

'Wardrobe' seemed an even worse conglomeration, the walls lined with glass-fronted wardrobes full of miscellaneous garments in no particular order.
Velvet doublets — Mozartian satin jackets and breeches — Empire dresses — hessian tunics — breastplates — Wagnerian robes — uniforms...
Laundry baskets full of stockings and gloves, frilled shirts and peasant smocks — wire frames for bustles and ruffs — laced bodices — waistcoats...
Tea chests of shoes — buckled — buttoned — high heels — low heels — wooden heels — silk and suede leather — velvet slippers — embroidered slippers — boots and boots — parasols and hats and hats and hats...
Not a single cushion.

Sergei had nearly had an apoplectic fit when he had seen the size of the cushion bearing his crown.
'This is the cushion for the glass feet for tales of fairies,' he roared.
'This is not a cushion for the crown of the Tsar of all the Russias...'

Stefan was despatched to find a larger cushion.
'I suppose I shall have to go and buy one,' he said.
'I shall go to Ferramis. They must have lots of cushions...'

Ferramis was the most exclusive furnishing store in Milan.
The deferential assistants wore white gloves and winged collars,

accustomed to dealing with the very wealthy and famous — the arrogant and demanding, who expected perfection and all their wishes attended to at once — now — sooner than now.
Everything was exquisite — fine workmanship and materials.
Santini probably shopped there.
The crystal candlesticks which had recently appeared on Guido's table probably came from there.

He would use scissors.
Long-bladed — sharp-pointed scissors.
His best hair-cutting scissors.
They would make the perfect dagger...

Erica had found a collection of cloaks, thrown in a heap — all different colours — red — midnight blue — black — embroidered with gold thread — fur trimmed — short and long...
'These are just great,' she said, picking up a long one of jade green satin, draped it round her shoulders.

It would be easy to hide a knife under a cloak — or even a sword — to come up to Santini in a crowd, stab him through the heart and vanish...

'I suppose I shall have to go and speak to the divine Isotta,' he said.
'Get velvet,' said Erica. 'Red — or purple. We can sew on gold braid and tassles and all that stuff. When this opera is over we should all be given at least six months holiday. A full scale production of Aida would have been less trouble... It would be easier to deal with a herd of elephants than these fat-headed Russians...'

'Things should get better once the first night is over,' said Stefan. 'I hope...'

'My God!' said Erica, throwing the cloak back on the heap.
'The first night — Is there ever going to be a first night...?'

The ballet opened to ecstatic reviews.
'A revelation..!'
'At last a breath of fresh air to blow away the dusty cobwebs of convention...'
'Bravo..!'

Guido was singled out for special praise.
'An electrifying performance..!'
'Quite superb..!'
'An eclectic mixture of subtlety and passion...'

The first night party a glittering occasion.
A bizarre gathering of theatricals packed solid in the sumptuous bar of the Plaza Hotel.
Stefan unable to move — wedged between an aged 'Carmen Miranda', her hat an imitation bunch of grapes and vine leaves, swinging banana earrings and a gold lamé kaftan, and a young woman in a flesh-coloured body-stocking with a collar of porcupine quills, her hair resembling a floor mop — watched Santini enter, immaculate in charcoal grey, accompanied by two hefty men in black wearing 'shades', their jackets misshapen with hidden weaponry — who cleared a pathway to the bar where the Director in a maroon velvet mandarin jacket was drinking champagne with the composer, who looked like a camel, with bulging eyes, bulging forehead and a little sandy beard.
And Guido in pale blue silk.

He watched Santini shake them all by the hand — he could not hear what they were saying.
The 'fruit basket' was telling him about a meeting she had had with Salvador Dali — 'We ate on the floor — his wife, at least I think it was his wife, was a very strange woman — We had goat's cheese — fried goat's cheese I think — very strong — They seemed very fond of goats...'

Santini was bending close to Guido — murmuring in his ear — and Guido was smiling — a rapturous smile...

He took the Samurai sword in both hands, and with one swift movement cut off both their heads — the necks gushed blood — a fountain of blood — and the heads toppled to the ground still smiling.

Guido was 'utterly exhausted', 'completely drained' in desperate need of rest — He just 'needed to sleep', have a glass of milk and go to bed...
Of course he was lying.

The lights in Santini's penthouse burnt long into the night.

There was no way he could get at Santini — no way he could destroy this filthy grey animal...
The flats had surveillance cameras in every bush and tree.
The security guard, housed in a bullet-proof glass box, was surrounded by consoles showing every inch of the building.
He carried a gun.
The fire escapes were locked and alarmed against intruders, with only the tenants and the Fire Brigade holding keys.

Vomit collected in Stefan's throat.

Santini's hand brushed Guido's neck, and Guido flushed with pleasure — laughed — and catching sight of Stefan, waved, and beckoned.
Santini turned, and for one long moment they looked straight into each other's eyes — Santini's stone grey — venomous.
Stefan, safe behind his dark glasses — smiled — a pleasant friendly smile...

This would have been a perfect occasion for the cloak-style assassination.
Among this crowd of eccentric oddities a cloak would pass unnoticed.
He could have made his way through the crowd and thrust the sword right through Santini.
Or he could have come up from behind, and stabbed him in the

back — but then he would not have had the pleasure of seeing his face contort in agony as the blade cut through the flesh, splintering the bones — severing artery after artery...

That would certainly have wiped the smirk off Guido's face.

Now he smiled with genuine amusement.

Santini's latest toy would soon be a rigid corpse in the morgue — identifiable only by the label tied to his big toe...

He would have to go away — would have to leave Milan — leave Italy...
He would take a long holiday.
Nobody would think it strange that he wanted to get away from the city where his lover had been so brutally killed.
He just wouldn't come back.
He had plenty of money.
He had always been careful with his money.
He had considered going to Egypt — or Morocco — but on the whole the Arabs were an unsavoury lot — dirty and dishonest, sandwiched between sea and desert. Nothing but sand separating them from the African hordes — bent on slaughter and tribal domination — plagued by drought and disease — armed to the drunken teeth with kalashnikovs and bazookas...
Definitely not a good idea...

He would go to South America.
He would go to Brazil.
He could easily vanish in Brazil — like so many before him — unobtrusively absorbed...
No problem at all.
Nobody would find him there.
He would have a good time — make a new life.

Santini had turned his back, placing himself in front of Guido so that Stefan could no longer see him.
The bodyguards, right hands in pockets, surveyed the room with

blank, black lenses.

Stefan dropped his gaze.
He did not want to appear conspicuous.
The 'fruit bowl' was talking about Monte Carlo — So different
nowadays — There used to be such wonderful parties — no
wonder poor Zelda had a drink problem — wonderful food —
wonderful clothes — wonderful people — proper music to dance
to...'

Stefan continued to smile — his mouth stretched thin — saliva
gathering at the corners — his temples throbbing with fury.
He said 'Excuse me...' and bowing politely turned to leave.
As he pushed his way through the crowd of the hairy and
non-hairy, the dressed, half-dressed and almost non-existently
dressed, he heard her say —
'What a charming young man...'

19

The photographs had not come out well.
In fact they were not good at all.
Really rather bad — very bad...
Somehow he had moved the camera so they were slightly out of
focus — blurred — several had mysterious red lines at the side.
The colour was very strong.
The Signora highly coloured — fleshy and bulbous.
Unaccountably there was one with Tina supporting the vase of
lilies — anxious and shiny.

The Signora had been most insistent that photographs were
important — essential to the painting of a portrait.
She had paid for the film, and for having it developed, and was
looking forward eagerly to seeing the results.

He spread them out on the café table.
He had been sketching all morning in the theatre, and Erica had

suggested they get a coffee.

The day was warm.
They sat at a table outside on the pavement, their feet in the sun.
Erica had not referred to the unfortunate episode in her flat again.
It was as if it had never happened.
She chatted amicably, asking the waiter for more chocolate on her cappuccino.

'Oh dear,' she said, and started to laugh. 'They're pretty awful aren't they...'

She keeps asking to see them,' said Peter. 'I don't know what to do...'
'Tell her they didn't come out,' said Erica. 'Say there was something wrong with the camera — She really does look awful — she's gross...'

'She's OK,' said Peter.
He felt uncomfortable — she was alright really — she meant well.
Underneath the ostentatious exterior, the posturing and preening she was a simple woman.
Rather pathetic.
She would probably be much happier with a big family — lots of children clambering about, wiping their sticky fingers all over her...

'She's a bourgeois parasite,' said Erica. 'The worst sort of snob — No Class...'
She picked up the photograph with Tina, sullen and worried, clutching the precarious vase of lilies.
'And who is this? One of her minions?'

'That's the maid,' said Peter.
'An exploited servant,' said Erica.
'I don't think so,' said Peter. 'She's quite kind really — a bit stupid — but kind — she's a bit bossy — but I don't think she exploits

Tina — at least she gets plenty to eat...'
'How do you know she gets plenty to eat?' said Erica.

Peter didn't answer.
He was sure the Signora wouldn't ill-treat anyone — she wasn't like that — she just wanted to appear grand — it was all show — like wearing too much jewellery — trying to impress...

Erica gathered the photographs together, and shuffled them like a pack of cards.

'I think you'd better stick to painting,' she said. 'I should just say they weren't any good — Throw them away — You don't need them anyway — Your sketches are super...'

20

Stefan stood against the wall, hidden by the buddleia, which, untrimmed, had grown long-branched over the wall in front of the concrete boxes that made up the flats where Guido lived.

'Don't come before midnight,' he had said.
'It's such chaos after the show, and I have to get changed and take my makeup off — and now people come round to say 'hello' and get my autograph.' And he giggled. 'I'm famous now, caro mio. Fancy people wanting my autograph...'

'Fancy,' said Stefan.

And there was Santini waiting — always waiting — always there — proffering gifts and flattery — beckoning him into a jewelled cage.
Vain — foolish — greedy Guido...

Santini's car was parked further up the street, the metallic predatory shape dull under the dim street lights.

Light glowed from behind closed blinds in Guido's flat.
He had only put on the subdued side lamps.

He was filled with disgust.

Tomorrow it would be over.
The golden boy a bloody carcass.
No more lies — no more deceit — the 'exhausted' one would
never wake again — his head would 'ache' no more —
It would all be over.

He had taken great care with his beard.
It was grey and curly — flecked with black — he had also given
himself thick grey eyebrows.
A black trilby pulled low on his forehead.
An old man stared back at him from the mirror.
An old bearded man.
He wore his black leather jacket — black jeans — socks and shoes
— black leather gloves with popper fastening at the wrists...
No blood would be visible.
No blood could penetrate.

Just before midnight Santini emerged.
Smooth as always — smooth and silver-suited.
He walked with arrogant assurance to the car — triggering the
motor into instant action — the headlights briefly illuminating
the houses on the corner, before the red tail lights vanished in
the darkness...

Stefan's hand clutched the sharpened scissors in his pocket.
He watched it go — cursing this vermin — this rat — carrier of
plague and pestilence — and turned to enter the flats.

Signora Basati had pulled the curtain across the half glass door
of the room in which she slept and ate and watched TV. It hung
limply — shabby and brown — unwashed for years. She had the
room in return for cleaning the stairs, putting out the garbage,
replacing light bulbs in the hallways and sweeping the entrance.

Stefan could hear her television as he trod quietly past her door.

He mounted the stairs slowly — one step at a time, and paused on the landing outside Guido's door before inserting his key.

Guido was coming out of the bathroom, a white towel round his waist.
The golden fleece of hair darkened with water.

He did not know how many times he stabbed him.
He drove the scissors in with all his strength — over and over again.
Guido did not utter a sound.
The look of astonishment — the open mouth, which he sliced with the first blow.

Blood soaked the white towel — the floor — the white rug — spattered the walls — the tall vase of pampas grass.

He breathed noisily — rasping — as if he was gagged.
It sounded in his head, a strangled silent screaming...

He stepped over Guido's inert bloody body and went into the bathroom and washed the scissors thoroughly in the basin.
He left silently — leaving the door unlocked — descending the stairs quickly this time, two at a time.

Out in the street, gulping fresh air — it had begun to rain.
He ran.
He didn't look back.
His heart a piston engine out of control.

Signora Basati opening the door to let in her cat — scratching and miaowing — he was getting too old for all this night life — noticed the grey-bearded man running up the street — Running very fast for an old man.
She picked up the cat, it's tail thrashing, and carried him back into her room.

As soon as he was far enough away, Stefan stopped running and removed the beard and eyebrows, shoving them in the pocket of his jacket with the scissors, and continued walking briskly — not hurrying — towards the station.

He went slowly up the wide marble steps and slowly to the locker where he had left his clean clothes that morning.

It was about twenty to one and the station was almost deserted. There were two policemen drinking coffee outside the all-night café — an old woman in striped woollen leggings asleep against a newspaper kiosk, her belongings spilling out of assorted filthy split carrier bags — an anxious group with suitcases staring at the empty 'Departures' board, and a bald man in a smart overcoat sitting on a bench eating a bar of chocolate and reading a magazine.

He went through the glass doors to the Albergo Diurno and paid for a shower — calmly and politely...
In the white-tiled booth, smelling of disinfectant and steam, he stripped off his clothes carefully, and stuffed them into a black plastic bin bag he had put in with his clean clothes.

There was no blood on his body or his hands.
The thick clothing and heavy gauntlets had protected him.

He lathered with the liquid brown soap and dried vigorously with the scratchy white towel, and put on his clean clothes — jeans and denim shirt with button-down collar, and his navy blue knitted jacket.

Coming out of the station he turned north, and made his way up the dark street to the concrete high-rises — gaunt soulless barracks — with dim security lights on the landings. The lower walls scrawled with graffiti and obscenities.
It was too late for the urchins who daily jostled for scraps with the scrawny dogs, their ribs sticking out of their fur, by the line of battered refuse bins at the back of the building in the yard

stinking of urine and rotting vegetables.

He lifted the lid of one of the bins, and dropped in the bag of blood-soaked clothes.
Tomorrow the dustcarts would come and take everything to the municipal incinerator.

He made his way back to the main road to catch a bus.

Suddenly he was hungry — very hungry — a strange new sensation.
He was never hungry — never really hungry — eating seldom and sparingly.

He went into a trattoria in the Piazza Meda which was still open, and ordered lasagne and a carafe of red wine — eating fast — rubbing the plate with bread — soaking up the last of the red sauce with the white crumbs — draining the dark wine...

21

The young man asked for Stefan.
Erica had just tipped a box of trimmings onto the already cluttered table, searching for braided buttons for the boy 'Prince's' tunic.

He stood in the doorway, his hair a carrot red cockatoo peak — stiff with hair spray, freckles standing out on his distraught white face.
He wore a gold chain round his neck with a cross, and one gold cross earring.
He spoke with difficulty, as if fighting back tears.

Erica wasn't sure where Stefan was.
She thought he had gone to see Sergei, who was agitating about his headgear — a sort of Russian helmet with a gold spike.
The young man had started to cry.
His face crumpled into a pink freckle-specked sponge.

He sat down on a stool, his head bowed, tears dripping onto his jeans.

Erica had swept the trimmings back into the box.
She could hear Stefan calling out 'Ciao — see you later...'
He came through the door, and, seeing the young man weeping on the stool, came to a sudden halt.
The young man lifted his head and whispered 'Guido — somebody has killed Guido — somebody has killed Guido — Guido is dead...'

There was a horrified silence.
The colour drained from Stefan's face. He swayed, and clutched the side of the table.
Erica, momentarily paralysed by this extraordinary announcement, moved quickly to take his arm and help him to a chair.

'What do you mean Guido's dead?' he said. 'What do you mean someone has killed Guido? Who has killed Guido..?'

He recognised this idiot — one of the corps de ballet — a red and white spotted mushroom in the idiotic woodland scene.
The whole ballet was idiotic.
Guido as some kind of ecological spirit had been idiotic.

'I don't believe you,' he said. 'Of course he's not dead — He can't be dead...'

He had given a lot of thought to how he should react when he heard of Guido's death.
He did not know how or where he would receive the news, but he had to be prepared.

He had to suppress the feeling of euphoria — the light-heartedness — the relief...
He had to show shock — horror — devastation — revulsion — anger...
A broken man in a state of collapse.

He couldn't weep — he was incapable of weeping — it was impossible — He had never wept — never shed tears...
He would bury his head in his hands — stunned and mute with grief...

The young man started to sob uncontrollably. 'He was stabbed — in his flat — someone stabbed him — the Theatre is full of policemen asking questions...'

Stefan had thought too what he would say when the police questioned him — for, of course, they would question him.

He would say that Santini had been pestering Guido to leave him — and was very angry and threatening when he refused. That he had offered him all kinds of inducements — gifts — money — had invited him on his yacht — given him the use of his many cars — chauffeured or unchauffeured — but that Guido had turned him down — Guido was not interested...

'I don't believe you,' he repeated. 'He can't be dead...'

It was easy to look pale and haggard.
He had had hardly any sleep — no sleep really.

When he had got home he had cleaned the scissors meticulously — taking special care with the screw where the blades crossed.
He washed them in soap and water, and soaked them in disinfectant.
He boiled them in a saucepan with vinegar, and polished them until they shone, before replacing them in his work box.

From his window he could see over the roofs of the city.
The spires of the Cathedral floodlit — the stalagmite figures — probably martyred saints — or something suitably religious — thinly silhouetted against the night sky.
The greenish light of approaching dawn shone on the bare boards of his floor, splintered and inexplicably stained with pale amoebic shapes.

He had bought two black steel-framed chairs and a zebra-striped bedspread to augment the meagre furnishings.

He had taken down the wormeaten crucifix from the peeling pink wallpaper over the bed, and shoved it at the back of the kitchen cupboard with the miserable collection of dented saucepans and broken cutlery.

He had lain down on the lumpy bed and dozed a little until the light changed from bog green to lemon yellow, and he went down into the Spring sunshine to buy hot rolls for breakfast.

'It isn't true,' he said. 'It can't be true...'

The young man continued to sob. 'It is true — Somebody killed him — somebody stabbed him...'
'Who would want to kill him?' said Erica.
She was still standing — speechless — shocked — holding the 'Prince's' jacket. 'Nobody could have wanted to kill him — It must have been some lunatic — a burglar — perhaps he surprised a burglar...'

'Santini,' said Stefan, speaking very slowly. 'It was Santini — Santini killed him...'

'What would a brigand like Paul Santini have to do with Guido?' said Erica.
'What do you think..?' said Stefan, his voice breaking.
'Oh God, Stefan... I'm sorry... I didn't know Santini was — er — like that — I'm really sorry — Perhaps he resisted...'

'Of course he resisted,' said Stefan. 'Of course he resisted...'
He buried his head in his hands.

He was genuinely tired now — immensely tired.
Now he could go home and sleep — a dreamless satisfied sleep.

22

Tina had a white lace collar on her shiny black dress, and a white lace apron.

The dress didn't fit her.

She attempted to tiptoe across the hall, a shapeless black bolster. Her thick ankles bending against the sides of the uncomfortable black shoes.

At the other side of the hall, absurdly out of place among the mirrors and illuminated niches of posturing figures, the Commissario in shirt sleeves, his bull neck scarlet above an unbuttoned white shirt, shouted down the phone.

Peter had never met the Commissario.

He was never there when he came.

He filled the hall with his physical presence, emanating heat and pent-up energy.

'Who let the poxy bastards in?' he was shouting. 'She had no right to let them in... What about the cordon..? Why wasn't there a cordon..? Well get down there and find out what's going on... incompetent imbeciles...'

Tina tapped nervously on the door of the drawing room and whispered 'Signor Gaspare — Signora..?'

The Signora was wearing a yellow trouser-suit and a lot of pearls. She had overdone the pancake makeup, her face an unbecoming shade of orange changing abruptly to white at the neckline, and startling black eyebrows.

She shooed Tina away.

'Don't bother with coffee,' she said. 'Just stay in the kitchen...'

She put a finger to her lips and beckoned him in, closing the door very carefully.

'I am so sorry,' she said. 'It is chaotic this morning — I completely

forgot you were coming. We will have to cancel the session...'
She waved at him to sit down.
'Benito is very upset — there has been the most dreadful murder
— and somehow the press got to know first and have taken some
dreadful photographs — Benito is furious — of course they will
not be able to print them — Not until he says so...'
She sat down herself in one of the leather armchairs.
'It is one of the dancers from the ballet at the Teatro Massimo
— the lead — the star — Guido Cenni — such a beautiful young
man...'

Shock caught Peter unawares.
His stomach lurching upwards.
A black wave momentarily blotting out the Signora — flooding
his head with a deafening roar.
Guido dead — Guido murdered...
Stefan still as death — that dangerous stillness — the smile that
moved his lips and never reached his eyes...
'Spooky,' Erica had said. 'Very spooky...'

The Signora twisted the ends of the silk scarf tied loosely round
her neck.
'We went to the first night of this new ballet everybody is talking
about — We are always invited to first nights — my position you
know — Benito didn't want to go — He hates first nights — and
he particularly hates ballet — It was quite unusual — modern —
but very interesting — We didn't go to the party afterwards — It
was at the Plaza — Of course we were invited, but Benito has to be
very careful where he is seen — He has to think of his reputation
— It got wonderful reviews...'

Stefan had brought all the newspapers to the Russian Café and
dumped them down on the table.
'50-50,' he had said. 'Half of them think it is amazing — Guido is
amazing — the production is amazing — the music is amazing,
and half of them think it's a lot of pretentious rubbish and that
the music is excruciating...'
He had laughed — at least he had bared his teeth — 'I don't know

what I think — What does one think of a lot of fruit dancing about..?'

'Somebody from the theatre found him — they went round when he didn't answer the phone — the door was open...'
She fished a tiny square of lace handkerchief out of her jacket pocket and dabbed her eyes.
'Such talent,' she said. 'Such a waste — cut to pieces — hardly recognisable — horrible...horrible...'

Stefan's long boneless fingers holding the bone-handled fruit knife — expertly dissecting a pear — paring a thin curling ribbon of yellow rind from the cheese — stabbing it upright in the tub of paté — all in one seamless motion, as if he was about to perform a conjuring trick and produce eggs from the sleeves of his jacket — strings of sausages from his pockets, or, with a roll of drums, bunch after bunch of paper flowers out of thin air — or stab you through the heart...
'That's terrible,' he said. 'What a terrible thing...'

The day had started so well.
He had got a letter from Lucia.
A proper letter.

Apart from the occasional postcards of London buses — postboxes — policeman — and other famous sights, he had received very few letters — hardly any at all...
Dora was holding the post in her hand when he went downstairs.
'A letter from England,' she said accusingly, as if he had committed a crime.

It was a long letter.
She and Teresa had moved to the above address.
A flat in West London with two bedrooms.
They now had their own room.
It had central heating, a blue bathroom and a telephone (the telephone number as above, under the address...).
They had given up their jobs at the restaurant, and were working

on the 'Check In' desk of Alitalia at Heathrow Airport.

She went on a lot about the job — the hours — the pay — the smart uniforms...
She was taking driving lessons.
Things were really good...
Now they had their own place he could come and stay.

He had sat on the bed and read it several times, taking it to show Bridget.
She had got a part time job in a bookshop, and was getting ready to go to work.
'We should celebrate,' he had said. 'Let's go out for supper tonight...'

He was glad he was sitting down, and although he desperately wanted to leave, to get out in the air, he felt unable to get up. His knew his legs would not support him.
'Who could have done such a dreadful thing?' said the Signora.
'Who would want to kill such a beautiful talented young man..?'

Stefan's breath smelling faintly of aniseed as he leant across the table. 'Dancing fruit,' he purred — smiling the smile that did not reach his eyes. 'Have you ever heard of anything as ridiculous as dancing fruit..?'

He danced, his body strangely elongated, the long arms dangling at his sides, across the Signora's eau-de-nil carpet — a black figure — predatory and threatening...

'Benito is so very upset,' said the Signora.
He was still bellowing down the phone.
'He can't stand the sight of blood, and he has to go and look at the body — it gives him dreadful heartburn — but it's his job — he has to look at bodies...'
A car drew up outside.
The Commissario stopped bellowing.
There were murmured greetings.

The front door slammed, and the car was gone with a skidding scrunch of gravel as it reversed sharply out of the drive.

'We have to go to a reception tonight,' said the Signora with a theatrical sigh. 'I suppose he'll be very late — He's always very late — It is not easy being married to a policeman — ' she gave a little strained laugh. 'Even a *very* senior policeman — particularly a *very* senior policeman — they have so many responsibilities...'

23

'So you have never met Signor Santini?'
Commissario Fratelli perched gingerly on one of the rickety chairs in the work room.
Erica had cleared some of the clutter off the table and had fetched coffee.
A young policeman sat on another chair with a notebook.

'No,' said Stefan, wan and red-eyed — he had perfected an excellent method of reddening his eyes — pulling down the lower lids and rubbing them vigorously.
'No — I never met him — I have seen him around a lot — he was always coming to the theatre...'
He sat on the edge of the chair — hands clasped tightly in his lap.
Sitting on the edge of the chair made him seem distressed — anxious.
If he sat back it would give the wrong impression.
He would appear relaxed and at ease.
He had to strike a balance between grief and apprehension.

The Commissario, corseted in his uniform, looked at him with close-set black foxy eyes, inquisitorial above the prominent bridge of his imperious Roman nose — incongruously haughty and fierce with the heavy jowls and bull neck.
Fourteen kilos lighter he would be an impressively handsome man.
It would not do to underestimate him.

'But you never met him..?' he said. 'Even though he was trying to persuade Signor Cenni to leave you..?'

'I never met him.'

'Signor Santini is a very rich and powerful man...'

'Guido and I were very happy together — He didn't want to go with Santini...'

'And you didn't meet at the first night party?'

'No,' said Stefan. 'He was with Guido at the bar — we just acknowledged each other...'

'Why were you not at the bar with Signor Cenni?'

'I couldn't get through the crowd — It was very crowded...'

'And Signor Santini?'

'His bodyguards forced their way through...'

'And you are sure Signor Cenni did not respond to Signor Santini's attentions? I understand he visited Signor Cenni at his apartment on several occasions...'

'How do you know that — ? Who told you that — ?' Stefan was agitated.

'The concierge — She had seen him coming and going — A man like Santini is not a man who goes unnoticed — He parked his car outside — A large expensive car is very noticeable too — especially in such a street...'

'I didn't know that,' said Stefan. He looked at the floor. 'Excuse me — I feel sick — excuse me...,' and he got up quickly, pushing back the chair roughly.

'Calm yourself, Signor Lucca — I am sorry we have to ask so many questions — but you must understand we wish to apprehend Signor Cenni's murderer as soon as we can...'

Stefan sat down again.

'I didn't know Guido was seeing Santini,' he said. 'I had no idea...'

'So you wouldn't have killed him yourself — ? In a jealous rage perhaps — ? You could have seem them together — Perhaps he taunted you with it?'

Stefan shook his head in disbelief.

'I had no reason to be jealous,' he said. 'I didn't know he was seeing Santini — I don't believe he was seeing Santini — We were very happy together — Why should he be seeing Santini..?'

'Signor Santini is a very powerful man, Signor Lucca,' said the Commissario. 'He tends to get what he wants...'

24

Stefan ordered a second vodka.
Peter was still sipping his first.
Stefan had insisted they had vodka.

They had just got back from Guido's funeral.

Outside the sun shone weakly between showers.
Inside the Russian Café it was dustily dim — the small-paned windows never let in much light.
At the next table two men were playing dominoes.
They had turned on the green-shaded light and looked very sick.

Erica had said they had to go to the funeral because of Stefan.
He had not been near the theatre since Guido's death.
'He doesn't answer the phone,' she said. 'I hope he's alright...'

Bridget was horrified by the murder — she kept saying 'Poor Stefan — how terrible — who would want to kill someone like that..?'
Peter mumbled something about mad people — crazy people — seeing Stefan's mirthless smile — the plasticine hands suddenly dripping blood...

Daniel knew a cellist in the ballet orchestra who had a car — it is difficult to be a cellist without a car — who would give them all a lift.
Bridget couldn't go because she was working.
'I didn't know him anyway,' she said. 'Such a terrible thing — Poor Stefan...'
So Erica, Daniel and himself went in Frederico's battered Fiat.
The funeral was outside the city, at a village off the road to Monza.

They drove past stained concrete blocks of flats, breaker's yards toppled with rusty wrecks of cars, and shacks made of rotting planks where the really poor lived — bare-footed children playing in the mud and rubbish — and took a small road through flat fields and clumps of trees to the village where Guido's grandmother lived.

Nobody knew he had a grandmother.

Nobody knew anything about his family.

Even Stefan didn't know he had a grandmother.

Erica said had they seen the newspaper headlines that morning, 'Millionaire questioned over Ballet killing'...?

'I think they're questioning Santini,' she said. 'Stefan is absolutely convinced he did it...'

Peter pretending not to hear, watched a kestrel swoop to earth to grab its prey.

'They'll never hold him,' said Daniel. 'He owns everybody in Milan... Well, pretty well everybody...'

'He was always hanging round the theatre,' said Frederico. 'Came to all the rehearsals — visited him in his dressing room — sent masses of flowers...'

The car bumped and shook on the rough road.

'People like Santini never get caught,' said Erica. 'He can buy himself out of anything...'

The church dominated the small square.

It was already full of cars.

They had to park down a side street.

It was not a very attractive church — just large.

The bell was tolling, and people jostled to get in front of one another.

There were a lot of people — photographers — a camera crew — important-looking people in camelhair and mink and earnest people in anoraks and headscarves.

'How to become famous overnight,' said Erica. 'Get yourself murdered.'

25

All the village seemed to be in the Church, a solid block of black-veiled heads and ill-fitting black suits — so were the entire Ballet Company in an assortment of colours, as if someone had emptied a jar of boiled sweets.

'I expect they are hoping to be seen on the television,' said Erica.

The grandmother, a squat figure enveloped in black, scuttled down the aisle like a veiled black beetle — escorted by the mayor emblazoned with his chains of office.

They took their seats at the front with the Director of the Ballet Company, the Chairman of the Arts Board and other select dignitaries including Signora Fratelli in a splendid black hat.

The coffin and the steps leading to the altar piled high with flowers.

Peter remembered the stark misery of his mother's funeral — the cheap wooden coffin, the scattering of anemones trampled in the mud — the few scarecrow onlookers.

He looked round for Stefan, and saw him sitting at the back at the end of a pew, motionless, inscrutable behind his dark glasses, wearing a dark suit and black tie.

The pictures moved jerkily — black and white — a silent movie — the screams unheard — the blood a black rivulet on the white floor — and Stefan laughing — soundless laughter — bending his long black form over the inert body...

The organ played — the congregation sang the hymns and intoned the responses, the priest read from the Bible, and the candles on the altar guttered in the draught.

Stefan had preferred to go with some of the dancers. With them he could remain silent without awkwardness.

It would have been more difficult with Peter and Erica.

He had been out early to buy the newspapers, and read with supreme satisfaction that Santini was being questioned by the police.

There were pictures of him and Guido on the front page.

'Millionaire businessman Paul Santini, an ardent admirer of the victim, Guido Cenni, the highly acclaimed dancer at the Teatro Massimo, was a frequent visitor to Signor Cenni's apartment on the Via Cavalli, and was probably the last person to see him alive. Signora Bassati, the concierge, said she had seen them arrive together at about 23.00, but had not seen him leave. She had been watching television. Signor Santini is at present helping the police with their enquiries...'

It was all going to plan.

He sat at the back of the church, coldly observing this gathering of common riffraff — wallowing in a public display of phoney grief.

Snivelling hypocrites.

Of those who had known Guido, and there were many who hadn't known him at all, few had liked him — most had disliked and resented him. Disliked him for his vanity — the preening and posturing — and resented him for his success — his golden looks — his charm. Were in fact gleeful at his demise — though tragic of course — which gave them an opportunity, by fair means or foul, to take his place.

Now they wept and supported each other in an orgy of hysterical sentimentality, getting a cheap thrill from being in such close proximity to a violent death, possibly, even, a scandalous death.

Contemptible scum.

If they could see beneath the masses of fragrant blooms — beneath the lid of the polished oak coffin with the polished brass handles — could see the disfigured body — drained of blood —

the dreadful colour — the stench of putrefaction overpowering the sweet smelling blankets of flowers — then they would have reason to clutch each other — to faint — to throw up — to have hysterics...

'In the name of the Father, the Son and the Holy Spirit...' droned the priest.
Stefan bent his head, crossed himself and murmured 'Amen'.

'I have to get away,' he said. 'I have to get away from here...'
'Of course,' said Peter, and then, thinking this didn't sound sufficiently convincing, repeated it more emphatically. 'Of course...'

Stefan, looking at him through half-closed lids, felt a sudden trickle of comprehension — a tingling sensation in his veins.
He knew — Peter knew — the naive young man with the magic paint brush knew he had killed Guido.
Of course he couldn't really know — nobody could really know.
He wanted to laugh, to lean over and say 'Prove it then — Prove that I killed him...'
He repressed the laughter that welled up, bubbling in the back of his nose — laughing was out of the question — it would not even do to smile.
It was a pity he couldn't squeeze out a few tears.

He continued to look at Peter through half-closed lids.
He had known — guessed — all the time.
That was why he had been so evasive — his difficulty in expressing his condolences — his hesitancy in condemning Santini as the prime suspect.
It was not shock or reticence, it was because he believed that he had killed Guido.
He wondered what had made him suspect him — made him so sure.
Peter felt Stefan observing him and pretended to sip his vodka.
He didn't want the vodka.
He wanted to leave the café as soon as possible.

He didn't know what to say to Stefan.

There was nothing to say.

'This place is haunted,' said Stefan. 'It will always be haunted.'

He bowed his head, his voice breaking. 'I can't live here any more — I can't believe he is really dead...'

Peter said, 'It's hard for anyone to believe it...'

'Who could have done such a thing?' said Stefan piteously.

'Who could have done such a terrible thing to Guido..?'

Peter was silent.

How could he keep up this charade?

When Erica had said he was spooky she had been right.

He was spooky.

Strip away the grieving mask and expose a triumphant killer.

'I have to get away,' said Stefan again. 'I can't stay here...'

Peter avoided looking at him.

Perhaps he hadn't killed Guido.

Just because he was spooky didn't mean he was a murderer.

It could have been Santini.

Or someone else altogether.

Guido could have been two-timing them both.

Or it could have been a burglar — a crazy burglar...

So why was he so sure that Stefan killed him?

Because he was quite sure.

'Where will you go?' he said.

'I don't know,' said Stefan, twisting his plasticine hands.

'I don't know — I just have to get away...'

He had already bought his ticket.

He was to leave for Rio the day after tomorrow.

He had to go to Rome to catch his flight — eleven and three-quarter hours direct to Rio.

The midday flight would arrive at about 7.30 in the evening, Brazilian time.

It would be good to arrive in the evening.

He would take very little — just one bag — leave the rest behind so that it would look as if he was coming back.

The rent was paid until the end of the month.

The landlord lived elsewhere, and apart from collecting the rent, was totally disinterested in his tenants.

If the police searched the flat, and so far they had shown no desire to do so, they would find nothing.

There was nothing to find.

'I don't know what I shall do,' he said. 'I don't know what I shall do without him...'

26

'Where the hell is Stefan?' said Erica.

It was the day of the dress rehearsal, and Peter had been sketching all morning in the theatre — the Imperial staircase heavy now with bearded men in fur-trimmed velvet robes embroidered with gold thread — heavy robes fastened with gold chains.

They had gone across the square to get something to eat.

Erica ordered spaghetti. 'I'm starving,' she said. 'So where is Stefan? Isotta's going round the bend. She was sure he would turn up for the dress rehearsal. She had to get four students from the Drama School, who are quite hopeless, to replace him, and nobody knows where anything is, and everybody is shouting in Russian — It's compete chaos...'

'I think he's gone away,' said Peter.

'Did he tell you he was going away?' said Erica. 'When did you see him?'

I haven't seen him since the day of the funeral,' said Peter. 'He said he had to get away, he didn't seem to know where, and he didn't say when he was going...'

Erica forked up a long strand of spaghetti. 'Well, he never said anything to me. He hasn't been in touch with anybody at the theatre. He never told anybody he was going away. We thought he would turn up for the dress rehearsal. We thought he wouldn't want to miss the first night — probably go away afterwards...'

Peter ate some of his spaghetti. It was very good.

'How's the portrait getting on,' said Erica. 'How's the "fabulous Signora"?'

'Fine,' said Peter. 'It's going to be fine — it's nearly finished.'

At the last sitting the Signora had talked incessantly about the murder. Such a terrible thing — Benito had been up half the night with his stomach...

'It was horrific,' she said. 'Quite horrific — carnage — a frenzied attack — blood everywhere — the poor young man cut to pieces — the act of a madman. Between you and me, because I shouldn't really talk to anybody about it, but I know I can rely on you to be discreet, Benito thinks Paul Santini had something to do with it. The only two people that the concierge could identify were Santini and that poor young man, Stefan Cenni — he works at the Scala — I've seen him there — Poor young man — he must be heartbroken...'

Today the cake was sticky and fudgy. Tina had remembered the forks and the serviettes and the silver sugar tongs. She still walked painfully in the flat black shoes, putting the tray down carefully on the glass-topped coffee table.

'The thing that puzzles him,' continued the Signora, 'is that Santini never does his own dirty work. He is never caught smuggling or supplying drugs — he doesn't beat people up — he is not involved in shootings and protection rackets. He has is own little army of thugs to do these things. It is most unlikely that he would actually kill someone himself — but this was such a savage murder, it doesn't look like a professional killing. It's too personal... that's what Benito thinks...'

She cut him a generous portion of cake. 'I was going to get a fruit tart,' she said, 'but they only had pineapple, and I'm not very fond of pineapple... The concierge said she saw an old bearded man running away down the street when she let her cat in around midnight — she is a completely unreliable witness — but it could have been one of Santini's men...'

Stefan the bearded man — the perfect disguise.
Peter swallowed his mouthful of cake too quickly, and coughed.
He had probably left the city by now — gone forever — sunning himself on some distant beach...

'It was a lovely funeral,' said the Signora. 'Most tasteful — and so nice to see all his friends and colleagues paying their respects — such a talent — such a terrible thing...'

She was very pleased with the portrait.
She looked quite magnificent in the green and silver striped ballgown, with the tall white lilies behind her — a jewelled hand resting on the lid of the grand piano.
'A friend of mine wants you to paint her daughter — so I've given her your address and telephone number. Her daughter is a very plain girl, but I'm sure you will be able to do something with her...'

'You don't suppose Stefan did it do you?' said Erica, twirling up another large forkful of spaghetti. 'Killed Guido, I mean. He was always very strange — sort of sinister...'

Peter said he supposed it was possible — anything was possible.

'He could have done it in a jealous rage,' said Erica. 'When he found out about Santini. He told the police he didn't know they were seeing each other — but I didn't believe him...'

27

It had been quite a good flight.
A bit cramped.
Aeroplanes didn't cater for tall people — nowhere for their knees.

A child ran noisily up and down the aisle, screaming when it's mother tried to make it sit down.

It was a pity it was not possible to open the door.
It would be amusing to chuck the obnoxious brat out, and watch it fall, its arms, fat in the padded jacket, flapping hopelessly, as it plummeted towards the distant waters of the Atlantic.
It would be possible to smother it with one of the blankets handed out by the stewardesses so you didn't get chilled whilst sleeping — but that would not be so amusing.

The woman next to him fidgeted a lot, adjusting the seat — the light — the ventilator. She wore a nylon polo-necked sweater, a black canvas bodybelt and sensible brown lace-up shoes — her scalp visible under the thinning hair.
She called the stewardess for mineral water and complained about the food — a flavourless stew and synthetic chocolate cake — put on a frilly eye mask and slept, breathing noisily through her mouth.
Perhaps he could smother her too.

At least she hadn't tried to start up a conversation — pestered him with puerile questions — where was he going — ? what was he going for — ? how long was he going for — ? and so on and so on — automatically inquisitive without caring in the least what the instantly forgotten answers were.

And then it was there below them.

The towering figure of Christ — arms outstretched to embrace His people — that maggot life below — squirming in their obscene hovels — hollow-faced women with distended stomachs rocking chicken-boned babies, shrivelled and toothless as the old, who sat stooped and motionless on broken chairs waiting for food — thin soup and rough bread which scraped their bare gums. Half-naked children, scummed with sores, racing sticks on the rivers of sewage.

'Suffer the little children to come unto Me...'
They were much too undernourished to attempt the climb...

Bouts of violence — the flash of knife blades, and blood mingled with the excrement.
The struggle for survival in the punishing poverty — a rim of shame around a prosperous, thriving city...

'The Lord is my shepherd. I shall not want...'
This particular flock must have been overlooked — gone astray somewhere...
Christ's gaze fixed on the wondrous blue ocean and stretch of silver sand — not on the human vermin sinking in the slime beneath him.

Best send in some tanks — wipe them out — crush them — put them out of their misery — turn them into manure — they would make marvellous manure — and then plant a vineyard — vine-covered slopes instead of disease-ridden slums...

The 'fasten your seat belt' sign had come on.
The wings tipped.
They were coming in to land.
Within an hour he would begin his new life.

28

Tomorrow Daniel was leaving for Rimini and they were going out to supper at a restaurant that Daniel said was very good — very reasonable — but very good.

He had been there before with members of the Symphony Orchestra.

The sort of restaurant which had starched tablecloths and flowers — all that sort of thing — and super calamari fritti...

He had invited a whole lot of people — mostly musicians.

It was going to be quite a party...

They had spent all day helping to clean his room and pack his things.

He was leaving his winter clothes with Peter, and books with Bridget.

Dora had come to inspect the room — poking about, and peering into every corner, to find some excuse for not returning his deposit.

Arguing over the broken table leg, and a hole in the threadbare bit of carpet.

Bridget had had her hair cut and was wearing a smart black dress she had made.

She had to wear black in the bookshop.

The new hair style really suited her.

She was a very nice girl.

The sort of person who would never let you down.

She reminded him a little of Lucia — always making the best of things, however difficult and depressing they might be...

It was still light and the air had the lazy warmth of approaching summer.

A single pale star suspended in a lilac sky.

There were yellow tulips round the little fountain on the corner, and the flowering cherries, which lined the street, frothed with pink and white blossom.

'Look,' said Bridget. 'Look at the headlines...'

On the billboards leaning against the side of the newspaper kiosk, in bold, black letters he read, 'PAUL SANTINI CHARGED WITH DANCER'S MURDER...'

'Well — that's it I suppose,' he said.

It would fizzle out.

Santini would be acquitted through lack of evidence — if it even ever came to a trial.
Guido would be forgotten.
And Stefan?
Stefan would live happily ever after...

'Come,' he said. 'We'll be late.'

He took her by the hand, and they went together up the street, under the cherry trees, which shaken by a sudden gust of wind, showered them with pink and white confetti.

Proceed With Caution

She was always apologising. She could not remember when it had started, sometime when she was young. Henry found it so irritating. 'For God's sake, Louise,' he would say with measured exasperation, 'What are you apologising for now?'

Now she said 'Oh sorry' as the woman in a turquoise jogging behind her drove her trolley into the back of Louise's legs. The woman ignored her selecting a bar of white chocolate from the display by the checkout. Louise had forgotten the list she had committed to memory before leaving home. If she had brought it with her she would have lost it or left it in the car.

She wished Caroline was not bringing this new man for the weekend. What was she supposed to do about the sleeping arrangements? She had made up the bed in the spare bedroom, but dreaded Caroline's derisive comments. She thought her mother hopelessly old-fashioned. Louise didn't care how many men Caroline slept with, so long as Henry did not blame her for their daughter's behaviour. Henry did not believe in cohabitation before marriage, especially for his daughter. Henry blamed her for Caroline's belligerent attitude and left-wing views.

Louise was quite sure that Caroline's political opinions were far more right wing than her father's. She took after him, clever, dogmatic, and, although Louise didn't like to admit it, really boring. She was unyielding and unimaginative, deliberately clashing with her father. They had had terrible rows, before she left home. She now had her own flat in West Kensington.

She had told Louise to get some decent wine to go with the meal. Paul was apparently quite a connoisseur. Louise had had to ask Henry. She knew nothing about wine except it was red or white, sweet or dry. Henry was huffy, wanting to know why they had to go to all this fuss over some idiot boyfriend. Was it serious? Who is he?

Louise said she didn't know and had enough to worry about dealing with the food. This annoyed Henry even more, and he said surely there was no difficulty providing a few meals for her own daughter and her friend. He enunciated the word friend with sarcasm, and helped himself to a large whisky.

Now she stood miserable with her trolley, hoping she had not forgotten anything. Mrs Toynbee would have finished the cleaning by the time she got home. She had left a note about dusting upstairs and washing the kitchen floor. She was always apologising to Mrs Toynbee. She was so sorry to have to ask her to do this or that or the other.

This irritated Henry. 'You pay the woman. She is a cleaner, you don't have to say you're sorry asking her to clean' he would say, going on to complain that his study hadn't been cleaned for weeks, and the stair carpet was covered in bits.

Louise reminded Mrs Toynbee not to forget the study. She was inclined to sniff if it was suggested she had forgotten to do anything, and then she would bang about and slam a lot of doors.

Louise hoped that Paul was not a vegetarian or anything. Perhaps she should have got more vegetables and fruit. She reversed her trolley apologising again to the person behind and went to get more. She hoped he wasn't a vegetarian. Henry didn't like vegetarians. 'Poseurs' he called them. People should eat what they are given and be grateful that there was plenty to eat. When we were young there was a war on, no place for faddy trends. They only had two ounces of cheese a week.

Louise remembered the cheese. She took six different kinds. At least there would be a full cheese board. One hard, one soft, one blue, a brie, goats and garlic. That should keep them all quiet. She was bound to forget something however hard she tried. Caroline would say 'Haven't you got...?' She wondered what it would be. Salted butter, unsalted butter, cane sugar, freshly squeezed fruit juice, dark rye bread. She would find something, and then Louise, contrite, would apologise again.

Louise had met Henry at the annual Golf Club dance, which was held at the end of November. Louise's father was a bank manager, and also President of the Golf Club, so every year since her mother had thought her old enough, she had attended the Golf Club dance. That year she was twenty, and had completed her expensive secretarial course. A whole year had been spent going to college in Kensington, staying with her aunt, her father's sister who had a huge old-fashioned flat off Sussex Square. She had really enjoyed herself, and wanted to move out and have a flat of her own. She did not dare to broach the subject to her parents, so she continued to live at home and got a good job with a solicitor's — Clegg, Rutt and Clegg, in Colesbury. That year she had a really nice dress of blue taffeta with a very full skirt, and there was Henry. He was tall and nice looking, and paid much attention to her all the evening, claiming dance after dance, holding her in a tight embrace, getting refreshments, making flattering statements.

Clare had said sourly, when he had gone to replenish her glass again, that he worked in her father's bank, and was wasting no time in getting in with the boss's daughter.

Long after Louise realised that this had been absolutely true. Henry had not been in the bank long, and he was ambitious. Not for him the tortuous climb, taking many years to reach the top. He wanted a short cut, and that short cut happened to be Louise. This time she had to apologise to herself for being such a gullible little fool, taken in by his flattering attentions, believing that he was genuinely smitten, and believing that she too was in love.

Her mother, after an initial hesitation, was so pleased that her very average daughter was to be married to this personable, hard working young man, encouraged the relationship enthusiastically and insisted on his being promoted — they couldn't have their daughter marrying a bank clerk. Her husband agreed, so Henry received his first promotion before they were married.

Her father, a rather remote figure, had always shown kindness and tolerance in his dealings with her, bought them a house on the outskirts of Colesbury, and everything went ahead for the wedding the following June.

Louise, who considered herself to be absolutely average in every way — height, weight, intelligence, looks etc. — felt very humble that she was to marry a confident, handsome man of the world.

Now as she backed out of the supermarket car park, she knew she had just been a stepping stone.

Louise turned back the maroon satin counterpane. It was 4.30, everything was ready downstairs, the drawing room dusted, the casserole in the oven, vegetables prepared. Now she had at least an hour to rest before having to rise and smilingly greet Henry when he came home from work. She slid gratefully under the maroon satin eiderdown, thinking again what a good thing it had been that Henry had decided, when they had moved to this house, that single beds were more sensible. The furniture was darker and heavier than she would have chosen, but the room was large, so it wasn't too oppressive. The adjoining bathroom had a maroon coloured suite, also chosen by Henry. Thank goodness he had not chosen brown, or even black! Her left leg ached, and she moved to make it more comfortable. What on earth had possessed Henry to ask Charles and Ursula to join them for supper at the Golf Club tomorrow evening? Everybody, apart from Charles, and seemingly Henry, knew that Ursula had been having an affair with the Golf Pro for months. A nice enough young man with a perpetual tan and even white teeth. Charles' patronising remarks on Ursula's inability to improve her game, even with all the extra lessons he was paying for, caused some choking into drinks in the bar.

About two weeks ago somebody had taken it upon themselves to tell Charles. Ursula had telephoned in floods of tears, Henry had ranted on about ingratitude and wifely betrayal. Charles had insisted that Ursula should accompany him to the Club, a grey wan shadow, to present a good face to the world. This did not augur well for an evening of amusing conversation, or create the right ambience for Caroline's new man.

Louise was always surprised at her daughter's good looks. Tall, immaculate dark hair, casually elegant, poised, confident, the very antithesis of herself.

Paul was also tall, dark haired, bespectacled and beautifully suited. Standing by the fireplace they looked as if they were in one of the new television commercials. Henry did not approve of commercial television.

Caroline worked for a large stock broking firm in the City as some kind of financial adviser. Louise, who could hardly manage her shopping list, found all the mystique of stocks and shares totally incomprehensible. She understood Paul was also in the City.

As she put down the tray of glasses beside the bottles on the table by Henry's chair, he demanded to know what she had done with today's *Telegraph* — he wanted to show Caroline an interesting article about a new economic theory. Louise apologised. She must have taken it in the kitchen when she was tidying up the drawing room. She went to fetch it.

She strained the sprouts, put them in the oven to keep warm and washed up the saucepan, before picking up the paper to take it in to Henry.

She disliked the *Daily Telegraph*. Like everything else, it was Henry's choice. She couldn't imagine Caroline allowing someone else to choose what daily paper she should read.

The dinner went off without mishap. She had not forgotten anything. Paul was politely attentive to everything Henry said, eating slowly and pausing to listen, nodding and smiling briefly.

Henry and Caroline, tongues loosened with wine, argued loudly on the state of the country, Europe, the World!

After she had served coffee in the drawing room, she mumbled some excuses and retreated to the kitchen to clear up, thanking heaven for the modern miracle of automatic dishwashers. Then she crept quietly up to bed.

She was comfortable ensconced with a new Patricia Highsmith when Henry came into the room. He shut the door very quietly, and taking his jacket off hung it deliberately on the back of a chair.

'Do you realise what he is?' he asked in a low voice.

'Something in the City I think.'

'I mean what he IS,' he emphasised the last word whilst keeping his voice low.

'Well, I don't know exactly...'

'He is a JEW.'

'Well, there are lots of Jews in the City ...'

Henry made an explosive sound. 'He is a Jew. Don't you mind?'

'Why should I mind?'

'Good God woman, don't you mind your daughter cohabitating with a JEW?'

'Of course not!' For once she was not going to be browbeaten. 'Paul is successful, good-looking, well mannered and he went to Oxford, what more could you want for your daughter?' and then suddenly really annoyed, 'After all, we are hardly staunch supporters of the Protestant faith. We never go to church, and you think the vicar is a fool.'

Henry swore, and then picking up his pyjamas went angrily into the bathroom.

Louise decided to wear a long black skirt and black silk blouse, and risk being mistaken for a waitress. The waitresses at the Golf Club on a Saturday night were augmented by some of the daughters of Club members earning a little extra pocket money. They all wore black, but she really did not think she would be confused with somebody's daughter.

There had been no more said about Paul's origins.
Henry had been playing golf all day and had only come in at teatime to bath and change.

Caroline and Paul had got up late and gone driving in the country and had also come in at teatime.

Louise served tea and bought cake in the drawing room. Henry complained about the cake, a jam sponge. He did not care for jam sponges. Both Caroline and Paul had a slice, and she fetched some chocolate digestives for Henry. Caroline said she would have preferred Earl Grey, and filled her cup with hot water. Henry said it was scented muck, and avoided speaking to Paul.

Louise had been going to the Golf Club for as long as she could remember. Firstly in her father's luxurious leather-seated Bentley, then in Henry's second-hand Ford, graduating through the years to the purring dark green Armstrong Siddeley. Now she drove her own white Morris Minor. Henry hadn't wanted her to learn to drive, said it would encourage her to gad about. Gadding about was not really a suitable description of her activities, attending various fund-raising events. Coffee mornings, sponsored knits, jumble sales, charity lunches — the collected revenue intended for victims of drought, flood, famine, war, hurricanes, earthquakes — the list was endless.

These occasions caused her to apologise even more frequently — for being late, having to leave early, for being unable to acquire sufficient sponsors, bric-a-brac, old clothes, for making tough unattractive quiches and inexpertly iced sponges.

Henry said it was all a waste of time, a lot of well meaning nonsense. 'The poor starving beggers won't benefit,' he would say, whilst complaining that he didn't care for rhubarb and couldn't she manage to grow something else, what did they pay a gardener for? When she explained that there was a glut this year, he interrupted to enquire if it was usual for mashed potato to have lumps. She would apologise again, her feeling of inadequacy threatening to engulf her.

She went to Spanish classes at the Adult College on Wednesdays. There was not the remotest possibility that they would ever go to Spain. Henry thought the Spanish lazy and backward, not to mention dishonest and dirty, not much use for anything really, even their dancing was repetitive and raucous, 'all that strumming'.

She had thought she might change and try something more useful, like upholstery, but as she was incapable of making a pincushion without it falling to pieces, decided against it. So she tried to throw herself more enthusiastically into the fund-raising effort.

She had once suggested to Henry, earlier in their marriage, that she might learn to play golf. The suggestion was greeted with unconcealed horror, and dismissed as absurd. She never mentioned it again.

On Tuesday evenings, the Simpsons came to play bridge. Tuesday evening's game was sacrosanct. Louise hated bridge, she was no good at it. She had to keep apologising to her partner, usually the kindly Mr Simpson. Mrs Simpson was easily aggravated and inclined to impatient clucking. Mostly she dreaded partnering Henry. She always made the wrong 'call' or played the wrong card, or forgot what were trumps. Henry would say she was an imbecile, slapping his cards down on the green baize table top and getting them all another drink.

She was supposed to provide 'snacks', and had to apologise for them too.

Henry wanted to know if there was really no alternative to cheese balls and bacon flavoured crisps. Her attempts at homemade titbits were always disastrous, compared with the artistic little morsels other women conjured up, soggy and unappetising. More apologies were necessary. They had known the Simpsons for years, or, at least, Henry had. They were older and duller but 'Useful'. As Henry would say , 'Very useful chap, Malcolm.'

The Golf Club had changed over the years. Bushes and shrubs had been cut down to make way for a car park, discreetly hedged. There were still brightly flowered round beds in the green velvet lawn leading up the Club House. The low red brick building had been extended to include new shower rooms and a sauna. There was also a shop selling golfing accessories.

The old terraced bar overlooking the sloping mounds of the Downs remained virtually the same, the lighting was more intimate, the seating more comfortable.

As a child she had sat on the terrace, waiting for her father and mother, sucking fizzy lemonade through a straw, and eating a packet of Smiths Crisps with the square blue packet of salt.

They had come nearly every Sunday for lunch in the brown dining room, served by two miserable grey-haired waitresses, licking the points of the pencils anchored by a string to the belt of their aprons. They would have grey roast beef, hard roast potatoes, and small squares of Yorkshire pudding swimming in thin watery gravy. Apple pie with brick hard pastry, and thin watery custard. This could be followed by a stale mini-matchbox-sized piece of orange-coloured cheddar and two crumbling cream crackers. In the winter it was too cold to take their coats off, and the waitresses snuffled and sneezed, waiting to bring their food from the hatch that led to the kitchen.

This characterless dismal room had been transformed into a first class restaurant. Thickly carpeted in red, with velvet-seated chairs, pink table cloths, gleaming glasses and cutlery, vases of flowers from the Club's beautifully tended gardens. There were table d'hôte and à la carte menus, a bowing head waiter with a French accent, and a considerable wine list.

The old ball room, dusty and splintered, where she had met

Henry, and where her engagement party had been held, was now smooth parquet with a dazzling revolving glass ball, and low green leather chairs, a platform with spotlights and microphones for the band, and a glass-fronted bar.

The austere ladies' cloakroom with its grubby roller towels was now a pink powder room with brass taps and a hot air hand drier as well as disposable paper towels. There were also several comfortable chairs to sit quietly.

They were to meet Charles and Ursula in the Terrace Bar at 7.30. Louise was dreading the whole evening. Charles was pretty boorish at the best of times, and poor Ursula was just a mess. She was a very pretty woman who spent many hours at the hairdressers and in beauty parlours. She and Charles had no children. She was somewhat younger than Charles who treated her very much as if she were a pet dog, occasionally throwing her scraps, material or emotional. He was a firm believer that a wife should be silent and decorative, in complete agreement with all her husband's opinions. Henry was nearly as bad, except that he most certainly did not view her as a decorative asset. He was always criticising her appearance.

Charles and Ursula were waiting for them in the bar. Both had obviously consumed a considerable amount of alcohol already. Henry pompously calling the barman, ordered another round. Ursula was wearing a very short very tight décolleté midnight blue velvet dress and very high heels. She reeled slightly as she got down from the bar stool to shake hands. Charles' voice was already slurred as he greeted everybody effusively, slapping Louise rather forcefully on the shoulder, telling Henry what a wonderful little wife he had, and what a lucky chap he was. Henry, pretending he had not heard, asked what sort of round he had had today with old Griffiths.

They had a central table. Henry liked to show off, a central table emphasised his importance, implied wealth and success. Everybody had to be aware of them.

Caroline was looking particularly lovely. She was wearing a black lace long sleeved dress, wafting expensive perfume. She and Paul made a very distinguished couple.

Ursula was slowly tearing up her bread roll, forming it into little pellets which she arrange in a circle. Charles said he was thinking of taking Ursula to Florida for Christmas. They hadn't been to Florida. He had been told it was a place everybody should go to.

Ursula rearranged the bread pellets to form a star. Smiling sweetly she reached over and took Paul's roll and began to make pellets of that. 'Perhaps a garden,' she said absently. Louise wondered nervously if she was on tranquillisers, if so she should not be consuming so much drink.

She noticed Samantha, the Saunders girl hovering, waiting to take their order. She smiled weakly at her and whispered that they were not quite ready to order yet dear, and could she come back in a little while.

Henry was ostentatiously studying the wine list.
'They have quite a good cellar here,' he said to Paul.

Ursula was now making the shape of a fish with the bread pellets. Charles was talking business, the difficulties of climbing the long ladder to the top. He addressed Paul condescendingly, warning of the pitfalls to be overcome, the skill and dedication needed to reach the highest pinnacle. He was drunkenly insulting in the implication that Paul had a long way to go, a lot to learn before he could match his own achievements.

Caroline spoke. 'Paul is a Director of his firm already.'

Charles hesitated a moment, slurped a mouthful of whisky, and then raising his glass in a mock toast, congratulated him warmly on his success. 'Family firm is it?' he asked with a sneer.

Ursula was dropping bread pellets one by one into her drink.

'Certainly not,' said Caroline. 'Paul has a brilliant mind.' Henry's voice sounded precise and cold after Charles' drink-blurred drawl. 'Must be his Jewish blood,' he said. Ursula knocked over her whisky, now full of sodden bread pellets, staining the crisp pink cloth in front of her. She began to eat the pellets.

Caroline got up. 'Come on Paul,' she said, 'Let's go'. Paul, his face taut with anger got up too. He bowed slightly towards Louise, and then together they left the restaurant.

With a small moan Ursula slid silently under the table.

Louise hung her skirt and blouse carefully in the dark heavy wardrobe, and got into bed. Henry had just come in. She heard him bolt the front door and go into the dining room. Having a nightcap as usual.

With the assistance of several husbands, Ursula was removed from under the table and taken to the ladies' powder room, where she was violently sick. Beryl the Ladies Captain materialised, and briskly took charge. A large woman, she looked, in her bright fuchsia pink brocade outfit, rather like an overstuffed armchair. She sent Samantha to see if Dr Robinson was in the Club, he usually was on a Saturday night, posted mousy Irene Stone on the door to prevent all but genuine cloakroom users from entering and told Louise to get Henry to take Charles home, as he was obviously not fit to drive. She and John would take Ursula home with them and put her to bed. Charles was not in a fit state to look after anybody.

Henry was in the lounge drinking coffee. There was no sign of Charles. He did not look up as she sat down at the table. She told him that Beryl and John were going to take Ursula home with them, and that Beryl asked would he take Charles home as he was not fit to drive. 'Disgraceful behaviour,' said Henry, 'We'll be a laughing stock.' It's hardly our fault Charles and Ursula were so drunk,' said Louise, in what she hoped was a mollifying tone.

'Good God woman! Our daughter and friend walk out, our guests fall under the table. Charles has been sick in the rhododendrons, and John is walking him up and down the terrace trying to sober him up. I can't understand you.'

Louise said she didn't think it was a good idea that he had asked them in the first place, under the circumstances.
'What circumstances?'
Louise could sense that Henry was getting really angry. 'Well, with the fuss about Ursula ...'
'Ursula is an exceedingly silly woman, she always was and always will be, and I consider her exceedingly silly behaviour should be totally ignored. I don't know how Charles puts up with it, he is much too indulgent.' He got up abruptly and went out on the terrace.

Dr Robinson had been found, and pronounced Ursula alright. He said it was a good thing she had been so sick, as that would have cleaned her stomach out, and that she should be alright after a good night's sleep. She should have plenty of liquids, not alcohol of course. Ha, ha! Louise cringed. She had never cared for Dr Robinson. He always made awful jokes, his hands were none too clean and he was too familiar. Fortunately, Henry, though thinking him a very good chap, and a fair golfer, did not have a very high opinion of his medical expertise so Louise did not have to endure him as their doctor.

They got Ursula to bed in Beryl's spare bedroom, cheerfully decorated in floral chintz. Ursula, attired in one of Beryl's voluminous flannelette nightgowns, managed a cup of tea before slipping off to sleep. Whilst they were upstairs John had made a plateful of buttered toast, and they insisted she should stay and have some with another cup of tea. They were extremely kind. Beryl had a reputation for being loud and bossy, but she was most understanding, particularly about Ursula, referring to Charles as 'that pompous ass'.

John had driven her home.

Henry was in the kitchen sulkily fiddling with the coffee percolator when Louise came down next morning. She was still in her dressing gown. She had hardly slept, going over in her mind what she could possibly say to Caroline.

Henry would be playing golf as he always did on Sundays, and should be at the Club by 10.30. Naturally he expected her to be up before him to get the breakfast ready. She removed the leg of lamb from the fridge, and, carefully wrapping it in foil transferred it to the freezer. 'I'm sorry, I shan't be getting lunch today,' she said. 'I'll eat at the Club. Haven't we any more marmalade?'

Louise silently fetched the jar from the cupboard, and placed it with care on the table. She realised that nothing was to be said about last night, about Caroline, about Paul, or poor Ursula falling under the table, or Charles' drunken weeping. It was to be put aside, an unpleasant episode to be instantly forgotten, the outcome of which should not be discussed. It was to be put aside like yesterday's newspapers, never referred to again. She left the room.

She waited until the Armstrong Siddeley turned into the street, and she could be sure Henry had gone, and then she phoned Caroline. There was no answer, she must be at Paul's.

She phoned Beryl. Ursula had slept well, had had a cup of tea, and was sleeping again. Charles had phoned. He was playing golf this morning, but would call in after lunch to see if Ursula was well enough to go home. Beryl thought it would be a good idea if she came over and had a chat with Ursula. 'I think she finds me rather intimidating' she said cheerfully. 'Perhaps she would find it easier talking to you.'

Louise got in her Morris Minor and drove over to Beryl's.

John was out playing golf. Beryl had cancelled her game.

Ursula, purple-eyed and weary, wrapped in a homely knitted

cardigan of bright pink, lay against the pillows, miserably pleating the sheet with thin white fingers.

Beryl brought up a tray of tea and toast, and a soft boiled egg under a bright pink cosy, and tried to persuade Ursula to have something. Ursula nibbled a piece of toast, tears welling in her eyes. She didn't speak.

Louise sat quietly by the bed, feeling completely useless. She had no idea what to say to Ursula. After a while Ursula said she thought she would have another sleep, and much relieved, Louise patted her hand, arranged her pillows and left.

She didn't want to run into Charles. She never wanted to see him again.

At intervals during the day she tried phoning Caroline, but there was no reply, and after Henry came in, some time after seven, and gone straight to his study, shutting the door behind him, she didn't dare use the phone, in case he listened on the extension. She would phone in the morning as soon as he had gone to work.

Caroline received the call at her desk in her spacious, sophisticated office, carpeted in grey with a thin black geometric pattern, the furniture sparse and meaningful, glass and chrome, black leather armchairs, a large bowl of decorative fruit, regularly changed, as were the flowers in the tall spreading vase on a glass cabinet. A cona coffee machine sat discreetly in a corner on top of a teak fronted fridge.

She narrowed her eyes as she heard Louise's anxious voice, filled with contempt at her mother's resigned acceptance of her stifling domestic situation.
She crossed her legs and extricated her cigarettes from the Dior bag in front of her. She smoked Stuyvesant Menthol King Size, lighting her cigarette with a gold monogrammed lighter, a gift from a former boyfriend. Her legs were long and beautifully hosed, tapering into expensive Kurt Geiger shoes.

Louise was abjectly apologetic. Charles had been drunk, he had not known what he was saying. He was upset about Ursula. Henry had also had too much to drink. He had had several whiskies before leaving the house.

Caroline replied that drunkenness was no excuse, and she could not understand the connection between Charles' wife's infidelity and anti-Semitism. They had no need to worry. Neither herself or Paul were contemplating visiting them again in the near future. She also said she found her mother's feeble behaviour contemptible. How could she allow herself to be treated in this humiliating way? Had she no opinions of her own? If it hadn't been for Grandfather's money, Father would still be working at the bank's counter. It was about time she stood up for herself. 'For God's sake, have some spirit.' She stubbed out her cigarette viciously in the heavy crystal ashtray, and rang for her secretary.

Louise replaced the receiver feeling completely wretched. Caroline was right of course, she shouldn't allow herself to be treated like a doormat. Doormats get trodden on.

She was very unhappy, and very guilty about being unhappy. She had been brought up to believe that it was not right for someone of her class to be unhappy. It was ungrateful and unjustified, with all the advantages that life had bestowed on her. Unhappiness was not allowed. The inner admonition to pull herself together struggled with a strong desire to cry. Crying was definitely not allowed. She must make an effort to pull herself together. She must try to assert herself more. She had never had a very good relationship with her daughter. She had tried hard but had always felt that Caroline looked down on her, despising her weakness. She must start stating her own views and wishes. She must stop apologising all the time. It would be difficult, but she must try. She would start with little things and build up gradually to more important things.

She put her coat on and went out into the street.
The newsagent's was on the corner by the laundrette.

Mr Reynolds greeted her politely.

'Yes, it is a really lovely morning,' she said. 'As from tomorrow would you deliver *The Guardian* as well as *The Daily Telegraph* to number 22?'

Mr Reynolds said that would be a pleasure, and would she like a copy of today's?

'Oh, yes please,' said Louise, and thanked him. 'I think I'll take the new *TV Times* as well.'